SCANDALOUS

THE ALPHA BODYGUARD SERIES

SYBIL BARTEL

Books by SYBIL BARTEL

The Unchecked Series
IMPOSSIBLE PROMISE
IMPOSSIBLE CHOICE
IMPOSSIBLE END

The Rock Harder Series
NO APOLOGIES

Join Sybil Bartel's Mailing List to get the news first on her upcoming releases, giveaways and exclusive excerpts! You'll also get a FREE book for joining!

SCANDALOUS

THE ALPHA BODYGUARD SERIES

Bodyguard.

Babysitter.

Chauffeur.

Not what the hell I thought I'd be doing with my life.

Especially not for a spoiled Hollywood actress on location in Miami Beach. But triple pay and carrying a gun had its advantages. I'd shove away paparazzi and screaming fans for a lot less. The Marines trained me to be Force Recon—intimidation and crowd control was child's play compared to four tours. This assignment should've been easy money.

But the doe-eyed starlet with the perfect ass dragged me down her rabbit hole. Living for the spotlight, she leaked the perfect scandal. I warned her making headlines wasn't in my job description, but she kept smiling for the cameras.

Now she was going to find out just how scandalous a bodyguard could be.

*SCANDALOUS is a sexy new standalone book in the Alpha Bodyguard Series.

DEDICATION

For My Family

CHAPTER ONE

Tank

CROSSING MY ARMS, I LEANED AGAINST THE BEACH WALL AND watched her naked ass run across the sand.

"Goddamn it," Tyler cursed through the comm. "Are you fucking kidding me?"

Halting before the water, she threw her arms out and shook her head dramatically before backing up.

She had a huge rack, but she was skinny as shit. "That a rhetorical question?"

"*Jesus Christ*," Tyler muttered. "I thought she was passed out."

"You seriously that naïve?" He'd been at this bodyguard gig as long as me. He knew better.

"Fuck you."

Ignoring him, I scanned the beach. "You better grab her." A crowd was growing.

"You do it," Tyler snapped.

Hell no. "I'm not her handler." I was, however, gonna stand there and watch the fuck outta her naked, tight ass.

Tyler growled in frustration. "Why the hell does Luna keep assigning me these crazy-ass bitches?"

"What's wrong, pretty boy, didn't get your dick wet tonight?" The female clients always went for him. He looked like a goddamn GQ model and smiled like a saint.

1

"Again. Fuck you," Tyler bit out. "Unlike your unprofessional ass, I don't sleep with the clients."

I smirked. "Who said anything about sleeping?"

Tires screeched and I glanced to my left. "Time's up. Paparazzi. Three o'clock."

A couple photogs spilled out of a van, yelling, *"Dreena! Dreena!"*

Audrina "Dreena" MacKenzie.

Hollywood's hottest actress.

Running naked as fuck across the sand in South Beach at—I glanced at my watch—oh-one-hundred, while her bodyguard, my coworker, stood watching.

I tossed the toothpick in my mouth and pushed off the seawall. "What the fuck you waiting for, Tyler? An invitation?"

"Fucking hell." He sighed. "Here goes nothing."

I watched him approach her sweet ass.

"Miss MacKenzie," Tyler clipped. "You need to come with me. Right now."

The second her name left his mouth, I knew he'd made a crucial error. "Wrong approach," I warned.

"Ohhhh." Dreena turned on him. "Hurry! *They're drowning.*" She flailed her arms.

"No one's drowning, ma'am." Tyler took another step toward her.

"STOP!" she screeched, her arms going straight out in front of her, hands up.

"Told you," I said into the comm. "Wrong approach."

Tyler turned his head slightly. "What the fuck do you want me to do?" he whisper-hissed.

"Pick her ass up." Fireman style.

"Fuck you, Tank." He looked back toward the spoiled

actress. "It's time to leave, Miss MacKenzie. The paparazzi are here. You need to get back to the hotel and put some clothes on."

Her fuckable mouth opened and she let loose at the top of her lungs. "We're all drowning!"

The paps rushed across the beach, and a crowd came out of nowhere. Camera phones, flashes, shouting. *Dreena! Dreena MacKenzie! Oh my God, she's naked! Is she drunk? Dreena!*

"Fuck this shit." Tyler finally threw her over his shoulder.

The spoiled little actress let loose with a bloodcurdling scream.

I shut off my comm for a second then turned it back on when I saw she'd stopped screaming.

"I'm drowning! We're drowning! You have to row!" Her cries carried across the beach.

"Ma'am," Tyler ground out, ignoring the cameras pointed at them, "we're not drowning."

"YOU HAVE TO ROW US TO SHORE."

If I wasn't watching the shitshow unfold with my own eyes, I wouldn't fucking believe the spectacle I saw next.

Tyler started rowing. Legit mime paddling with the arm not hanging on to her.

"We're rowing, ma'am, we're rowing." Tyler's arm kept going like a fucking fish outta water. "Almost to shore. Hang on. I got you."

I cracked a smile. "Fucking priceless."

"Coming at you, Tank."

"No fucking way." I shook my head.

"Your vehicle's closer," Tyler argued.

"Keep rowing!" the hot mess of an actress screeched.

Tyler rowed some more. "Open the back," he ground out.

I crossed my arms. "I'm off duty."

"Open. *The motherfucking back!*"

Half to fuck with Tyler, half to take in the hot mess over his shoulder, I stood there a moment and watched him carry her toward me. Her long hair tangled and hanging everywhere, her bare ass over Tyler's shoulder looking like it was made for sin, her legs long enough to wrap around my waist—I'd fuck her.

"Now!" Tyler bellowed as he passed me.

I hit the key fob, and a few yards behind me, the back of the SUV opened.

"We made it, ma'am. We're safe on land." Tyler threw her ass in and slammed the back shut as the paparazzi descended on us like a fucking swarm of gnats.

I got behind the wheel, and Tyler jumped in the passenger seat. The paparazzi's camera flashes kept going off like a red carpet event, lighting up the interior despite the limo-tinted windows.

I cranked the engine and floored it, pulling into the nighttime traffic in South Beach.

For two whole seconds it was dead quiet in the back, then movement in the rearview mirror caught my attention.

She sat up and looked around like a caged animal.

"Round two," I warned.

Tyler turned in his seat. "Oh fuck. Lock the doors, *quick.*"

She reached for the back release as I hit the lock button. When she realized she couldn't get out, a keening filled the car and she started to thrash.

Tyler looked at me like he couldn't believe what was happening.

"Bad day at the office, dear?" I deadpanned.

4

"You're not fucking funny."

I smirked. "Says the asshole who rowed his way across South Beach."

He tipped his head toward the back. "What the fuck am I supposed to do with that? I can't carry her into the hotel like this."

I glanced in the rearview mirror again. "Why the hell did you let her out of your sight in the first place?" Seeing her tits bounce around like she was being fucked made my cock twitch.

"I was tired, okay? We'd been up since three a.m. for a last-minute scene retake she had to do that wound up taking all day. She kept powering Red Bulls, then switched to alcohol, and by ten p.m. she was fucking hammered at Club Frenzy, dancing her ass off. A couple hours later, when she finally told me she was done, I got her in the Escalade and she started acting weird. I asked what the fuck she took, but all she said was she needed to sleep."

She let out a loud-as-fuck animal noise, like a horse neighing.

Tyler raised his voice and spoke over her like this shit was normal as fuck. "She was a stumbling mess on the way to the room. I got her in bed, she looked like she passed out face-first, so I shut the door. Five minutes later, I was on the couch with my eyes closed and the door to the suite bangs shut. By the time I threw my boots on and called for backup, she'd streaked down the hall to the elevator. The doors closed before I could grab her, so I ran my ass down twenty flights only to see her sprint through the hotel lobby and take off across the street toward the beach. That's when you showed." He looked over his shoulder, shook his head, then slumped in his seat. "Why the hell are you here if you're off duty?"

"I was just leaving the office when your call for back-up came in. Thought I'd come by and watch the sideshow." I shook my head. "Which, by the way, was epically fucked. Hundred bucks says you're viral by tomorrow."

His groan was drowned out by the actress who'd graduat-ed to roaring like a lion.

My cell rang through the car's Bluetooth. I turned up the volume and answered. "Tank."

"*Jesucristo*, why the hell am I seeing naked photos of our client all over the fucking internet?" André Luna, our boss and owner of Luna and Associates, practically yelled. "Wait. Did I just hear *a lion*?"

Tyler rubbed a hand over his face. "That's the client, boss."

"She's making animal sounds?"

Tyler glanced at me as he answered Luna. "Yes, sir."

"What *the fuck* is going on?" Luna asked, incredulous.

Tyler sighed. "Acid, I think, sir."

Luna swore again in Spanish. "First, we're gonna discuss this shit tomorrow. Second, contain this mess, Tyler. Contain her, contain whatever the hell you have to. Your ass is already all over social media. Get out of sight, you hear me? Your face plastered all over the internet makes you useless to me."

"Copy that," Tyler answered, sounding exactly like you would when you'd had your ass handed to you by the boss.

"Tank," Luna snapped. "You're up."

Fuck that. "Not unless you wanna pay me overtime." I'd just come off another job.

"I'm charging her agent triple for this shit, and I'm call-ing her publicist. I don't deal with fucking junkies. Keep her behind closed doors until we can unload her ass tomorrow. And yes, you're making overtime on this, plus the overage I'm charging her agent."

I wasn't an idiot. I'd take the money. "Done."

"Congratulations," Luna said sarcastically. "You got a new client."

CHAPTER TWO

Tank

CIRCLED THE BLOCK HER HOTEL WAS ON A FEW TIMES. BY THE FOURTH pass, the paparazzi were gone and the actress had apparently run through all the animal sounds she knew. She was quietly staring out the back window.

Tyler glanced at her. "At this point, I don't know if we're lucky she's quiet, or if we should be concerned as fuck."

The latter. "Next pass, I'll drop you off."

"Copy that." He fished a key card out of his pocket and handed it to me. "It's the west penthouse. Her schedule's on the desk. She's done shooting, but she has press engagements. She's got something at noon today, but I don't know how the hell she's gonna make that."

I took the card. "I'll handle it."

"Fair warning, not that you couldn't already tell, but she's a fucking handful."

I glanced at the naked twenty-three-year-old in the back who'd been acting since she was a kid. She was too fucking young for me, and she was goddamn mess, but her long honey-blonde hair and sexy-as-fuck body had my damn cock half-hard.

I drove into the hotel's underground parking and pulled up to Tyler's company SUV. "She's a handful because she's spoiled as fuck." I hadn't seen any of her movies, but I knew there were a shitload of them. And career actresses were always a pain in the ass as clients. She was lucky Tyler was her detail and not me when she'd made a run for it. I would've spanked the fuck out of that sweet ass of hers.

Tyler snorted. "No shit." He got out of the Escalade. "You want me to help you get her up to the suite?"

"I got it."

"Good luck." He couldn't close the door fast enough.

I waited till he pulled away, then turned in my seat.

She was still staring out the back window.

I didn't even know if she was cognizant we'd stopped. "Audrina," I clipped, authority in my tone. "Look at me."

Not turning, she trailed a finger down the window. "I don't do drugs."

Right. "I told you to look at me, Audrina." I used her full name because I hated Dreena. I wasn't one of her groupies.

Her hand pressed against the glass. "The colors, they're like a waterfall."

"Turn around," I commanded.

She finally listened. Her eyes dilated as fuck, her gaze on me, she looked right at me but she didn't see me.

Shit. "You want me to take you through that hotel lobby up to your suite or do you want to come to my place?"

Her gaze strayed back to the window. "I never noticed colors before."

"Answer my question." She wasn't in any condition to make the decision, but I wasn't not gonna ask. "Lobby and your hotel suite or a private residence?"

"Nothing's private." Her voice dropped. "Nothing, nothing, nothing."

No fucking shit. "Not when you run naked across South

Beach, it isn't."

Her hands went to her breasts and squeezed. "Skin," she whispered.

Jesus fuck. "Hotel or condo?"

She dragged her fingers down her body and spread her own legs. Her head dropped. "So lonely. Everyone's drowning." She touched her shaved pussy.

Fuck me. "Audrina," I warned.

She groaned like a goddamn porn star.

"Hey!" I barked.

Her head snapped up then wavered, but her eyes met mine.

"You come in my car, I'm gonna spank the ever-loving fuck out of you," I promised, giving no fucks about impropriety. "You hear me?"

"Yesss," she hissed, her head falling back. "Spank me."

Fuck this. I wasn't carrying her orgasming ass through a hotel lobby with security cameras. "Condo it is."

"Yes," she moaned. "Condo, condo, condo."

I shot off a text to Luna, telling him I needed her agent's and publicist's numbers, then I threw the vehicle in reverse. Pulling out of the parking garage, I hit the street with her un-buckled, moaning ass in the back.

The first turn I took, she rolled and hit the side of the car. Her grunt did nothing to tame my hard-as-hell dick. Adjusting myself, I stepped on the gas and flew through all the lights. I was at my building in eight minutes. Eight minutes of listening to her make sounds no man wanted to hear unless he was di-rectly responsible for them.

I pulled into one of the parking spots under the building and killed the engine. "Stay," I ordered as I got out. Taking my shirt off as I walked to the back, I powered open the lift gate.

Her hair everywhere, her face flushed, she would've been fucking gorgeous if she wasn't high as shit. Not to mention, backing away from me on all fours.

"Come here," I ordered, holding my shirt out. "You're putting this on."

She shook her head, and hair stuck to her mouth. "That's drowning."

"That's the rules," I corrected.

We looked at each other, and for a split second, I thought I was getting through. Then she let out a high-pitched squeal like a damn cat.

Fighting for patience, I tried another tactic. "Do you want to drown?"

Her head shook like a pendulum.

"Put on the shirt and you won't."

Her head stopped shaking, but she didn't move. She eyed the shirt.

I went for broke. "Water's rising, you need to put this on."

Slow, like a wounded, untrusting animal, she crawled toward me.

I didn't do comfort. Ever. I dominated and fucked women, then I left before the sun came up. I didn't have time to fucking coddle, let alone cuddle. But for a single second, the way she was looking at me, I thought about picking her up. For what, I didn't know. She was unfuckable in this state.

I impatiently waited as she crawled the final few inches toward me, then I threw my shirt over her head. "Good girl," I muttered, slipping her arms through, not knowing what the fuck had gotten into me. "Can you walk?"

I didn't get the last word out before she launched herself at me. Her arms wrapped around me in a death grip, her legs

11

went around my waist, and she buried her face against my neck. A split second later, she was crying.

Jesus fucking Christ.

I caught her with an arm under her bare ass before I yanked my shirt down on her and tucked it under. Closing the lift gate, I locked the vehicle and strode to the elevators. Despite her huge tits, there was no weight to her. I'd be surprised if she was a buck ten soaking wet.

Thinking of her soaking wet made my dick come back to life, and I pounded my fist on the call button. Waiting for the elevator, stepping inside, riding up eighteen floors, I didn't say shit.

I listened to her cry.

I'd never thought about a woman crying before, because I was immune. Tears had zero effect on me. Ask any of the women I'd walked away from who'd pulled that bullshit. Sobbing was drama I didn't need. But this young-as-hell woman in my arms wasn't sobbing.

She was fucking weeping.

Weeping like shit hurt deep.

I didn't utter a word as I unlocked my condo and walked inside. I didn't speak as I carried her to my bedroom. And I sure as shit didn't say anything as I peeled her off me and dropped her on my bed.

But when she started to crawl away, I barked out a command.

"*Freeze*. You're staying right there."

The weeping stopped and she froze.

On all fours.

With her bare ass facing me.

My head cocked, and I issued another order, "Lie down."

She lay down.

Goddamn. "You gonna stay, or do I have to handcuff you to the bed while I shower?"

She curled in a ball.

My dick hard as fuck because it didn't get the memo that she wasn't being submissive, she was high as shit, I stood there for thirty seconds, waiting.

Besides her chest rising and falling with each breath, she didn't move. At the minute mark, I figured she'd gotten the message. Locking the bedroom door just in case, not that'd it do anything except slow her down for a few seconds, I strode to the master bath and turned on the shower. Two fucking minutes in my arms and I smelled like her. Yeah, it was ocean and alcohol and sweat, but it was also pussy and perfume. And that was enough to make me want to wash that shit off before any more deviant thoughts entered my head.

I checked on her in the bedroom before I stripped down, but she still hadn't moved. Kicking my boots off, then my clothes, I got in the shower with a raging hard-on. I needed to get fucking laid soon and get this shit under control.

Not wanting to take the time to jerk off, I was in and out and walking back to the bedroom with a towel around my waist in under three minutes.

Bed empty, she was gone.

"Motherfucker." I spun in a circle.

The bedroom door was still locked, the floor on the opposite side of the bed was vacant, and the slider to the balcony was still closed.

That left the closet.

I hit the light in the walk-in and found her rocking in the back, her knees to her chest. Her hair was pushed back, and black streaks of makeup from her eyes ran down her face.

Jesus. She looked like the poster child for say no to drugs.

"All right, let's go." I was done with this shit. "You're getting in the shower."

Of course she didn't move.

I scooped her up and walked right back in to the shower and set her on her feet. She started to shiver. I tossed my towel to the floor just outside the shower and turned on the water full blast.

Shock hit her face, her mouth opened, and her back arched like needles were piercing it. Thank fuck she didn't scream or start with the animal sounds again, because after being up for twenty hours, I wasn't in the mood for anything except my bed or fucking. The latter of which wasn't happening.

"We're getting you cleaned up," I muttered, tilting her head back into the spray.

Her hands flew to my waist in a death grip, and she closed her eyes.

I wet her long hair, then dumped a handful of my shampoo on the top of her head. "Wash," I ordered.

Still fucking silent, her eyes still closed, her hands still on my waist, she didn't move.

Goddamn it.

In the single most cock-blocking shower with a woman I'd ever had, I washed her fucking hair.

Then I washed her.

Every goddamn inch, because apparently I was into torture.

With nothing left but her face and the makeup that hadn't washed off, I took her hand and placed the bar of soap in it. "Do your face."

Water running down her body, her eyelashes wet, she looked at me. Really fucking looked at me.

Then slow, just like in the back of the SUV, she came at me.

Except this time she didn't look terrified.

Her lips hit me midchest and she licked me.

CHAPTER THREE

Audrina

OH MY GOD, MY HEAD.

It was pounding like I was on a construction site and someone was relentlessly hammering on my skull. I couldn't remember a worse headache.

Why the fuck did I drink so much last night?

And why the hell did I leave all the damn lights on?

I raised my arm to put my hand over my face, but halfway through the motion something caught. A metal clanking sound rattled the silence, and a split second later pain bit into my wrist.

What the…?

I opened one eye.

Oh my God.

I was fucking handcuffed?

Belated panic set in, and I opened both eyes, picking my head up.

White sheets, fluffy pillows, thick white comforter, and a wall of glass looking out over sparkling turquoise waters.

My head fell back and I inhaled.

Okay. I wasn't in jail. That was good. One less thing for my asshole agent to be pissed about. Although…. No, don't even think it. Jail would be bad, even if it did destroy my career and get me off this fucking merry-go-round. Beds in jail wouldn't be this soft. I rolled my head and inhaled again. Or smell this good.

Because *damn*, it smelled really good.

But not hotel good.

No bleach, no disinfectant, no sterile this-is-supposed-to-be-clean-but-they-are-still-used-sheets distinctive smell. I knew that smell. I'd lived that smell for more years than I could count. After back-to-back movies for the past decade, I was intimate with hotel sheet smell.

This wasn't that.

This was…

Oh no.

No, no, *no*.

My heart suddenly in my throat, I slowly rolled the other way.

Holy.

Fucking.

SHIT.

He was huge.

A giant beast of a man with unbelievably huge muscles was asleep next to me. And holy fuck, he was hot. Scary as hell looking, but oh-my-God *hot*.

And apparently naked.

With the sheet only up to his waist, he had chiseled abs, a screen-worthy jawline, and strong cheekbones. He wasn't just naked and hot, he was every bad decision I'd never made but wished I had gorgeous.

Stupidly, I mentally ran through every A-lister I knew, but I already knew this guy wasn't Hollywood. He was too… masculine. And his dark brown, almost black hair was practically shaved in a neat buzz that screamed military, not movies.

His chest expanded with a long inhale, but he didn't open his eyes. "You're staring."

Oh, *my God*.

Sleep rough and deep, his voice was more vibration than baritone, and it went straight between my legs.

I wanted to taste him.

Actually, I wanted to crawl on top of him and ride every ounce of sexual energy he was giving off while drowning in his scent and listening to his voice forever.

And I didn't have sex. Like ever.

Okay, that wasn't exactly true. But ages sixteen to eighteen didn't count. I was young and stupid then and I'd spread my legs for a slimy prick of a costar who'd fucked every groupie he could get his hands on behind my back. But since then? I'd been smart. I'd kept my legs closed. Unless… last night….

Oh God.

Panicked, I looked down.

Naked as the day I was born.

Damn it, damn it, *damn it*. I was going to be really pissed if I'd screwed him and didn't remember a single minute of it. But more, I was going to be seriously pissed at myself. Jeez, why the hell couldn't I remember a damn thing from last night?

"Relax, sweetheart." Mistaking my silence, he gave me his sexy-as-hell voice again. "I didn't fuck you."

My nipples hardened to the point of pain when he said *fuck*. "But you managed to handcuff me." I should be seriously pissed about that. Infuriated, actually. But all that was happening was a growing ache and pool of moisture between my legs that not only said I hadn't been well used last night, but screamed I needed to get my hormones under control and tell my libido to fuck off.

"I needed some sleep." He opened one gorgeously green-and-brown eye and looked at me. "Didn't want you running across South Beach naked." He paused. "Again."

Again? *Naked?* Fuck. FUCK. I mean… shit, I worked out every day and went vegan two years ago to stave off any resemblance to a natural woman my body might be inclined to adopt. I didn't have anything to be ashamed about walking around naked, unless this was the Renaissance. Then I'd look like a starving pauper, but it wasn't fifteen hundred, or whenever the Renaissance was. It was Hollywood and it was cutthroat. Unless you looked like a twelve-year-old boy, had no tits, could sing better than Whitney, and were willing to take ridiculous roles no female with a brain would ever touch, then you didn't work in Hollywood.

So, I shamelessly worked and took that multimillion-dollar paycheck. And apparently ran naked across South Beach.

Shit.

Shit.

"Did my ass look good?" That's the first thing my publicist would ask me.

The sexy-as-hell tank of man lying next to me opened both eyes and his head as his eyebrows shot to his forehead. "That's what you're worried about? Your ass?"

"Yep." Nope. Well, maybe if he was looking.

He laid his head back down and closed his eyes. "It's a great fucking ass. Needs some meat on it, but still fuckable."

"Gee." Dick. "Thanks." I changed my mind. He wasn't sexy as hell. He was crude.

"Not that I need to tell you how your ass looks." He reached to the nightstand on his side without opening his eyes. Like Superman, his hand landed unerringly on a cell phone.

He picked it up, tossed it, and it landed in the exact middle of my chest. "You're little show's on every news channel from here to Dubai. Check out your ass for yourself. Passcode's one-one-nine."

I stared at the phone on my chest and stupidly wondered what his contacts list would look like. I envisioned a lot of female names. Ones like Candi, Brandi, and Mandi. He looked like he went for the fake-breasted, exotic dancer type. Or any girl he could use and toss aside an hour later. Shoot, ten minutes later for all I knew. Unable to restrain myself, I peeked at him again. Okay, maybe more than ten minutes. But I wasn't going to think about that.

Sighing, I tossed his phone on his mountain of a chest. "Where's my cell?"

"Fuck if I know." His eyes still closed, he put his phone back on the nightstand. "Probably with all of your shit at your hotel suite."

I tugged on my still handcuffed wrist. "And why am I not back at my hotel suite?"

He did the open-one-eye thing again. "You don't remember fuck-all from last night, do you?"

I had to admit, it was kind of nice having someone talk normally to me. No Miss MacKenzie this, no ma'am that. And he wasn't shy. At all. He didn't stumble over words or say stupid tongue-tied shit. Which made me wonder... "Do you spend a lot of time around actors?"

He smirked and closed his eye again.

I took in the length of him and wondered how big his dick was. "That wasn't an answer."

"It was a stupid question."

It suddenly occurred to me that maybe he wasn't tongue

tied because I wasn't his preferred gender of choice. "Okay, how's this question? Do you like to fuck men or women?" Hell. "Or both?"

Slow, like a turning tide, his mammoth chest rolled to face me as he moved an even bigger arm, bulging muscles and all, under his head. His heated gaze met mine, then it slowly dragged down my face to my lips and drank me in before sliding even lower to my chest and devouring me.

I felt like I'd just been savored, used, and spit out, all without a single touch.

"I fuck women," he rumbled. "Hard."

Ohhh God. Wet city. My mouth ran away from me. "Yes, but do you do it well?"

"If I fucked you, you wouldn't have to ask."

I let out a snort I was sure was not attractive by any means, but it was a nervous tic I'd never been able to fully break. "Cocky much?"

The side of his mouth tipped up. "Cock being the operative word."

A single half smile and my entire body tightened with need. I wanted to hate how fucking sexy he was, or at the very least be alarmed by a stranger in my bed, but the sad fucking truth was that my life was nothing except strangers. Actors, agents, publicists, fans, security, costars, I didn't know any of them and none of them knew the real me.

At least this stranger wasn't pretending to be nice, or faking professionalism only to gawk. Instead he was being almost normal. Cocky as hell, but still, normal enough to make me forget my empty stomach and hunger pains long enough to remember how long it'd been since I'd had sex.

Not that I wanted to let on for one second that I was

thinking about him or his muscles.

Putting the years of acting classes to good use, I managed to keep my expression this side of disinterested and firmly in the bored camp. "Operative word, huh?"

He didn't hesitate. "My dick's big, and I know how to use it."

Hungover, deranged, out of my mind—I didn't know what my excuse was, but the words were out of my mouth before I could stop them. "How big?"

"You'll never know."

I opened my mouth to say something sarcastic as hell, but he sank the blow even lower with a smirk.

"Unless you remember last night."

I shifted my legs and desperately tried to remember even a single detail about him from last night, but all I had was vague impressions of strong arms and sand and shitty feelings of being trapped, which was a constant for me anyway. Besides, this beast of a man had just said we didn't fuck, and my pussy felt as empty as it always did, so I was betting on no sex, but that didn't mean I, or we, didn't do something else.

The thought alone had me salivating.

And now I wanted to remember this beast of a man from last night more than anything. Except everything after the club was a fog, and now that I was thinking about it, that was seriously fucking fucked-up.

Colton Bradley Payne fucked-up.

Colton I-have-more-drugs-than-a-pharmacy-and-I-always-forget-my-lines Payne.

That *motherfucker.*

"I don't remember last night," I ground out, putting two and two together. Colton drugged me. I knew he did.

The sexy hazel-eyed beast of a man leveled me with a look. "Then you're not gonna know how big my dick is."

It was instant. All my Colton anger transferred into Mr. Muscle anger. "First of all," I snapped, attempting to hold up one finger, but only managing to get my wrist lynched by the damn handcuff again. "You said we didn't fuck. Second of all, uncuff me. And third of all, do it fucking quick because I need to find Colton Bradley Payne."

He stared at me a moment, and his expression didn't change, but he looked at me like he couldn't believe I'd just said fuck. Which I got, a lot. I was Hollywood's brightest child star before I was Hollywood's darling, and anyone who didn't actually know me was always surprised to realize I wasn't the cherubic thirteen-year-old with virtue anymore.

Indignant, I glanced pointedly at my restraint. "Are you going to uncuff me?"

"Depends."

Ass. "On?"

"Is the spoiled Hollywood actress asking, or the chick from Kansas?"

So he'd read my fake bio. So fucking what? "It makes a difference?" I was stupid enough to bite.

He eyed me. "Girls from Kansas don't usually streak across South Beach."

I had no idea what people from Kansas did. "I'm one and the same," I lied. "Uncuff me."

He ignored me as his eyes narrowed. "Why do you need to find your prick costar?"

I yanked on the cuff twice for dramatic effect. "Because that motherfucker drugged me last night and I'm going to kick his scrawny, capped-teeth ass, right after I kick yours for fucking

23

around with me."

The tank of man stared at me as the lines between his eyes deepened. "We didn't fuck."

I was riled up enough to ask the stupidest of all stupid questions "Why not?"

Throwing back the sheet, he rolled and got out of the bed. Six and a half feet of muscled gladiator stood to his full height in nothing but formfitting black boxers that did little to hide the massive, *massive* cock he was sporting.

My breath hitched, and I forgot about Colton Bradley Payne, running naked on a beach, and being hungry. I even forgot about being handcuffed. All my blood rushed south, my pussy clenched in needful pain, and I became the one thing I despised most in the world.

Needy.

A throbbing, aching, mindless need so intense, my world reduced to a series of single-action screenshots.

He bent.

I heard a zipper.

My mouth watered.

He straightened.

I pulsed between my legs.

He strode to my side of the bed.

His intense stare landed on me.

I sucked in a breath and fought to come back to reality, but it was impossible. My heart threatened to explode as he took my hand, held it in his huge palm, and used a key to unlock the handcuff.

Then he did the last thing in the world I ever would've expected a man like him to do.

He gently massaged my wrist.

Every stroke of his fingers sent electric shock waves up my arm, then down my body, going straight to my neglected pussy. Four years of self-induced celibacy suddenly felt like a lifetime, and I was thinking I wanted to know what he could do with that giant cock when his deep voice broke the magical silence of my fantasies.

"We didn't fuck, because I don't fuck my clients." He dropped my hand and walked out of the bedroom.

CHAPTER FOUR

Tank

THIRSTY AND HORNY AS FUCK, I WALKED TO THE KITCHEN AFTER lying to her about fucking clients. Not that I had, but there was a first time for everything.

She followed.

"What the fuck does that mean? *Client*," she demanded, spitting the last word out.

I grabbed a water and took my time turning around. Shit. Wrapped in my top sheet, no makeup on, her hair everywhere like she'd been fucked all night long, she was hot. She was also lucky I had some fucking scruples.

I tipped my chin at the sheet trailing on the floor. "You gonna make my bed after tearing it apart?" Housekeeper didn't come until next week. I fucking hated making beds.

"Who," she growled, *"are you?"*

I almost smiled. "Your new bodyguard."

"Where's Tyler?" she demanded.

I studied her for a second, looking for the telltale signs. "Gone." I knew Tyler hadn't fucked her, but that didn't mean she didn't want to fuck him.

"I want him back."

"Tough shit. He's reassigned," I lied.

She slapped my cell down on the counter and shoved it toward me. "Then call him and get him *un*-reassigned." She glared at me like she thought I'd actually act on a fucking word she'd said.

Hot or not, she wasn't the one paying my fee. Her agent was. And he was pissed as hell at her little stunt last night. My orders were clear. Keep her hidden until he and her publicist could spin her junkie jaunt into a PR opportunity of epic proportions. Until then, she was here and I was ground zero.

I opened the fridge and took out bacon and eggs.

"What are you doing?" she demanded.

"Making breakfast." I grabbed orange juice and butter. "You put my bed back together, I'll let you eat."

"I'm a vegan." As if on cue, her stomach growled.

I looked at her sideways. "Because you don't want to eat Bambi, or because you want to stay unhealthily blockbuster thin?" I'd washed every inch of that body last night. She needed twenty pounds on her, at a minimum.

She made the snorting sound again. "Whatever."

"Answer the question." I had fruit. I could probably make a smoothie or some shit. It wouldn't have protein, but it'd hold her until I could get some groceries delivered.

"All right, fine. It keeps me thin, okay? Is that what you want to hear?"

I refrained from shaking my head. "Go put my bed back together and get dressed." I threw the bacon in the oven and washed my hands.

"And what clothes am I supposed to wear? Apparently you forgot about that *minor* detail when you kidnapped me and brought me here without anything to wear, or my cell phone so I could call my people and escape."

I pulled a pan out for the eggs and spared her a glance. "Not my fault you ran out of your hotel buck ass naked."

For half a second, she looked stricken before she squared her shoulders. "If I did, there was a reason for it."

"Tell that to the press." I didn't give a shit. "Go make my bed. Food'll be ready in a few."

"What the hell am I supposed to wear?" she practically screeched.

I purposely didn't turn around again to look at her. "There's a closet full of shit, pick something."

"Of yours?" she asked incredulously.

"You see anyone else livin' here?" Fuck, she was easy to rile. "Yeah, mine. Pick something, make my bed, and get your spoiled ass back here for breakfast."

"You can't speak to me like that. *I'm your boss.*"

This time I did look at her. Half my mouth tipped up, and I winked. "Your agent's my boss, and I'll speak to you how I speak to everyone else. Directly." I wasn't in the Marines anymore, and she wasn't my CO. I'd speak any damn way I wanted. Giving her my back again, I tossed some butter in the pan and cracked eggs into a bowl.

For two seconds she didn't say shit. Then her attitude came roaring back.

"Don't cook my eggs in that butter," she snapped before huffing back to my bedroom.

Christ almighty, she needed to be fucking spanked. I set the coffee maker and whisked the eggs. Fifteen minutes later, she showed back up as I was plating the food. Her hair was up in a bun with what looked like one of my pens from my desk stabbed through the middle of it, and she was wearing one of my plain black T-shirts that hit her midthigh.

She didn't look like the polished chick on movie trailers that starred in every blockbuster movie in the past five years.

She looked like a woman who'd just been fucked. Saying she was hot was an understatement.

I put the plates on the island next to the napkins and forks I'd already set out. "Coffee or water?"

"Coffee, no cream, almond milk if you have it, and one packet of Stevia."

Fucking brat. I poured black coffee and set it in front of her before sitting down on one of the stools.

She got up on the stool next to mine, crossed her legs, then looked at the coffee with disdain. "Where's the milk?" She glanced at my junk. "And how come you don't have to put clothes on?"

"Drink it black. I already have clothes on." I saw the way she'd looked at my cock earlier. She needed to look some more. I ate two pieces of bacon at once.

She stared at me and her stomach growled.

"Eat. Tyler says you didn't eat shit yesterday before you started pounding alcohol." I gave her a warning look. "Heads up, that's not happening on my watch."

"*Heads up*," she mimicked me. "You get me fat and the studio will sue you for millions."

I pushed my stool back, went to the freezer, and grabbed the pint of vanilla ice cream that'd been there a month. Taking a spoon from the drawer, I dug out a giant scoop then dumped it in her coffee, spoon and all.

She looked at me like I'd lost my fucking mind.

"Cream and sugar." I threw the pint back in the freezer.

She stared at her coffee while I sat back down, but she didn't move.

Jesus fuck.

I stirred the damn coffee, melting the rest of the ice cream, then dumped the spoon on the counter. "There you go. Drink. Your studio can fuck off. Every man in America will thank me for putting weight on you."

Her head popped up. "You think I'm too thin?"

"Yes." Everywhere but her tits.

She blew out an exasperated breath. "No one's *ever* told me that."

"Quit Hollywood, gain thirty pounds and a perspective, then talk to me." I ate half my eggs in one forkful.

She did the half snort, half laugh thing again. "No one quits Hollywood. It quits you."

The shit about drowning last night clicked into place. "Quit if you want to quit. You don't have to drown in that bullshit." She had to have a shitload of money by now.

"I'm a star," she said sarcastically as fuck. "Who said I was drowning?" She picked up her coffee and took a tentative sip.

"You did, last night. Repeatedly." I ate the rest of my eggs.

She took another sip of her coffee and was quiet. Then after a moment, she asked, "What else did I say?"

I ate my last piece of bacon and pushed my plate away. Then I stared at her. She was fucking pretty without makeup. "It wasn't what you said." I was still fantasizing about her rubbing one out. The animal sounds I could've done without.

She swallowed, then stared straight ahead. "Okay, what did I do?"

"Straight up, you don't remember shit?" She was all over me in the shower. Washing her and not fucking her had been a new kind of torture. I wasn't a stranger to delayed gratification, but fuck.

"No," she clipped.

"Nothing?" Because in the shower, there were a few

minutes when I was convinced she knew what was up, including my dick.

She shook her head.

"What'd you take?" I wasn't gonna lecture her, but come the fuck on.

She picked her fork up and pushed her eggs around. Taking a deep breath, then letting it out slow, she put her fork down. "Short answer is I don't know. The long answer? I didn't drink that much. So the fact that I barely remember anything, including how I wound up naked next to you in bed when I've been celibate for four years, tells me I was drugged. And since Colton Bradley Payne is a walking pharmacy for every and anything, I know it was him."

I was gonna handle that costar prick of hers later, but right now I was zeroed in on the other bomb she dropped. "Four years?"

"Yes."

Damn. "On purpose?"

"Yep." She took another sip of coffee.

I picked her fork up, stabbed some eggs, and held it to her mouth. "Eat."

She looked at me. "You're bossy."

"You don't know the half of it. Open that sweet mouth before I force it open." She was lucky I was a master at restraint.

Her eyes narrowed. "You'd do that?"

"Without hesitation." And I'd enjoy every fucking second of it.

Understanding dawned. "No way."

"Yes way."

She tilted her head and her bun slipped. "You're into that kinky shit?"

31

"Take the bite, Audrina."

The second I said her name, something flashed in her eyes and her face went pale. Then the air between us took on a whole new level of intensity.

I stared at her.

A dozen ways to make her submit ran through my head, and I forced them all down. Knowing I shouldn't, knowing I was a fucking fool for opening this door, I grasped her jaw. "You remember me saying your name last night." I was only half guessing. "You liked it."

She swallowed and shifted in her seat, but she didn't say shit.

"There's two ways you can eat this breakfast." I paused, making sure she felt the pressure of my grip. "The second way, you're not gonna like," I warned.

"What's the first way?" she whispered, eyes wide.

"Open your mouth, Audrina."

She opened.

I fed her the bite, but I didn't let go of her. I forked another and held it up.

Still chewing, she stared at me, but she didn't open her mouth.

"You gonna try and play this out?" If she wanted to test my sincerity, I was all for it.

She swallowed, then shook her head as much as she could while I was holding on to her chin. "No."

I fought a smirk. "Good. Open."

She opened her mouth and took the bite, chewing and swallowing quickly.

I repeated the process, but when I held the next bite up, I didn't put it in her mouth. I told her what I was going to do.

"I'm gonna handle Payne."

Her pulse jumped, and she tried to pull back. "How?"

I held firm, but kept my tone casual. "When was the last time you ate bacon?"

"I—I don't remember."

"Pick up a piece," I ordered, putting some force into my command.

Her eyes strayed from mine for only a second. She took the piece of bacon between two fingers like it was dirt, then looked back at me, expectant.

I held her gaze. "Take a bite."

Her chest rose and fell as uncertainty clouded her expression. "What are you doing?"

"Feeding you." Testing her.

She stared at me a moment. "There's more to it than that."

No fucking shit. "I'm taking a decision off your plate." And making her submit.

"Why?"

"Because that's what I do."

She frowned. "I didn't ask you to do that."

She didn't ask me for shit, but it still didn't change the fact that she needed a good fucking. "You need an outlet."

Her eyes narrowed. "What's that supposed to mean?"

"What are you in control of in your life, besides what you put in your mouth?"

"I'm not anorexic," she said instantly.

I hadn't thought she was, but now I was fucking thinking about it. "Eat the bacon, Audrina."

"Don't use my name as a weapon," she snapped, dropping the bacon on the plate.

"I'm not." I didn't have to. She'd just told me more than

I needed to know. She was afraid of losing control when she already had none.

"Bacon isn't good for you," she added defensively before brushing her hands off on my shirt as it rested over her thighs.

My sick self thought about making her wash my shirt… while she wore it. "Neither is a decade of back-to-back films." Still holding her jaw, still holding the fucking fork, I was losing patience. "This once, I'm gonna give you a choice. Eat the eggs or the bacon."

She instantly took the bite of eggs.

I set her fork down. "What's the problem with meat?" She'd either lied earlier and really didn't want to eat Bambi, or she was afraid of the calories.

She pulled out of my grasp and dropped her gaze as she reached for her coffee. Then she lied to me. "Nothing."

I calculated my next move. "What else has Payne done to you?"

"Besides be an utter ass and forget all his lines? Nothing." Holding the mug with both hands, she took a sip of coffee. "What's your name?"

"Look at me." I didn't like not having her eyes on me when I spoke to her.

Before looking up at me, she took another sip of her coffee to show me she thought she was in control.

It didn't fucking work.

Looking vulnerable as hell, her hair falling out of its make-shift bun, the sun landing on her through the wall of windows in my condo, she was beautiful. Beautiful and young. Too damn young for me. I gave her my nickname. "Tank."

She blinked. Twice. "Your name is Tank?"

For a split second, I actually contemplated telling her

my real name. Mentally kicking my own ass, I nodded once. "Why'd you choose the eggs over the bacon?"

She stared at me a moment, then she went for her coffee. "My stomach will revolt. I cheated once, after I'd gone vegan. I ate a steak. I was sick for two days." She picked up her fork. "I don't have time to be sick."

Someone knocked on the door.

"Finish your eggs." I ate a piece of her bacon and stood.

"Who's here?" she asked nervously.

"Your agent."

The switch in her demeanor was instant. Her face dropped, her shoulders sank and she closed her eyes.

A protective instinct that went way fucking past professional hit me, and I was suddenly on high alert. I grasped her chin as a second knock came. "Tell me what I need to know, right now," I demanded.

"Nothing," she said, miserable.

"I don't have to open that door." And I wouldn't if there was a problem. Her agent sounded like an asshole when I'd talked to him last night. He'd seemed older, but that didn't mean he hadn't taken advantage of her, or fucked her over in some way. "If you don't want to talk to him right now, you don't have to."

She grasped my hand, then looked at me, really looked at me, and what I'd bet money was the real Audrina MacKenzie came out. "Thank you. That's honestly the nicest thing anyone has said to me in a really long time."

I wasn't nice. I wasn't anything close to fucking nice. The only reason I'd send the agent packing was because despite the thousand obvious reasons why it was the worst idea I'd had in the past decade, I wanted to fuck her. Not just fuck her, but dominate the hell out of her. Every deviant way I could think of. So no, I wasn't nice, or well-intentioned. I was self-serving.

"The agent," I reminded her.

She dropped her hand and her gaze and pulled out of my grasp as she stood. "It's fine. I'm used to it."

Christ. "Used to what?"

"What's about to come." She walked toward the front door.

CHAPTER FIVE

Audrina

H E GRABBED MY ARM. "YOU'RE NOT OPENING THAT DOOR."
For a split second, I thought he meant he wasn't going
to make me see my agent, Jerry. I turned to look up at him
to tell him it was fine, I'd have to face the music sooner or later,
but he set me against the wall in the hallway.

"Wait," he ordered.

Goose bumps raced across my flesh as I watched his huge,
muscular body move down the hall toward his bedroom. The
memory of his intense stare and his hand on me as he fed me
made me shiver. No man had ever looked at me like that. Not
even in a movie. I didn't even know a single actor who could've
pulled that kind of intensity off. Which was a giant warning
that I was in over my head, but I was too busy fantasizing about
the most dominant, most masculine, most infuriating man I'd
ever met, and dangerously forgetting every reason why I swore
off men.

I was trying to convince myself that just because he'd offered to send Jerry away didn't make him trustworthy when he
came back down the hallway dressed. Black polo, black cargos,
black combat boots, he was shoving a black gun in a holster on
his waist, and he looked almost hotter than when he was parading around in nothing but his underwear.

Forcing a screen-worthy smile as my traitorous stomach

fluttered, I straightened my shoulders and looked at the insignia on his shirt. "Are all the bodyguards at Luna and Associates ridiculously ripped?" My previous bodyguard, Tyler, was a few inches shorter than Tank and had about thirty pounds less of muscle, but he'd still been ripped by Hollywood standards—by any standards, actually.

Tyler had also been movie star handsome. I'd told him he should be an actor, but he'd only laughed. I couldn't picture Tank laughing. I couldn't even picture him in a full smile. That was the other huge difference between him and Tyler. Tyler had actually been nice, polite even. Tank wasn't polite. And striding toward me, he didn't even look cordial. He looked pissed off and battle ready, and I wouldn't wish him on my worst enemy.

"Give me a timeframe," he clipped, moving past me in a wave of masculine scent I wanted to bottle and sniff every night for the rest of my life.

"Timeframe for what?" There was something wrong with me, because all I could think about was that he was even hotter pissed off.

He stopped at the door as Jerry pounded on it again. "How long you want your agent here?"

"Funny." I laughed without humor.

I'd made Jerry. He'd gotten me my first break, but I'd earned every contract after that because I'd worked my ass off and done everything right. Jerry was set for life from the money he'd made off me and the subsequent A-listers who'd flocked to him hoping to get a piece of the magic he claimed he'd created for me. He was rich beyond his dreams because I'd been too stupid and too young to negotiate a better contract with him, but he acted like every breath I took was because of a privilege he'd provided.

I was over it.

I'd been over it. I'd been planning for the past year to fire Jerry after this movie. I was sure he suspected what was coming, because his asshole-ness had upped to a new level and he'd been riding me hard about signing the deal for the next movie, but I'd outright ignored him.

Looking completely unamused, Tank stood by the door with his hand on his hip. "There was nothing funny about the question."

"More like ironic," I explained. "Jerry's a class-A asshole, and he'll stay as long as it takes for him to rip me a new one for whatever I did last night, then lecture me how he made me, and try to strong-arm me into signing the next deal, which I won't do. So, however long that takes." I waved my arm toward the door. "Let Mr. My-Shit-Doesn't-Stink in and you can witness it all for yourself." Apparently being drugged with who knew what the night before caused me to lose all professionalism around my new bodyguard, because I'd just aired more dirty laundry in ten seconds than I had in ten years. "Or if you're really smart, you'll quote me and sell that to TMZ for a mint."

My new tank of a bodyguard frowned and opened the door.

In a perpetual state of pissed off and bulldog fueled by life-threatening amounts of caffeine, Jerry pushed his way through the door with barely a glance at Tank.

Aiming for me, his pointer finger already out, his suit rumpled from probably an overnight flight, Jerry let loose before both feet had crossed the threshold. "What the hell do you think you're doing, MacKen—"

The last part of my last name died on his lips as Tank grabbed his hand and twisted, putting him in an arm bar.

Jerry's face twisted with shock as he was incapacitated by my new favorite bodyguard.

"My place, my rules," Tank warned with lethal calm. "Speak to her in a civil manner or not at all."

I smiled. Grinned, actually. "Hi, Jerry."

Jerry's shock turned to rage in zero point two seconds. "Do you know who I am?" he yelled at Tank.

"You berate, harangue, or intimidate her, you're no one. You speak to her like a fucking human being, you're her agent. Make a choice." He didn't raise his voice, but Tank's message was still one hundred percent clear. Fuck with me, you'll get fucked by him.

I went all squishy inside.

Jerry's face turned beet red as he growled out an answer. "Fine."

"Tone," Tank warned.

"I said, *fine*," Jerry snapped.

The elevator across the hall from Tank's still open front door dinged and the doors slid apart.

Tank moved.

Swinging Jerry around, still holding him in an arm bar, Tank drew his gun as my publicist, her assistant, and Colton fucking Payne looked at us.

"Oh," Janette, my ever-calm, always understated publicist whispered.

Colton smirked. "Is this a bad time?" Pushing his way past Janette and her assistant, Corrine, he gave me a snide look as he walked right in to Tank's place. "Because we can come back when you're..." He dragged his gaze lecherously down my body. "Dressed."

My hatred focused on Colton, I didn't see Tank move.

A giant muscled arm shot out and the barrel of Tank's gun pressed into Colton's temple.

Colton instantly threw his hands up. "Hey, hey, hey, dude. *Relax.*"

This time, Tank's tone did change. It turned lethal as hell. "You've got one fucking chance to answer my question." Still holding Jerry's arm twisted behind his back, Tank's nostrils flared. "What did you drug her with last night?"

Janette and Corrine collectively gasped.

Colton went white as hell. "I didn't—"

"Safety's off," Tank warned. "Give me one reason not to pull the trigger, *intruder.*"

"Okay, all right!" Colton's voice pitched high as fuck. "I did it, okay? But it was harmless, just a little acid. No harm, no foul. Just a trip, man. She needed to relax. She wanted it. It's cool, it's cool."

"She *what?*" Tank growled, pressing the gun even harder against Colton's head.

Colton's arms went straight up as he locked his elbows. "Okay, okay! Maybe she didn't ask for it, I get it, I get it."

Anger surged. "You fucking piece of shit, Colton. I *never* do drugs. I told you that the first hundred times you tried to push your pharmacy of shit on me." I swung my glare to Jerry. "I told you he needs a fucking intervention before he kills someone!"

His face pinched in pain, his arm about to snap behind his back from Tank's pressure, Jerry didn't say shit.

"What a fucking joke both of you are." I was disgusted with all of them. Except the man holding the gun.

His aim never wavering, Tank lowered his voice. "You do that again, to her, to any woman, you're answering to me, Payne. Understand?"

"I'm cool, it's cool. I get it. We're good, man. All good." Colton tried to nod.

"Correction, we're not good. We never will be. Remember that." Tank glared at him for two heartbeats, then he holstered his weapon in a move so natural to him, so clearly a part of his everyday life, it made every action movie I'd ever worked on seem like the cheapest of imitations.

Releasing Jerry's arm, Tank swung his intense stare toward me. "Who stays?"

Janette, ever the optimist, raised her hand. "Um, I think I need to. And my assistant, Corrine. We need to, um...." She trailed off as she looked between Colton and me, before looking back at Tank. "With your permission, we'd like to come in and discuss strategy."

Tank didn't take his eyes off me. "It's Audrina's call."

At the mention of my full name, four pairs of eyes turned from Tank to me.

"What?" I asked sarcastically. "No one realized the great Dreena MacKenzie has an actual real name?" Un-fucking-believable. Turning toward the living room, I gave them all what they wanted. "They can stay."

The sooner I got this over with, the sooner I could call my lawyer.

I was done.

So fucking done.

CHAPTER SIX

Tank

F IT WEREN'T FOR THE AUDIENCE, I WOULD'VE BEAT THE SHIT OUT OF the little prick actor. Then I would've beaten him again. That fucker needed to pay.

Drugging women.

I was fucking enraged, and that was a goddamn bad sign.

Looking ten years older than when he'd pushed through my front door, the agent followed Audrina into the living room. The pussy actor rushed to keep up with the agent like it'd protect him from me.

The publicist, who I'd called last night to tell her what the fuck was up, looked at me with reservation. "Thank you again for calling me and giving me a heads-up. It's much easier to do my job when I can get ahead of these things."

I tipped my chin in response but every one of them could fuck off for all I cared. My job was to protect the actress. If that meant from her own people, so be it. I saw the look on her face when I mentioned her agent. And now that all these fucks were here, I could only imagine the bullshit they were gonna unleash so they could spin the drugging into some kind of cash flow for themselves.

Fucking disgusting.

I slammed my front door shut, then followed the publicist and her mouse of an assistant into my living room. The agent was standing over Audrina as she sat cross-legged in the corner of my couch, and the fucking prick junkie was staring out at my view. Normally I would never intrude. My job was to be invisible, but seeing Audrina sit there as her agent tried to intimidate her, I made a decision.

Glaring at the older prick, I moved to the end of the couch where Audrina sat and crossed my arms before tipping my chin at the chair behind the agent. "Have a seat."

Without comment, but giving me the eye right back, he sat. "Dreena," he stated, inhaling like he needed patience. "You have publicity interviews lined up every day, this could not have come at a worse time," he lectured. "The studio is all over me, and if I thought for one second that you were going to—"

"Do I need to repeat myself?" I warned. "She didn't do shit."

His nostrils flared, but he kept his eyes on Audrina. "Janette is going to pull you out of this mess, but you need to do exactly what she says."

As if on cue, the publicist sat down on the couch and took papers out of her briefcase. "Okay, here's the plan. You and Colton are a couple. You had an argu—"

"NO." Audrina shot to her feet. "No way in *hell* am I pretending to be with that asshole!" She threw Payne a scathing look before glaring back at her publicist. "Everyone knows he fucks anyone and everyone, not to mention he's an addict!"

"Sit down," the agent clipped.

The publicist held her hand up. "I get it, I do, but this will help both of you and the studio," she said quickly, before rattling off the rest of it. "Colton's agreed to rehab after the movie releases and you'll escort him. In turn, he'll publicly admit to giving you something... *recreational* that you weren't prepared for, then you hold hands and announce your support for each other and make nice-nice. He walks into rehab, you shed a few tears and a week later everyone will forget about it and hopefully the studio won't sue."

Jesus fucking Christ.

"How about *I* call my lawyer? *I* press charges. *I* sue his ass. And *he* goes to jail?" Audrina spit out. "He *drugged* me!"

The agent dropped his head to his hands. The publicist drew her lips into her mouth. The assistant stared at her shoes, and the fucking junkie sighed like he was bored.

I'd never thought about being proud of a woman before, but in that moment, not only did I vote for Audrina's plan, I was proud as fuck that she'd stood up for herself.

The agent looked up at her, and the second I saw his expression, my muscles tightened.

"Did you get a blood test?" the fuck asked.

Audrina blinked. "What?"

"Blood test," the agent repeated. "Did you get one? Can you prove he was the one who drugged you? Can you prove anyone drugged you? How do we know you didn't take something yourself and you're just blaming him?"

You could hear a motherfucking pin drop.

Itching to slam my fist into his face, instinct yelling at me to get her away from these assholes, I was about to open my mouth and kick them all out, when the gorgeous blonde I'd slept next to last night turned to me.

Calm and totally fucking collected, she raised an eyebrow. "Can you please take me to the hospital?"

I didn't fucking delay. I threw my arm around her shoulders and led her to the door.

"Wait one goddamn second!" the agent bellowed.

"*Dreena*," the publicist frantically called.

My keys and wallet already in my pocket, I opened my front door.

"*MacKenzie*," the agent snapped in a furious growl.

"Let her go," the junkie scoffed. "She's bluffing."

I rushed her out my door and down the hall, past the elevator. I shoved the door to the stairwell open then scooped her up.

Her arms wrapped around my neck, and she looked behind us. "They're going to follow us."

"Let them." I carried her down the first flight, skipping the last two steps.

Her arms tightened around my neck. "You left them alone in your condo."

"What are they gonna do? Steal my bacon and eggs?" I went down another flight.

She glanced at the stairs below us then looked back behind us. "Guns, ammo, money, I don't know."

"I keep that shit locked in a safe they'll never find." I took us down another flight. Two more and I could cut to the other end of the building.

"I was half kidding."

"I wasn't."

She tightened her hold on me. "Why the stairs?"

"Elevator would've taken too long." I fucking liked her holding on to me.

"I can walk."

"I'm faster and you have no shoes." Another flight.

"They'll just take the elevator and be waiting for us in the lobby."

"We're not going to the lobby." I hit the lower level that had the service elevator that went directly to the garage. Exiting the stairwell, I carried her across the length of the building, then set her down in front of a set of double doors as I pulled my keys out.

"What are you doing?" She looked nervously behind us.

"Service elevator." I opened the door, let her through, then closed the door behind us and hit the call button. Pocketing my keys, I pulled my cell out and dialed Luna.

He answered on the first ring. "What's up?"

"I need Audrina MacKenzie's personal items removed from her hotel, and I need a call ahead for a VIP at Memorial."

"*Mierda*," Luna swore in Spanish. "She okay?"

"Precautionary," I clipped, not wanting to say more until we were in a secure location.

"Copy that. Hold on." He held the phone away and called to someone, then came back on the line. "Tyler's on his way to her hotel now. Do you need to get her to the hospital ASAP or do you want her shit first?"

"Personal items first." She needed to put some clothes on. "I'm coming in. Tell Tyler to meet us in the garage." I wasn't bringing her up the elevators or into Luna and Associates in only my T-shirt where a minimum of ten ex-Marines would be working.

"Copy that," Luna confirmed. "Give Tyler twenty. I'll call ahead to Memorial once you get here."

"Thanks. I've got another issue." I glanced at her, but she wasn't looking at me. "Do we still have access to the security cameras at Club Frenzy?"

"Last I checked, why?"

"I need the feeds pulled from last night. Colton Payne was with Audrina. He admitted to drugging her. I want the footage if it exists."

47

"Jesucristo," Luna muttered. "I'm pulling them up now. I'll let you know what I find. Anything else?"

"I need the four people in my condo gone and my access code to the lobby changed." I never should've given the agent prick my access code last night, but he wasn't sure when he'd get in and I hadn't been willing to risk leaving her alone to let him in. I could've changed the code myself, but I had my fucking hands full. Literally.

"I'll send Sawyer to your place and text you the new code once I program it. I'll make a copy of any footage I find from Frenzy and text it. For the record, I hope she goes after the asshole."

"Ditto. Thanks."

"De nada. Call if you need anything else."

"Copy that." I hung up and the elevator arrived.

We stepped inside, and I hit the garage level button.

She looked up at me. "So, you could've gotten my clothes all along."

I didn't answer. I stared straight ahead, because she was right. I could have, but I didn't. And after seeing how she was treated by those people, I was man enough to admit I was a fucking tool for it.

CHAPTER SEVEN

Audrina

H E SILENTLY STARED AT THE ELEVATOR DISPLAY FLASHING THE FLOORS as we descended.

"Not saying anything?"

He didn't respond.

That's what I thought. Jerk.

I was stupid enough to think back in his place he'd felt something for me past the bodyguard slash client thing when he'd stood up for me with Jerry. I hadn't even cared if it was purely lust, or an itch that needed scratching, I was feeling the same thing. I was *so* feeling it. But now that I knew he could've gotten my clothes last night and purposely hadn't? Then he'd *handcuffed* me? He was no better than the rest of them.

He was a stupid bodyguard, for God's sake. Fuck him and his muscles and his bullshit about pretending to care if I had control over anything in my life or not. Fuck his little food game and his ridiculous statement about putting weight on and everyone would be happy. Fuck all of his bullshit.

Fuck him period.

The elevator doors opened, and quicker than I could protest, he scooped me up.

"Hey!" I snapped. "I can walk."

"Not in bare feet across the garage you can't."

I hated him now. I hated how he smelled like soap and

spice and musk. I hated how he picked me up like it was nothing, and I hated the way he'd looked at me upstairs. I hated that
especially, because I was feeling shit I shouldn't, and I'd been
stupid enough to think he was into me.

I wasn't going to make that mistake again.

I was going to focus on my plan, not the stupid bodyguard
carrying me to an SUV that looked exactly like the one the previous bodyguard had driven.

Dumping me in the front passenger seat without ceremo-
ny, the bodyguard started to close the door, but I held my hand
out. "I need your phone, and I need two minutes of privacy."

A muscle ticked in his jaw, but he pulled his phone out of
his pocket and handed it over.

I took it and reached for the door handle, half expecting
him to stop me, but he didn't.

His expression somewhere between pissed off and professional disinterest, he rounded the front of the vehicle and stood
in front of the driver's door with his back to me and his hands
clasped in front. His working bodyguard stance was something
I'd been seeing since my first big movie break, reminding me the
tank of a man standing there was nothing but a paid employee.

I punched in the code he'd given me earlier, then dialed a
number I knew by heart.

On the fourth ring, my lawyer picked up. "Stanislas."

"Peter, it's me, Dreena."

Peter exhaled. "I saw the footage. Are you okay?"

"I'm fine, but that's why I'm calling. I need to up my
timeline."

"First, as your lawyer, I need to ask if you are of sound
mind to make this decision right now."

I refrained from telling him to go fuck himself. "I said I'm fine, but just so you know, I was drugged last night. Colton Payne admitted to it in front of witnesses. I'm on my way to the hospital to get some tests done, so I have proof. The security company I have watching me here is working on getting footage from the club to back up my story."

"What security company?" he asked, suddenly all business.

"Luna and Associates."

"Who hired them?"

"Jerry, I'm sure." He hired all my security. He did everything, actually.

Peter quietly cursed. "Okay, first, you need to get them on your personal payroll immediately. I don't want them under Jerry's influence. Second, I need a contact at Luna and Associates. I'll follow up with them. From here on out, I'll take the lead on this. List me as the contact at the hospital and make sure a copy of everything gets forwarded to me. You know the drill, don't say anything to anyone, the press least of all."

"I'm not going to say anything." I may have been walking away from my career, but I wasn't stupid.

"Good. Who are you with right now?"

"Just me."

He paused. "You're alone?"

"No." But I might as well be. I didn't have friends. I didn't even have anyone in my life that wasn't in the business. "The bodyguard assigned to me is waiting outside the car while I talk to you."

"What happened to your phone?"

"I should have it back shortly, so you'll be able to contact me on that in a few." If the bodyguard came through. "While I head to the hospital, I need you to pull the trigger on the plan and send the notifications. Let me know once it's done, and we'll take the next step." Despite everything that was about to happen, for the first time in more years than I could remember, and despite being in a borrowed T-shirt in a stranger's vehicle in a city where I didn't know anyone, I could breathe. Actually fucking breathe.

"Dreena." Peter switched back to fatherly mode and drew my stage name out.

"Audrina," I corrected, feeling more like myself than ever before.

"Audrina," he repeated before pausing. "I know we've discussed this at length for a year, but I have to ask. Are you sure this is what you want to do? This could prevent you from ever working in this industry again."

This was why I'd hired a New York attorney, and not one from LA. Besides the fact all the LA attorneys knew all the managers, agents and publicists, they also knew all the other gossiping actors in the business. But Peter wasn't Hollywood. He didn't say I would never work in Hollywood again like the name itself was the Holy Grail. He said *industry*, because that's exactly what it was. An industry. *One* industry.

Peter hadn't even tried to dissuade me from my plan when I first brought it up. Instead, he'd spent countless hours going over every current contract I had, the ramifications of what could happen, the countersuits I might get thrown at me, the way he would handle each one, and all the contingencies he could think of.

After he'd exhausted all the possibilities without once mentioning who'd I'd piss off, or what people would say, or how it would look, he meticulously went over the financials. He told me how to live so I'd be set for life, even if we had to fight counter lawsuits for a decade and lost millions.

This was why he was worth his weight in gold.

"Peter," I said with more confidence than I'd ever felt, "I'm sure."

"Okay, then we're a go." I could hear the smile in his voice. He lived to lawyer, like I used to live to act.

"We're a go," I confirmed.

"One last detail before you hang up. Do you trust the current bodyguard, or do you need new security?"

I knew what he was asking. Was Tank's alliance with Jerry or me? "You know I don't trust anyone except you."

He let out a small laugh. "Appreciated. But can we trust this current security company, or should I find you a new one?"

I replayed Tank's arm bar on Jerry and drawing his weapon on Colton. While I didn't trust him, I knew he didn't like either of those jerks, and that worked for me.

"We can trust Tank."

"Tank?" Peter asked skeptically. "That name isn't giving me a lot of confidence. Put him on the phone."

"Yeah, well, if you saw him, you'd understand the nickname."

Peter chuckled, and it was somehow reassuring. With everything that was about to go down, I wanted someone who was sane enough to laugh at the absurd, and Peter Stanislas was as solid as they came in that department.

"Okay, get him in the car and put the phone on speaker. I want you to be a part of this conversation."

"Got it. Hold on." I put the phone on speaker and leaned over and knocked on the window.

Tank turned and looked at me.

I made a come here gesture, and without hesitation, he got behind the wheel, his eyes on the phone still in my hand.

When he closed his door, I introduced him to Peter. "Tank, this is Peter Stanislas, my attorney. Peter, this is…" I looked at Tank, but he didn't offer his real name. "This is Tank."

"Mr. Tank," Peter began.

"Gunther," Tank corrected.

"Thank you. Mr. Gunther, as my client has relayed to me, she was drugged last night and you are on your way to the hospital to facilitate some tests to confirm her well-being and any evidence of any illegal substances she may have unknowingly ingested last night."

"That's correct," Tank answered.

"Mr. Gunther, in light of recent events and the highly sensitive nature of this issue, I'd like to terminate your contract with her agent and employ you on behalf of my client, Audrina MacKenzie. If that is amenable to you, I will discuss terms with your supervisor."

Tank didn't hesitate. "Agreed. André Luna is the principal and owner of Luna and Associates." He rattled off a number. "That's his direct line. You can discuss contract terms with him."

"Excellent, thank you. Additionally, I would like Ms. MacKenzie removed from the hotel she was staying at and relocated to a more secure venue while she is in Miami. I will make a few phone calls and get back to you within the hour for alternate housing for her."

"No need. We have corporate apartments and several safe houses we can move her to, or she can continue to stay in my condo, where she was last night. It's a secure location, and the access codes have been changed so neither her agent or publicist can gain entry."

Peter paused for a half a second at hearing where I'd been

last night. "Yes, well, the decision of where she stays is ultimately up to Ms. MacKenzie. As long as she is safe and the paparazzi are not able to gain access, then I will defer the decision to her."

"Understood," Tank acknowledged, scanning the garage. "Anything else?"

"Not for now. Do you need me to call ahead to the hospital to secure a private admittance?"

Tank turned his intense stare on me. "Already handled."

"Thank you. If anything else comes up, this is my personal cell phone. I can be reached at any time. Please, do not hesitate to call should you need anything."

"Copy that," Tank answered crisply, not taking his eyes off me.

"Excellent. Ms. MacKenzie, I'll be in touch."

"Thank you, Peter." I hung up on my lawyer, and my old life.

CHAPTER EIGHT

Tank

S HE HUNG UP AND HANDED MY PHONE BACK TO ME WITH A muttered, "Thanks."

Tipping my chin once, I forced myself to look away from her and the change in her body language as I started the Escalade and checked the rearview mirrors. The last thing I wanted to deal with right now was the fucking paparazzi.

I backed out of the parking space.

She crossed her arms. "You're not saying anything."

I spun the SUV around and headed up the exit ramp. "What did you want me to say?" The anger and determination in her expression before the call to her lawyer had morphed into something I couldn't decipher.

"You're not working for Jerry anymore."

I never worked for that prick. I worked for Luna first, myself second. Everything after that was fucking relative. "Your point?" I checked the street for any asshole with a camera before I pulled out.

"Do you have a problem working for me?"

Besides the fact she was up to something and I'd bet my fucking Harley it was trouble? "Said I didn't."

She stared straight ahead for a moment. "You're attracted to me."

Bold as fuck, I'd give her that. "What gave you that

impression?" I asked only to fuck with her.

Dropping her guarded expression, she turned halfway in her seat. "Oh, come on. Mr. Kinky Dominant Handcuff, now you're going to pretend to be professional?"

I turned down the street the Luna and Associates offices were on. "Never claimed I was professional." I glanced at her. "But I'm good at what I do." There was a difference.

She did the half snort, half smirk thing. "He says humbly."

I drove into the underground parking at Luna and Associates and pulled into a spot. Keeping the engine running, I turned to her and gave her the fucking truth of the matter. "There's a reason it's called close protection. If I was your detail last night, you wouldn't be in this situation. Castigate my methods all you want, but the simple truth is you wouldn't have been out of my sight for two fucking seconds." Not at the club and not in public anywhere.

"What, you would've danced with me at the club?" she asked, incredulous.

I stared at her. Hard. "You wouldn't have needed to go to the club."

"What's that supposed to mean?" Her tone was all attitude, but she'd leaned back in her seat as she asked the question, putting more distance between us.

"Exactly what I said." Catching movement out of the corner of my eye, I glanced in the rearview mirror as Tyler pulled into the garage behind us. "Wait here." I got out of the SUV and walked to the back.

Tyler pulled up behind us, got out and grinned. "How's the zoo impersonator?"

I wanted to forget those fucking animal sounds last night. "You got everything?"

"Yeah, all four suitcases and her giant purse." He walked to the back of his SUV. "Three of the suitcases weren't even opened."

I tipped my chin toward my SUV and gave him fair warning before opening the back. "She's inside."

"Yeah, figured. She seen the videos yet?"

"Not that I know of." I opened the lift gate and we transferred her shit from his SUV to mine.

Audrina turned to watch us, but she didn't say anything.

"Take care, Ms. MacKenzie." Tyler smiled his pretty boy smile at her after loading her last suitcase. "Hope you enjoy the rest of your stay in Miami."

To my utter shock, she apologized to him. "I'm sorry for the trouble I caused you last night, Tyler."

"All in a day's work, ma'am." Tyler smiled again. "No worries."

Day's work, my ass. Her little stunt had plastered his face all over the internet, which was bad news for a bodyguard. I shut the lift gate, cutting off their little reunion.

Tyler eyed me, then chuckled. "In a hurry?"

I refrained from telling him to fuck off. "Taking her to Memorial."

He instantly sobered. "No shit? She sick? From last night?"

"Tox screen. She was drugged by her prick of a costar at the club." I leveled him with a look. "You see anything?"

"*Shit.*" Frowning, his hands went to his hips. "I got her drinks last night. Payne was around, yeah, but he had his own security. She danced with him, but I didn't see him give her a drink. I assumed she took something on her own."

"She didn't. He admitted to it."

"Damn it." He looked stricken.

"I need to get her to Memorial. Let Luna know we're on our way there."

"Copy that." He rubbed a hand over his head. "Fuck, I dropped the ball."

"Catch you later." I didn't say shit one way or another. We'd all had wild-card clients. It could've happened to any of us, but the fucking truth was, if you were smart, you discouraged a client from going clubbing. It was one of the hardest venues to guard. The second you walked through that door, nothing was in your control, the client included.

I got behind the wheel and waited for Tyler to pull away before I started to back out.

"I need to change before walking into the hospital."

Shit. My head space taken up with Payne's bullshit and Tyler's negligence, I'd fucking forgotten she was still in my T-shirt.

I pulled back in to the parking spot, now pissed I had to take her into the building, and her current state of undress would be on the security cameras. Which was a joke, considering that by now every guy at L and A had probably seen the footage of her naked ass while Tyler rowed his way across South Beach.

"You can change upstairs." I pulled my phone out to text Luna to see which of the apartments we kept for clients were vacant.

She glanced toward the elevators. "Not that I'm complaining, but walking into your company's office in a T-shirt with a bunch of muscled bodyguards isn't on my short list." She looked to the back of the SUV. "I'll get dressed in here if you could just grab me some clothes."

I shouldn't have liked the fact that she didn't want to parade her ass past the other men. "There're apartments upstairs.

You won't be walking through the office."

"Here's fine. I just want to be dressed."

Hollywood's hottest actress, her hair a mess, no makeup, and she wanted to throw clothes on in a company SUV. Not gonna lie, she threw me. "You don't want to do your hair or makeup?" She'd had that shit caked on last night.

"I'm going to the hospital, Mr. Gunther. Not the red carpet."

Not digging her using my last name, I opened my door. "What do you want?"

"Just grab me something," she snapped, out of patience.

My first thought was I wanted to spank the fuck out of her for barking an order at me. My second thought, a distant fucking second, was that I shouldn't give a shit that she was capable of being low maintenance, or that I was relieved I wasn't parading her into L and A.

Ignoring the shit in my head, I opened the back. Three suitcases looked new and one looked well-used. I grabbed the latter and opened it. It was full of movie scripts, and a couple pairs of shoes. I reached for one of the newer-looking suitcases and opened it. All clothes, all new, all with the tags still on, underwear included.

Mentally shaking my head, I grabbed jeans and one of the only shirts with long sleeves, because hospitals were cold as fuck. Picking out underwear I'd love to rip off her, I grabbed shoes and a hairbrush from the first suitcase, then snatched her purse and went back to the driver's seat.

"Here." I handed her the pile.

"Thanks," she muttered, dumping her purse and shoes at her feet and ripping the tags off the clothes without even looking at what I gave her.

She slid the underwear up her legs, but when she got to her hips, I looked out my window. As much as I wanted to watch her get dressed, I wasn't a total fucking prick.

"You've already seen me naked. You're turning your head now?"

I looked back at her. She had the bra and jeans on and was pulling the shirt over her head. "I also showered with you." Jesus, she needed some fucking weight on her. "You forget that too?"

She froze for half a second, then took the pen out of her makeshift bun. Blonde hair fell halfway down her back. "Apparently you're not that memorable."

I watched the slight shake in her hand as she picked up the brush and dragged it through her hair. "You enjoy lying?"

She covered her surprise with a smirk. "I'm an actor." She tossed the brush in the center console. "Take me to the hospital."

My cell vibrated with a text.

Luna: *Hospital's expecting you. Spoke with her lawyer, new contract. You're taking her to Neil Christensen's house in Golden Beach after. Double gated entrance, no press access. You'll stay there until we hear back from the lawyer. He said expect a week. Sending your go bag and groceries now. Anything else?*

I fired off a response.

Me: *She's vegan.*

Luna: *Copy that. Supplies on the way. Sending separate text with address and gate codes.*

A second text from him came in with the address, and I pocketed my phone.

"Ready?" she asked sarcastically.

CHAPTER NINE

Audrina

I HATED HOSPITALS.

But being able to walk into one and not be wheeled in was reassuring, even it if was through the delivery entrance and I was being escorted by a surly bodyguard and two hospital security guards.

A silent ride up in a freight elevator and we came out on a floor that looked mostly administrative. The two security guards led us to an office at the end of the hall then left us to wait. I sat in a chair across from a large desk while Tank slash Gunther stood by the window scanning the parking lot.

"Gunther, huh?" I didn't know if it was his first or last name.

He didn't comment. He didn't even look at me.

"Sounds German."

His hazel-eyed intense stare swung toward me. "It is."

I would be lying if I said my stomach didn't flip every time he looked at me. "That's your first name?"

"No." He studied me for a moment. "Falcon."

I blinked.

Falcon. Falcon Gunther.

I couldn't even wrap my head around that. Of all the names I could've imagined, the man in front of me being named after a bird would've never crossed my mind. It didn't fit. Yet,

I couldn't imagine him being called anything else. "Falcon," I repeated, just to feel the two syllables fill my mouth.

His unwavering stare pulled me in and used me up, daring me to say more. He spoke more without saying words than anyone I'd ever met. I didn't know if that scared me or intrigued me.

"There's a story behind that." There had to be. "Falcons are strong, they're birds of prey." He was named Falcon for a reason.

For a long moment, he said nothing. His arms crossed, his biceps stretching his shirt, he stood with his legs slightly apart like he was ready to attack. But then, with his voice low and quiet like I'd never heard, he began to speak.

"My mother was Seminole. On the way home from the hospital after I was born, she saw a falcon. She took it as a sign."

Three sentences and my Midwest upbringing felt insignificant. "That makes you Seminole." I knew next to nothing about Native Americans, but I had heard of the casinos the Seminoles owned in Florida. Colton, that asshole, had wanted to go gambling while we were here.

"Half," Tank corrected.

I focused on the other part of what he'd said. "I'm sorry you lost your mother."

He held my gaze. "It was years ago."

"And your father?"

"Alive and kicking."

"I take it Gunther comes from him?" I didn't know why I was grilling him, but the more I looked at him, his dark hair, his strong features, his hazel eyes, the more I foolishly wanted to know.

He tipped his chin once in confirmation. "He's German."

He looked over my head. "Company."

I turned in my chair as a very young, very attractive doctor walked in through the glass-paneled office door with his hand out.

"Ms. MacKenzie." He smiled like a fan. "I'm Dr. Erickson. I'm head of administration here at Memorial Hospital. It's a pleasure to meet you." His expression turned serious. "Although I am sorry about the circumstances." He leaned against the desk in front of me. "I understand you're requesting a toxicology screen?"

The manufactured concern, the way his eyes strayed to my chest, the too-close proximity to me—I instantly disliked him.

Either sensing my discomfort or just exerting his alpha dog, Tank spoke up. "Details were already provided of what we need. You have the contact information on where to send the results. She'll sign the consent forms, then a female will do the blood draw."

The doctor turned to look at Tank for the first time. "Yes, of course. And you are?"

"Her security detail."

The doctor looked back to me. "I do need to ask you a few questions, Ms. MacKenzie. Would you like some privacy?"

Not with him. "Mr. Gunther will stay with me."

"Yes, of course." The doctor stood and moved behind the desk to the computer. "I just need to verify some information." He typed a few strokes then asked me my date of birth, social security number, and address. Then he started in on the personal questions. After telling him I wasn't on any medication, I wasn't pregnant, I hadn't had unprotected sex since my last cycle, and about a hundred other intrusive questions about how I was feeling, he stood up and came out from behind the desk.

"Ms. MacKenzie, I must warn you about the limitations of a toxicology screen. If you were given LSD, the drug can pass fairly quickly." He held his hand up as I started to protest. "But it's my understanding we are still within a thirty-hour window, so if the drug is present, we should be able to get results."

Fucking great. "Terrific," I replied dryly.

The doctor gave me a fake concerned look. "Any other questions?"

"No." I just wanted this over with.

"All right, that should do it." He glanced at Tank. "I'll send in a nurse to do the draw and collect a sample. Then Ms. MacKenzie can be on her way."

Tank nodded once.

The doctor looked back at me and smiled. "I enjoy your films, Ms. MacKenzie. I do hope you feel better soon." He held his hand out.

I shook it and muttered, "Thanks."

With a nod toward Tank, he walked out.

I waited till the door closed after him. "Fucking creep."

Tank glared at the closed door, but he didn't say anything.

I exhaled. "You do this often? Take clients to the hospital?"

"When needed," he clipped, still standing exactly how he was when we first entered the office.

His stance, his short answers, his change in demeanor from breakfast—I got it. He was in protection mode, but I didn't like it. I was stupid enough to want back the man I'd woken up next to. I was so desperate for non-fame attention and friendship that I was replaying everything he'd said and done this morning and analyzing it, wondering if I'd wrongly tried and convicted him of being an asshole.

Worse, a single memory from last night of his voice saying

my name kept circling through my head on repeat. An hour ago, an image of him washing my hair had been added into the mix, and I was unraveling.

Which was exactly why I needed Peter to execute my plan. Immediately.

I glanced at the man named after a predator, and I needed a distraction, both from him and the thought of a needle going into my arm. Reaching for my purse, I dug for my cell. I'd been ignoring the fact that I'd run naked on the beach, but I had to face it eventually. From the few details Tank had told me, I knew I'd have hundreds, if not thousands of texts, voice mails, and social media message alerts.

My stomach constricting, my heart racing, I pulled my phone out.

A large hand covered mine. "Leave it."

His deep voice, quieter than usual, his proximity, not hearing him approach, all of it made my heart start to pound even faster. "I…" I suddenly wanted to cry. "I can't."

With surprising gentleness, he took my phone from me. "It'll wait."

The office door opened and an older nurse came in with a small mobile cart full of shit I didn't want to think about.

Cheerful and nice, she smiled at me. "Ms. MacKenzie, I'm just going to do a quick blood draw and collect a urine sample after you sign these forms." She handed me a clipboard and a pen.

I signed in the highlighted areas, then set the clipboard on her cart.

The nurse pulled out a blood pressure cuff and deftly shoved my sleeve up before taking my blood pressure. Then she put a thing on the end of my finger and laid stuff out on her cart. "Your blood pressure's a little high today, dear."

Breathing through my nose and out through my mouth, I tried not to look at the shit on the cart or think about the indignity of having to piss in a cup. "I'm not a fan of needles."

"Don't worry, I'll be quick." The nurse tied a tight thing around my upper arm then looked up with motherly concern. "Are you a fainter?"

A large hand closed over my shoulder. "She'll be fine."

"It won't take long at all." The nurse smiled.

Tank squeezed my shoulder. "Close your eyes."

Inhaling deep, trying to control my rapid breathing, I did as he said, and coldness touched my arm.

My eyes popped opened, I saw the needle, and I panicked. "*Wait.*"

Tank's hand moved from my shoulder to the back of my neck. As if he knew me, as if he knew my fears, he issued an order. "Eyes closed. You're okay."

"Just a quick pinch," the nurse warned.

She shoved the needle into my arm.

The pain hit and irrational fear raced through my veins. Suddenly, I was so light-headed, my ears started ringing. "Tank," I called, feeling like I was sinking.

"Hold her arm," Tank barked at the nurse.

Two hands grasped my arm, and a second later, I was airborne.

I gulped for air and opened my eyes, immediately seeing the needle in my arm again. "Oh God." My head spun.

Tank had his arms under me in a nanosecond, and he was cradling me to his chest, as he sat back down in the chair.

My vision tunneled.

"Lean her back, bring her legs up," the nurse calmly

instructed, her voice sounding like it was a million miles away.

My legs rose up as my head was gently lowered.

"Deep breath," Tank ordered, his face right above mine, his scent everywhere.

The hands on my arm moved. "Hold her still," the nurse instructed.

One of Tank's huge hands held the back of my head, while his other arm remained under my knees, holding my legs up as his hand wrapped around my thigh. "Breathe," he quietly commanded. "Almost done."

My lungs listened to him and I took a breath, then another.

"Almost," the nurse murmured.

"Keep breathing." Tank's legs under my back shifted slightly.

I took another breath and the ringing in my ears started to fade, but acute embarrassment seeped in. My voice weak, I pushed words out. "I'm okay. I can get up."

"No." Tank's hand tightened on my thigh. "Deep breath, right now."

I'd barely inhaled when I felt the pressure leave my arm and the nurse took the needle out.

"There you go, all done." The nurse pressed down hard on my arm before putting a Band-Aid on and folding my arm up. "Keep a little pressure on it for a minute." She patted my knee. "When you're ready, you can use the restroom in the hall for a urine sample." She handed me a small plastic cup with a lid.

Dying of embarrassment for first almost fainting and now holding a damn piss cup as Tank held me, I moved to get off his lap.

He pulled me closer. "Hey."

"I'm good."

"Look at me," he demanded.

I glanced up, and his beautifully stern expression made me want to simultaneously crawl in a hole and never get up. "I'm good."

He studied me a moment, then slow, as if his movements were a measure of my stability, he lowered the arm holding my legs, brought my head up, then helped me to stand. When I didn't waver or sway, he dropped his hands, but not his gaze.

My cheeks flaming under his scrutiny, embarrassment drowning me, I needed to get out of the office. "Be right back," I muttered, rushing out.

My head swimming, my arm smarting, I found the bathroom and did what I needed to do. A few minutes later, with a cup of my own damn pee, hating Colton even more, I went back in the office.

The nurse discreetly took the cup and tucked it onto her cart. "You're all set, dear." She glanced at Tank. "Get her some juice or something to eat, it'll help with any light-headedness."

Tank nodded to acknowledge her without taking his eyes off me.

The nurse pushed her cart toward the door. "When you're ready to leave, the security guards will escort you out the way you came in."

We both said thanks, and the nurse left. Then I made the mistake of glancing at the wall of muscle in front of me.

His stern expression made me instantly look away. "Thanks for...." I drifted off, gesturing toward the chair.

He grasped my chin and brought my face back to his. "You should've warned me about the needle issue, Audrina."

Every time I heard him say my name, something inside me shifted and a yearning for a closeness I'd never experienced grew. And not just closeness. Not just this feeling right now of gratitude that he'd held me and taken care of me. I wanted more. So much more.

I had a career most actors never dreamed of. I had money, fame, and brand recognition. I had movie producers lining up to work with me. I had famous men wanting to spend time with me. I had everything.

But I didn't want any of it.

I wanted the touch of a man who cared.

A smile meant only for me.

A summer evening under the stars with no cameras.

A month, a week, hell, a day without obligation.

I wanted country roads and Sunday drives.

I wanted holding hands and stolen kisses.

I wanted everything simple.

But the man who'd just held me, the man who'd been named by a mother who believed in the beauty of a predator, he wasn't simple. I stared at his full lips, his strong jaw, his stern expression—if a man born to be a warrior could be beautiful, he was beautiful.

But he wasn't simple.

Complex and dominant and commanding, and so intriguing he scared me more than what I'd asked my lawyer to do, Falcon Gunther was everything I needed to stay away from.

Before I did something stupid, like grasp on to his strong neck and beg him to make me feel not so desperate, I stepped back. "I'm sorry—" I didn't get the rest of the sentence out as I promptly ran into the arm of the chair and stumbled.

Large hands caught my arms, and I sucked in a sharp breath as the heat of his skin sank through the thin material of my blouse. Awareness shot through my body as one of his hands moved to my nape.

Oh God. "I-I'm good," I stuttered, trying not to breathe in the heady scent of his soap and musk.

His hand on my neck holding firm, his gaze burning through me, he watched me for two heartbeats, but he didn't let go.

The urge to reach for him overwhelming, I forced myself to look away.

Quick, precise, he gripped a handful of my hair. Angling my head, my body, he stepped into me as he tilted my head back.

Oh God, oh God, oh God. I wanted him to kiss me. *Please kiss me.*

Towering over me, a storm darkening his green-brown eyes, his voice dropped to a low warning. "Do not look at me like that."

As involuntarily as the breaths that filled my lungs, my tongue licked my bottom lip. "Like what?"

CHAPTER TEN

Tank

GOD FUCKING DAMN IT.

She knew exactly how the fuck she was looking at me.

"Like I'm your only anchor." It wasn't a statement, it was a warning. This woman wanted more than my mouth on her. Which wasn't something I did. Ever. I didn't kiss women. I bent them to my will, then I fucked them and left. No kissing. No attachments.

A shitstorm of emotions raced across her face before something close to calm settled in. I was stupid enough to presume her next words would be every bit the actress she was.

"Right now, you are my only anchor." Guileless, and with a trust I didn't fucking want, she laid her shit out there.

And because my dick had been hard since the damn shower last night, I bit out questions I had no business asking. "Boyfriend? Family? Support system?"

"No, I don't have anyone." No hesitation, she rattled off her response without blinking.

Fuck. *Fuck.* "Why?"

"Why what?"

"Why no support system?" I'd been around too long not to see the warning signs. Famous actress or not, a lonely chick was a lonely chick. Add a uniform, whether it was the service or Luna's damn logo polos, and you became a target. I wasn't above using a uniform to score, but a chick who clung to you? Not my scene and not fucking happening.

Her chest rose with an inhale. "Jerry and Janette were it." Her eyes a clearer shade of blue this morning without her pupils dilated as fuck, she stared at me for a moment. Then she dropped a bomb. "I just fired them."

Fuck.

I wasn't surprised she'd fired her asshole agent. Expecting the unexpected was how you survived. Shit rarely surprised me after Afghanistan and Iraq. Only a fucking fool would let himself get taken off guard after spending any time downrange. I figured something was up when she'd called her lawyer then he'd had her security contract switched to her control. But *fuck.* The ramification of Hollywood's it girl firing the team that managed her career while I was her security detail? That fucking threw me.

"You got someone else in place?" I had no business asking. My job was singular. Protect her from the paparazzi. I got paid whether she threw her life away or not. I didn't need to get involved.

She shook her head. "No."

Not involved. *Christ.* I had her hair in my fist, she was looking up at me with misplaced trust, and my dick was itching to get in her mouth and have those full lips wrap around it. Not to mention I was contemplating kissing the fuck out of her just to see what she tasted like. This wasn't a dangerous combination, it was a fucking catastrophe. *She* was a catastrophe.

A naturally submissive, sexy-as-fuck catastrophe.

She licked her bottom lip again.

Jesus, I needed to remember my fucking job.

I changed the subject. "Tunnel vision, ringing in your ears, light-headed, anything?"

She'd already almost passed out on me once, which hadn't made me fucking happy. In fact, it'd done the opposite. I was pissed as hell she hadn't told me about her fear of needles, or blood or whatever the issue was, but she clearly knew it going in and tried to mask it with bravado. Not that I didn't respect that, but her laid out on the floor wasn't happening on my watch.

She reached up and grasped my forearm in her small hand. "I'm good."

I knew the move. I knew every signal she was putting out, and they were all green lights. I also knew who the fuck I was. I didn't screw around with clingy women. I kept everything simple and clean. That meant no attachments and no bullshit drama. This chick was drama on steroids.

She was also begging for the kind of attention I knew how to give. She'd be exactly what I wanted between the sheets. Hell, she'd fit my needs like a glove, but fuck, I was a damn fool to even consider going there.

Shoving down thoughts about taking her mouth and wondering what her sexy bedroom voice would sound like when I fucked her hard, I dropped my hand to her elbow. "Let's go."

She planted her feet. "Do you have a girlfriend?"

Shit. "No," I clipped, digging myself deeper.

"Wife? Current or ex?"

Was she fucking crazy? "Read between the lines." I dropped her arm and stepped toward the door.

She followed. "Answer my question."

"No." Goddamn it, my cock liked sparring with her.

"No, you don't have a wife or no, you aren't answering?"

I stared at her because I could.

"I'm your boss," she said defiantly. "You have to answer my question."

A dozen ways to wipe that defiance off her face crossed my mind then traveled straight to my dick. "You're a lot of things, but my anything isn't one of them."

"I'm your client." She pointed out.

I switched tactics. "Do you know how old I am?"

Her face scrunched up in confusion, like I'd thrown her. "Thirty?"

I had no clue when she was or wasn't acting. Not when I didn't have my hands on her. Which wasn't happening again. "Thirty-four." Too fucking old for her. "Why didn't you go for Tyler?"

That made her blink. "The other bodyguard?"

"Yeah." Or any other asshole for that matter. I wasn't fucking fishing for compliments. I was stupidly trying to gauge how serious she was, because despite every warning sign, I was still thinking about what it would feel like to pound into her.

"The one who smiled all the time and called me ma'am," she stated, like I was dumb as fuck.

And the one who'd let her naked ass run across South Beach, which I was progressively more pissed about by the minute. But she didn't ask it as a question, so I didn't answer.

She exhaled like she was put out, then glanced around the office before her gaze came back to me. "Okay. You want the truth?" She didn't wait for a response. "Here it is. I don't do this." She pointed between us. "I don't sleep around. I wasn't looking for a man to satisfy some itch. I wasn't looking for anything except to keep my head above water until the day I decided I was done. Because you don't get to decide anything in this industry. Not what you say, what you wear, how you act, where you go, who you go with, what you make, or how you do it. None of it is in your control. I'm not a person, I'm a brand."

She stopped to take a breath and see if I'd say shit.

I didn't.

"But I'm not my brand." She held her hands up and spread them out as if reading a marquee. "Former squeaky-clean child star becomes Hollywood's darling." She snorted. "That isn't me. It never was, but I'm not dumb enough to fuck my gravy train with no end game in sight. So I made my own end game, and that's been my focus for four years. Not a thirty-second orgasm from some Hollywood prick more concerned about how he looked as he fucked me and what he'd get out of me than if I got off. So no, I didn't look twice at Tyler, or any other man." She paused. "Until I woke up hand-cuffed to your bed."

Bullshit. "Let's go." I turned toward the door.

"That's it?" she practically squeaked, her voice cracking with indignation. "That's all you have to say?"

I didn't buy one fucking word. Declarations were the half-assed attempts of the desperate to gain control over a situation they had no control over. She didn't think shit when she woke up handcuffed, except to wonder where the hell she was and who I was.

"You've been here long enough." I needed to get her the fuck out of here. "Time to move."

She let me take her arm as the same two security guards met us outside the office and escorted us back to the parking garage. By some stroke of luck, no one had figured out she was here, and we made it to the Escalade without incident—until I opened the door to the back passenger seat of the SUV.

She looked up at me with disdain. "Now I can't sit in the front?"

"I never should've had you in the front to begin with." Not with a high-profile client. The side and rear windows were limo tint, but in the front passenger seat she was visible through the windshield. "Get in."

She didn't move. "So this is how it's going to be? You lead me on, I pour my feelings out, then you relegate me to the back seat?"

"I'm your security detail, not your shrink." Unsecure garage, no backup, and vehicles coming and going, it was only a matter of seconds before someone recognized her.

She looked at me like she couldn't believe what she was hearing. Then she shook her head and her actress face slid into place. "You're an asshole."

"Confirmed and certified." I knew who the fuck I was.

CHAPTER ELEVEN

Audrina

I COULDN'T BELIEVE HIM.

Pissed, at him, at myself, at Colton fucking Payne. Hell, I was even pissed at Jerry despite it being my own damn fault for signing his stupid contract in the first place after my first agent told me she was retiring. But mostly, I was pissed at the mass of muscle in front of me who'd gripped my face and looked into my eyes like he saw me. Saw who I really was. Not Dreena, but me.

I was a fucking idiot.

This was exactly why I'd sworn off men. I had shit taste in them.

Glaring at a man named after a predator, I got in the back seat of the SUV.

He slammed the door and rounded the front of the vehicle like he was the king shit. I hated every single one of his dominant strides and his stupid handsome face. But I hated it more that I was wondering what the hell had happened between the breakfast he'd cooked for me and now.

All muscle and controlled movements, he got behind the wheel, started the engine and threw the car in reverse. "Seat belt," he clipped.

Immature and petty enough to ignore him, I crossed my arms.

He put the vehicle back in park and turned. "You want to play this game with me?"

I refused to look at him. "I don't want to do shit with you." Lie. I wanted to punch him. Maybe kick him.

"You gonna be pissed the rest of the day?"

I was going to be pissed for a lot longer than that. Men didn't turn me down. I turned them down. "I'm not pissed." He didn't get to have that satisfaction from me.

"You're lying. You're pissed I didn't worship at your feet with that little speech of yours."

I turned in my seat and hated all over again how damn handsome he was. "You're so fucking egotistical, it's disgusting." I sounded exactly as pathetic as I felt, like a jilted lover.

His cell phone rang through the speaker, and he hit a button on the steering wheel to answer. "Tank."

"Mr. Gunther, this is Peter Stanislas. I need to speak with Ms. MacKenzie, but she isn't answering her phone."

"That's because he took it from me," I bitched, throwing him under the bus.

A car pulled up next to us and two paparazzi spilled out with their cell phones and cameras.

"Audrina?" Peter asked.

Tank's massive arm reached over the seats, and in one quick, measured movement, he grabbed the seat belt, stretched it across my chest and threw it home. Jamming the gear shift into reverse, he stepped on it.

I glared at Tank. "Yeah, Peter, I'm here."

The huge vehicle lumbered back, and Tank spun the wheel. I would've been thrown into the side panel if I wasn't buckled in.

"You don't have your cell phone?" Peter asked, confused.

Braking as abruptly as he'd stepped on the gas, Tank threw the gearshift into drive and gunned it.

We were out of the garage before the paparazzi could get back in their car.

"I took her phone," Tank answered Peter. "She was a nervous wreck waiting for the blood draw when she pulled it out. She didn't need to see the video in that moment."

Peter cleared his throat. "I appreciate your concern for her well-being. I'm assuming you're finished at Memorial now?"

"Affirmative." Tank took a corner too fast.

Thrown against my seat belt again, I cursed.

"Audrina?" Peter asked, his voice laced with concern.

"What?" I snapped.

"Are you okay?"

Just fucking peachy. "Fine."

Tank smirked.

Asshole.

Peter cleared his throat. "Mr. Gunther, please return her phone and take me off speaker so I can confer with my client."

Tank pulled his cell phone out of his pocket, hit something on the steering wheel then handed me his phone.

Glaring at him, I took it. "Hi."

"Am I off speaker?" Peter asked.

I hated how Tank's cell phone smelled like him. "Yes."

"Are you all right? Do you need different security? Because I can—"

"It's fine." Apparently I was glutton for punishment, because the thought of getting rid of the asshole driving like he was auditioning for NASCAR made me want to cry.

"Okay." Peter exhaled. "You ready to go over this?"

No, yes, I didn't know. But it didn't matter, because I'd

already pulled the trigger. I piled on the lies. "More than ready."

"All right, let's start with Janette. She took the news well, and she wished you well once I explained what you were doing. She's signing the termination contract as it stands. She won't be an issue."

A small breath that wasn't enough air barely inflated my lungs. "Okay." I gripped the phone tighter. "And Jerry?"

Peter paused, then spoke in a rush. "It's worst-case scenario. He alerted the studio before I could. He's digging his heels in. Breach of contract, lost wages, claiming verbal consent on three more movie deals."

"That fucking liar," I spit out. "I *never* consented."

Tank looked at me in the rearview mirror.

I ignored him. "I'm not going to take this sitting down, Peter." I wasn't going to get sued by the studio because of an asshole agent I'd made.

"I know, I know," Peter appeased. "I reminded him he only has the contract for the current movie through its premiere and release. I told him everything we discussed, then I gave him the terms of our offer. He has forty-eight hours to sign the termination contract if he wants to get paid."

"He isn't going to sign it." I knew Jerry. He was too greedy.

"That's fine. We're prepared for that. This will just take longer."

And cost me more in legal fees. Which Jerry knew. "He's playing a game."

"Then you have a choice."

I knew what that choice was. Up the termination sever ance. I didn't even want to give him a severance in the first place, but Peter had said it would be the quickest and easiest way to get rid of him. I'd warned Peter that Jerry was a bully though. He wouldn't fight fair. Or ethically. "You know how I feel about that." I'd rather pay Peter's legal fees than pay Jerry another cent.

"Then we have our plan. We'll wait the forty-eight hours. In the meantime, we need to deal with the Colton Payne issue."

I didn't know what the hell to do about that. I hadn't seen any of the coverage or videos or what my fans were saying. Which, technically, I shouldn't care about. I was walking away from acting, but I didn't want to be sued by the studio if the movie tanked because of this. Colton could fucking take that responsibility.

"What did Janette say?" I hadn't anticipated needing her past this week. All the interviews she'd scheduled were set up. All I had to do was show up and smile. After that, I was supposed to be free.

"She didn't, except to say if you needed her again, she would be willing to work on an hourly basis if need be."

"She had a plan for how to handle this." But I'd been too fucking angry to listen to the details.

"Would you like me to contact her?"

A vicious headache started right behind my eyes. "No." I needed to learn how to handle my own affairs.

"You sure?" Peter asked.

I wasn't sure of anything except out was out. If I was walking away from Hollywood, I didn't need a Hollywood handler. If I was finally going to be myself, then this was it. This was the time to start.

Dreena MacKenzie was dead.

I was Audrina MacKenzie, a Midwest farm girl.

CHAPTER TWELVE

Tank

CONSENT.

What the fuck hadn't she given consent to?

My jaw ticking, I watched her in the rearview mirror as I drove to Golden Beach.

Gripping my phone, her voice defeated, she spoke to her agent. "Yes. I'll be at the interviews and the premiere."

She listened while her lawyer said something.

"I know," she enunciated. "I'll handle it." She paused. "I get it, Peter." She hung up and held my phone out without looking at me. "Here."

I took it. "What's going on?"

She looked out the window. "Nothing."

She was lying again. "What didn't you consent to?"

"What do you care?"

I shouldn't. But for some fucking reason, I did. Except before I could give her some bullshit answer, my cell rang. Glancing to see it was Luna, I bypassed the Bluetooth and answered. "What's up?"

"I went through the footage from Club Frenzy. She was right. Payne put something in her drink."

My knuckles tightened around the steering wheel. "No question?"

"No," Luna clipped. "The footage is grainy, but you can

clearly see the fucking pendejo taking a shot glass of something from his security detail, turning to dose it, then handing the glass to MacKenzie. She tosses the shot back and the fucker pumps his fist. No question he did it. You get the tox screen done?"

"Yeah." Fucking Payne was mine. Next time I saw him, he was answering to me.

"She should get the results in a few hours. In the meantime, I'm sending the footage to her lawyer."

"Copy me on that. I'll give it to her." She had a right to see that shit.

"Done. Anything else you need?"

"No. Almost to Golden Beach."

"Good. Her lawyer said she needed to lie low for a bit, but let me know if you need backup for any engagements."

"Copy that." I hung up.

"What are you going to give to me?" she asked from the back seat, her arms crossed.

"What didn't you consent to?" Besides the fucking shit Payne had dosed her with.

"Nice try." She snorted. "You work for me, remember?"

"Careful," I warned, unprofessional as fuck.

"Of *what*?" Hollywood attitude seeped out of her. "Asking a question you actually have to answer?"

I didn't say shit. I stopped at a light and glared right back at her in the rearview mirror.

"What are you going to do?" she taunted. "Quit?"

"Keep pushing, and you'll find out," I promised. I'd wipe that smug-as-fuck look off her face, and she wouldn't like one damn second of it.

"Fine, don't tell me about your cryptic conversation." She

turned toward the window.

My cell vibrated with an incoming text. Glancing at it, I saw Luna sent the video clip. I pulled it up and held the phone over my shoulder. "Watch this."

"I don't need to see my naked ass." She pouted.

I took note of her defensive tone. "This you need to see."

With a look of irritation, she snatched the phone. Ten seconds later she looked furious. Her fingers swiped across the screen a few times, and without a word, she handed the phone back.

I pulled up to the security gate at the development for Christensen's house and entered the code. Following the GPS, I drove to his place and entered a second code for his gate. Scanning the grounds as I pulled around the driveway, I wasn't impressed. Unless he had perimeter security, anyone could scale the six-foot wall surrounding the property, not to mention the place was completely accessible from the beach.

I threw the Escalade in park and cut the engine.

She reached for her door.

"Wait," I commanded, before getting out of the SUV. Scanning the hedges, the grounds, the driveway we'd just come up, I didn't leave shit to chance. Rich as hell gated communities weren't immune to paparazzi or meddling neighbors.

Once I was satisfied no one was around, I opened her door.

Not making eye contact, she held her purse and slid out of the SUV.

I took her elbow and led her to the house, mentally reminding myself to find the fucking garage door opener so I didn't have to park in the driveway. It wasn't until I had us in the house, door locked, that she spoke.

"I sent the video to my cell."

I tipped my chin, catching her drift. Taking her cell out of my pocket, I handed it over. "Stay. I'm grabbing your bags."

She didn't say shit as I went back out through the garage. Five minutes later, the SUV was in the garage, her bags were in a guest room, mine was in the master because it had a bigger bed, and she was standing in front of the fridge, door open.

She took one of those small-ass carrots and crunched half of it before closing the fridge. "I need my schedule."

"Where is it?" I remembered what the nurse said about feeding her. Pushing her out of the way, I opened the fridge.

"I don't know." She leaned against the counter, watching me. "Your pretty boy bodyguard had it last."

Fuck. I grabbed veggies and tofu and dumped them on the counter, then I pulled my phone out and fired off a text to Tyler. A few seconds later, he responded that he put her schedule in her purse. "Check your purse." I took a pan out.

She went to the island separating the kitchen from the open plan living room and dug through her massive bag. Unearthing some paperwork, she stared at it a moment then pulled her phone out and sat at one of the stools to make a call. "Peter, it's me. I need a favor...."

I found a cutting board and started chopping carrots, broccoli and onions.

"I know, I saw, but this isn't about that," she said to her lawyer. "I need you to call Janette, get her on hourly, and tell her to cancel all my interviews except *Miami Morning*."

I silently groaned. *Miami Morning* broadcasted to a live audience outside every morning it wasn't fucking pouring rain. It was a shit venue to deal with.

"I know, I don't care," she continued. "There's nothing in

the contract about the interviews being mandatory, only the premiere, and I'll be there." Her voice turned hard. "But if that fucking asshole Colton is anywhere near me, I swear to God, Peter, I will make a scene. *A big fucking scene.* Tell Janette that. Have her relay the message. Colton doesn't know who he messed with."

Throwing the vegetables in the pan, I cursed.

Her head popped up and she looked at me. "What?" she challenged.

"Leave Payne to the lawyer." And me.

She gave me the fucking smirk again. "You're a publicist now? You know how to handle my career?" Her eyes narrowed. "No, Peter, I'm talking to Mr. Gunther," she bit my last name out sarcastically. "He seems to think I asked for his advice. That, or he's suddenly an expert on how to handle a Hollywood scandal."

My nostrils flared. "Hang up."

She glared at me. "I fucking get that, Peter. Just call Janette and tell her what I need. Take care of that and Jerry, and I'll handle the rest." She hung up and practically kicked the stool away as she got down. "I'm going for a run." She took off toward the guest room.

Goddamn it.

I turned off the burner and went after her. Pushing the bedroom door open, I walked in like I owned the place. "You're gonna eat, then we'll discuss your exercise routine." The last thing she needed right now on an almost empty stomach after giving blood was a fucking run.

"Screw you." She tossed the banged-up suitcase on the bed and fumbled with the lock.

That's when I saw it.

Shaking hands and quick breaths.

Attitude, language, hands, storming off—I put it all together in about half a second.

Stepping up behind her, I reached around her small-as-fuck body and grabbed her wrists. "Take a breath."

She jerked like I'd burned her. "Let go!"

I crossed her arms against her chest and pulled her in tight. "Take a breath," I repeated.

"What the fuck are you doing?" she screeched, struggling against me.

"My job." Lowering my head to her ear, increasing my grip, ignoring the sweet scent of her, I dropped my voice. "You're not the first person to have a panic attack."

"I'm not panicking!" Her whole body shook. "I'm Dreena MacKenzie!"

I should've let her go, she was more goddamn trouble than she was worth, but I fucking didn't. "Inhale to the count of three and hold it."

"Or *what?*" She kicked at my shin. "You'll pull your gun on me too!"

I spun her around, gripped her hair and glared at her as I gave her a fucking dose of reality. "I've dealt with armed Marines who were having a panic attack with their goddamn finger on the trigger because they couldn't reconcile the amount of death in front of them. You want to lose your shit over a phone call and a Hollywood reputation, be my guest. But don't think for a single *second* you're more special than all those men and women fighting for your freedom."

She choked on a sob, and the fight in her body left. "I'm not panicking."

"Yes you are." I'd seen it too many times to count.

Her whole body trembling, she fought for a breath. "I'm sorry."

"Don't apologize to me." I tamped down my irritation. "Own your shit, and take a breath before you hyperventilate."

Her chest rising and falling like she was sprinting, she tried to shake her head, but my grip was too tight. "I'm good, I'm fine."

"Cut the bullshit, Audrina. Inhale to the count of three. One… two… three."

She inhaled.

"Now hold it." I counted backwards from five. "Exhale through your mouth."

Her chest deflated as her hands landed on my forearms.

"Again," I commanded, counting to three. "Hold it." I counted down from five.

She listened to my instructions, and we repeated the process three more times before the shake in her limbs turned to a tremor and her breathing evened out somewhat.

After another round, she'd calmed down enough for me to lay it out. "You want to go for a jog, we'll do it after you eat and after the sun's down, but that isn't gonna help you run away from shit."

"I'm not running away."

I stated the obvious. "You fired your agent and your publicist, and you have no backup."

Her gaze fixed on her hands on my arms, and her fingers tightened. "That's not running away. It's calculated. And I have Peter."

There was only one reason she'd fire her team but keep her lawyer. "You walking away from your career?" I told myself I didn't give a shit what she did. I didn't care what any woman did, let alone a client. I got paid either way. But the question was out of my mouth before I could filter it.

She didn't answer.

Still gripping her hair, I tilted her head up. "Eyes on me, Audrina."

Slow, distressed, her gaze traveled up my face, and if I didn't know better I'd say she was giving me a performance.

"Yes," she admitted. "I'm walking away."

CHAPTER THIRTEEN

Audrina

WHAT THE HELL WAS I DOING?

I couldn't tell him my plan. I couldn't tell anyone. Not yet. I needed to keep my mouth shut and my shit in check. I was close, so close. A few more days, a week tops, then I could fall apart, or run, or do whatever the hell I wanted to do because my life would be my own, and no one could tell me otherwise.

I tried again to pull out of his grasp, but his stupid fucking hands were bigger than my head, and I wasn't going anywhere until he decided I was going somewhere. And that right there should've been enough to staunch the river of disastrous desire that overflowed every time he so much as looked at me, let alone touched me. Or did what he was doing right now, which was pretending he gave a single fuck about me or what I did.

Reaching for and trying to channel some self-righteous anger, I threw out attitude, because I didn't know what to do with his silent stare. "That's right. I'm walking away from a once-in-a-lifetime opportunity. A seven-figure paycheck per movie career, and I'm doing it all on my own. I planned it, I'm executing it and I committed to it. I don't need a bodyguard turned life coach. I can breathe and stand and make decisions all on my own, so you can let go."

He didn't move. He didn't even blink. His steadfast gaze

locked on me, he stared.

"*Now*," I snapped.

"How long?" he asked.

"What?" What the hell was he talking about?

"How long did you plan this?"

His heart wasn't pounding out of his chest. His hands didn't shake. His pulse wasn't hammering at his neck. Slow and steady, opposite of me, he breathed and stared and held on to me.

For some reason, his calm only made me angrier. "Did I miss the bond fest where we ate too much ice cream, made friendship bracelets and swore to be besties?" He wasn't my friend. He wasn't even an acquaintance.

"You don't plan, execute and commit," he said, completely ignoring me.

What *the fuck* was he talking about? "This is relevant how?"

"You commit first," he stated, no intonation in his voice.

"No fucking shit, Einstein." I wasn't stupid. "I committed to this plan over a year ago." As soon as the words left my mouth, I cursed my stupidity. "That was on purpose."

He didn't insult me by rubbing it in. "If this was planned, then why are you panicking?"

My heart rate a little slower, the awful tightening in my chest not so bad, my lungs taking deeper breaths, I hated that I'd been panicking, but I hated more that he'd called me out on it. I still hadn't seen the video of my shit last night or checked all the fallout on social media, and the old me, the person I was trying to cut off at the knees, was panicking about that.

Half my brain was telling me I needed to get in there ASAP. Manage damage control, watch the video, scour the gossip sites, see what my fans were saying, see what my haters were saying, see what the hell kind of spin Colton Asshole Payne was putting on it or if he'd started rumors that we were a couple.

That half of my brain was overpowering any sense of rightness I'd felt in pulling my own proverbial trigger. So when I saw the footage of that asshole giving me a shot he'd put drugs in, and his smug-as-fuck expression followed by his fist pump like he was actually going to get me in bed or worse, I'd lost it.

I'd tried to run. I'd *needed* to run.

But a six-and-a-half-foot giant tank of a man had been in my way.

He was still in my way.

Mustering every ounce of training I'd gotten over the years from all sorts of whacked directors, I schooled my expression and went for shock value. "From publicist to bestie to life coach. What's next, *Falcon*? Fucking?"

Just like I thought it would, his expression went stone cold when I said his name with equal parts disdain and sarcasm. It was a low blow, unconscionably so after he'd laid out his story, but I didn't care. I told myself I was done giving a shit what people thought of me.

Except seeing his face shut down did something to my stomach. And my chest. And I didn't like it. At all.

"Let go of me," I snapped.

Silence.

His eyes searching my face, his grip just as tight as before, he didn't move.

Idiotic, suicidal, I egged him on. "Go ahead," I seethed, wrapping my arms around his massive neck and going on tiptoe. "Do what every other man in America wants to do." I pressed into his impossibly hard body. "Kiss a movie star." I bit out every ugly word. "Take from me like every other fucking person on the planet."

All at once, his expression went slack, his shoulders dropped and he let go of me. "You done?"

Yeah, I was done. So fucking done. With him, with acting, with fame, with pressure, with assholes who put drugs in my drinks, I was fucking *done*. But I was also stubborn enough to do the stupidest thing I could think of.

"I'm just getting started." I launched myself at him.

My arms went around his neck, my legs around his waist, and I desperately, pathetically did to him what I accused him of doing to me.

I took from him.

I forced my mouth over his and I kissed him.

For one horrifying, confidence-slaying moment, he remained stone still. A wall of muscle, he didn't even flinch. As if my weight on him, my assault, was nothing, he stood perfectly, impossibly *still*.

A cry, part anguish, part anger, and all humiliation erupted from the ashes of my dignity, and I lashed out. My arm pulled back, my hand fisted, and I aimed. *"I hate you."*

He moved.

One of his huge hands caught my fist as the other gripped a punishing handful of my hair.

Then his mouth slammed over mine.

His tongue, huge and thick and dominating, drove into me. Taking my shocked gasp, stealing my breath, still holding my fist, he bent my arm behind me. Incapacitating me on every level, he pushed my arm into my lower back, forcing my hips against his.

One controlling, perfectly executed grind of his hips, and I felt every inch of his giant cock between my legs and on my stomach as he thrust his tongue.

He didn't kiss me.

He devoured me.

And I fucking melted.

Clawing at his neck, grinding my hips, moaning, I wanted him to fill my empty core or I wanted to die. There was no in between.

"Fuck me," I begged, out of my mind, forcing words around his unrelenting possession of my mouth.

For five glorious seconds, he tightened his hold on my hair and shoved his tongue deeper. Air rushed past my heated body, and the resulting shiver only made my dripping core wetter.

Yes, I thought. *Yes, yes, yes.*

Until my ass hit the cold top of the dresser.

His grip on my arm behind my back dropped, and his mouth ripped away from mine. The pressure on my scalp ceased, leaving an unbearable tingle as a rough, calloused hand wrapped around my throat.

My lungs, deprived of oxygen, automatically reached for air and I inhaled.

Slow, like coming awake when I'd never been alive, my eyes traveled up the chest of a tank and my gaze came into focus. I took in the formidable beast of a man in front of me as he stood staring at me.

His expression hard and impenetrable, his storm-colored eyes locked on me, his lips wet, he waited.

My stomach dropped.

"Hi," I whispered, forcing a swallow.

"You do not," he started, his voice low and threatening, "fucking kiss me."

Desire surged between my legs and my traitorous core

pulsed. Hoping, praying, for attitude-laced words, I opened my mouth.

The pressure on my throat increased.

I snapped my mouth shut, but not from fear or pain. Oh no, it was worse, *so* much worse. My mouth shut, and my legs rubbed together as I choked down a groan because my body wanted to do anything and everything this dominating asshole tank of a man told it.

I wasn't humiliated or blindingly angry.

I didn't even give a shit about my dignity.

I was out of my mind desperate, salivating for him.

And he was denying me.

No recourse, not even sure I wanted one, I dropped my gaze.

His thumb pressed under my chin and lifted my head as he barked out an order. "Look at me when I'm talking to you."

I did. Instantly.

"You don't take," he warned.

"Okay," I whispered, hungry for something I didn't understand.

His nostrils flared.

Hope surged like a victory party low in my belly, and a dangerous thread of brazenness unraveled. Emboldened, I licked my bottom lip.

It was the last thing I should've done.

His expression locked down, his hand dropped, and he walked out.

CHAPTER FOURTEEN

Tank

FUCK.

Submissive little bitch.

But fuck.

I never should've fucking kissed her. I didn't kiss chicks, and I sure as hell didn't fucking kiss needy ones.

Goddamn it.

I strode into the kitchen and grabbed the rice out of the cupboard. I didn't think she'd follow me, but the scent of her wet pussy and the sound of her light footsteps ate up my six. I filled a pot with water and threw it on the stove. Her doe-eyed, desperate gaze burned a fucking hole on my back, but I didn't spare her a glance. My dick painfully hard, I grabbed a knife and turned on the broiler. It wasn't until I was cutting shit up that I felt the air shift.

"Sit your ass down," I barked, not turning around.

I didn't have to look to know she fucking complied.

Reaching into the fridge, grabbing a bottle of some sort of premade fruit-blended drink, I held it out behind me. "Drink," I ordered.

The weight of the plastic bottle left my hand, and I let go.

Hearing the twist of the cap as she opened it, I fought a smirk. Dominating asshole one-oh-one, reward them when they do what you say. Then I ignored her for the next twenty minutes as I made food. I didn't look at her, I didn't give her any tasks, I didn't fucking speak.

I cooked. She watched. I calculated.

Fucking her would be an epic mistake. She was too god-damn vulnerable. She'd attach herself to me faster than I could give her an orgasm. I fucking knew this. But I was still thinking about a tight pussy that hadn't been touched in four years, and that smart mouth. I wanted to fuck that mouth. I wanted to fuck the incorrigible right out of her.

Shoving down the way she'd instantly gone submissive on me, I turned the burners off on the stove and plated the rice, sautéed vegetables and tofu I'd broiled. Grabbing a couple of forks, I walked around the island and sat, putting the plates down.

Still sitting on the island, she looked over her shoulder at me.

I didn't make eye contact. "Get over here and eat." Fucking hungry, I took a huge bite.

She hopped down without comment and came to sit by me, but she didn't pick her fork up. She stared at her food.

Jesus fuck, not this shit again. "Eat," I ordered.

She turned to face me. Out of the corner of my eye, I saw her chest rise with a steadying inhale. "Answer a question, and I will."

Mentally shaking my head, I took another bite. Any other woman, I would've told to fuck off. But other women didn't talk to me like she talked to me. My height, my size, my scowl, they either ran the other way or did exactly what she did when I got my hands on her. They submitted.

Curiosity getting the better of me, I relented. "Ask."

"Do you like me?"

A bite halfway to my mouth, I froze for a fraction of a second. Then I chewed slowly and kept my eyes off her, because it was all part of the game. "You don't strike me as the insecure type." I took another bite, not knowing if I should be fucking disappointed in her lack of confidence, or watching her for whatever game she was trying to play me with.

"This isn't about insecurity," she countered.

Bullshit. She was wondering why I'd said what I'd said. Horny as fuck, bored with talking, I dropped my fork and grasped her nape. Then I put my eyes on her.

She fucking drank me up like she was starving.

Deliberately, I picked her fork up, stabbed some tofu and brought it to her lips. Lowering my voice, I tested her. "Open your mouth."

For two heartbeats she stared at me.

Anticipation surged, wondering if she'd comply, but ultimately hoping she wouldn't. I bent women. I made them cave to my commands, then I gave them the mind-blowing orgasms they wanted. But it was never a challenge. It hadn't been for years. In fact, I couldn't remember the last time a woman had been a challenge.

That alone should've been a warning. But add in the fact that I wanted this young-as-fuck, spoiled, too thin, hot mess of a woman to be my own personal fuck toy, and I should've been calling Luna to tell him to pull my ass off this assignment.

The only smart move was to disengage.

But I didn't fucking do it.

I increased the pressure on the back of her neck, I touched the food to her lips, and I actually put fucking effort into my command. Stroking her neck, taking the threat out of my tone, I dropped my disinterested expression and let her see how goddamn much I wanted her. "Eat the food, Audrina."

"No."

I couldn't fucking help it, I smiled.

Deadly serious, she pushed my hand away. "Did I pass?"

"Pass what?" I dropped her fork and picked up mine, pretending I didn't know exactly what the hell she was talking about.

"Your test."

"Eating isn't a test, it's a necessity." I briefly scanned her body. "More so in your case."

"I fucking get it, you think I'm too skinny." She picked up her fork and jammed it into a piece of broccoli. "But you still didn't answer my question."

I tipped my chin toward her plate. "Eat all of that and I will."

She shoved the bite in. Then three more in rapid succession.

I glanced at her as her cheeks distended like a fucking squirrel's. "Swallow."

She choked down the food in her mouth. "You'd like that, wouldn't you."

Like she wouldn't believe. "Depends."

She did the snort thing. "On what?" She took another bite.

"If you knew what the fuck you were doing before you swallowed." Not that I gave a shit. I'd get off on teaching her exactly how to take my giant cock down her throat.

She choked.

I grabbed her arms, raising them over her head as I pulled her to her feet. "Easy, easy. Breathe through your nose."

"Water," she rasped.

I grabbed two bottles from the fridge and handed her one. Tears in her eyes, she chugged half, then anger contorted her angel face. "You're a bastard, you know that?"

I was a lot of things, but a bastard wasn't one of them. Not technically. "Eat your food, don't inhale it." I sat back down.

She didn't move. "Fuck you. Answer my question."

Fighting another smile, I picked up my fork. "I'm not paid to like you." I'd never let a woman tell me to fuck off before, let alone multiple times. No clue why I was letting it happen now.

Incredulous disbelief washed across her face. "Were you *paid* to kiss me?"

I almost lost the battle with another damn smile. "No."

Her hands went to her hips. "Exactly. You wanted to kiss me."

"Sit the fuck down and eat." My tongue in her mouth had made me soft. I didn't want to kiss shit. I wanted to eat. My food and her cunt.

Looking almost smug, she sat. "I'm not sitting because you told me to. I'm doing it because I'm hungry and I want to."

Right. I didn't say shit.

"I saw that. I saw that smirk on your face." She took a bite.

She didn't see shit. "You'll see what I want you to see."

"Oh." She laughed through the word. "Okay, *sure*, Mr. I'm-A-Tank, I can control everything. Well, guess what? You can't control me."

I abruptly stood and kicked the stool out behind me. Before she even had a chance to fucking blink, I'd grabbed her around the waist and lifted her skinny ass to the counter. Stepping between her legs, I took two handfuls of her thick fucking hair I couldn't keep my hands out of and crashed my mouth over hers.

She didn't gasp. She didn't push me away. She didn't even hesitate.

Her legs and arms went around me, and she asked for it. "Oh my God, *more*."

I shoved my tongue into her mouth like I wanted to drive my cock into her cunt, and I fucking dominated. Every stroke, every flex of my muscles was a goddamn lesson in control. I controlled her mouth. I controlled her body, and I controlled her desire. I decided what she fucking got from me. If she wanted a piece of me, I topped. Period.

God-fucking-damn it, I topped.

Always.

Except this time I wasn't.

A hundred-pound sass mouth with giant tits and eyes to die for had grabbed my ass, pulled me on top of her and was fucking writhing underneath me.

And I was letting her.

Grinding my hips, dry humping her jean-clad pussy, kissing her like this was more than a hard cock and a wet cunt, I play fucked like a goddamn amateur.

But I wasn't a goddamn amateur.

Fuck.

That.

My tongue down her throat, both my hands went to the waist of her jeans, and I yanked. Hard. The material stretched over her nothing hips as I jerked the jeans and her lace underwear down and off her legs in one pull.

I ripped my mouth from hers and shoved her legs to her chest. Her ass came off the counter and the sweet smell of cunt hit me. I barely had time to appreciate the sight of her wet pussy laid out for me before I barked out the only question that mattered. "You want more?"

"Oh my God, yes. *Yes.*"

I shoved my face into her cunt and licked.

Goddamn.

I growled, and she moaned, loudly.

I didn't hold back. I didn't make her work for it. I latched on to her clit and pulled the greedy flesh between my teeth as I shoved first one, then two fingers inside her tight-as-hell pussy.

"Ahhhh," she screamed.

I bit her clit, then sucked hard.

Her pussy clamped down. "Tank!"

I stroked her G-spot once, one fucking time, and she detonated like a goddamn IED. Pulsing, shaking, crying out, her hands gripped at my hair.

I thrashed my tongue against her clit one more time, then pulled both my mouth and my fingers out of her still coming pussy. Grasping her knees, I loomed over her.

Ruthless, controlled, I didn't allow myself to register her hooded eyes, the just-fucked mess of her hair or the relentless throbbing of my dick. Wet cunt all over my mouth, I glared at her.

Then I fucking laid it out. "This?" I thrust my fingers deep into her pussy and rubbed her G-spot. "I control."

CHAPTER FIFTEEN

Audrina

OH MY *FUCKING* GOD.

His too-thick fingers rubbed a spot I'd only ever heard about as my pussy clenched so hard around him, I started to come again. Or I never stopped. I didn't know what the hell was going on with my body. No one had ever touched me like he just did.

I didn't even care that he'd said he controlled me.

I was a wanton mess under his abrasive touch. Except that wasn't touching. He'd assaulted my body like I was the enemy and he was the conqueror.

Before I could come again, or finish coming, his thick fingers left my aching core.

Without another word, he righted his stool, sat back down, and picked up his fork. Shoveling in a bite of the tofu he'd cooked, he stared at his plate.

My bare, soaked pussy throbbed inches from his face and his food.

Oh my God.

Oh my God.

Desire leaked out of me, and I closed my eyes. Every second of his attack and what it meant and what he'd been doing—it hit me like a freight train.

I had no dignity.

Zero.

None.

And no amount of attitude would save face. Not with him. Because everything he'd just done was calculated. That wasn't passion or even lust. He was proving a fucking point. I didn't even know if his dick was still hard, or if I was the one who'd made it hard in the first place. Maybe I was just another warm body to his emotionless game of fuck and control. Or control and fuck. It didn't matter what order it was, it was a game to him. That much I got.

But what I was going to do next, I didn't know.

I figured I had two choices. Slink away and pretend it'd never happened. My pussy pulsed in protest at the thought. Or turn the tables on him... if I could.

It wasn't even a choice.

Before I could analyze my self-destruction, I reached for the front of my top. Still lying on the granite island countertop, naked from the waist down, I unbuttoned my blouse.

I didn't look at him, and I didn't go for a sexy striptease. I knew it'd have zero effect. Instead, I efficiently went through the buttons, slipped my arms out then lifted my back and un-hooked my bra. Pulling it off, I tossed it to the floor.

For three whole heartbeats, I lay there naked.

My pussy wet, my nipples achingly hard, my breath rag-ged, I reached for a character, any character, because I didn't know who the fuck I was as I sat up.

I couldn't even comprehend the woman who picked up her plate of tofu and stir-fried vegetables then spread her legs wide.

A stranger. That's who I was.

Because it was a stranger with her legs wide, her breasts heavy with desire, and her pussy wet and clenching on air who did the unthinkable next.

Completely naked, she straddled the tank of man's plate in front of her and scooched in close. The scent of her desire stronger than the smell of the food, she held her plate up under her chin.

Then she became me.

Every dirty, pathetic, consuming inch of hungry need I had, I embraced.

Ravenous, my eyes locked on a predator, I spread my legs wider.

Then I picked up a handful of food with my bare hand and shoved it into my mouth.

CHAPTER SIXTEEN

Tank

J ESUS FUCKING CHRIST.
Not for one goddamn second did I think she would do what she did.

Legs spread, pussy wet, she straddled my plate and gave me a front-row view of her cunt. Which was fucking ballsy in and of itself after her little striptease, but then she picked up her plate and went for broke.

Holding it under her chin so I still got the full fucking view of her tits and pulsing pussy, she grabbed a handful of food and in a spectacular display of fucked-up, she shoved it in her mouth like a goddamn animal.

For one fucking heartbeat, I froze.

This woman wasn't Hollywood's highest-paid actress. She wasn't a drugged-out mess running naked on the beach. And she sure as hell wasn't the woman who told her lawyer to fire the team who managed her career.

This was a woman asking to be fucked.

Dominated and fucked.

And *goddamn* I was turned the hell on. More than I'd ever been in my entire fucking life. But it'd be a cold day in hell before I let her know that.

Pulling my shit together, I put a forkful of rice and tofu in my mouth and choked it down. My gaze steadfast on my plate, my dick throbbing, I kept my expression Marine hard and locked down.

Two more bites I didn't fucking taste and my plate was clean. Unlike hers. Rice falling all over, she kept grabbing handfuls and bringing them to her mouth as shit dripped down her chin and fell all over the fucking place.

My cock throbbed to get into that wet cunt, but my sick mind was thinking about flipping her over and spanking the shit out of her while I made her lick up her mess on the counter.

Lucky her, I didn't do either. My giant dick would destroy that small pussy, and I was damn sure she'd never been spanked. Instead, I stood and picked up my plate, vowing to never give her utensils with any meal I cooked her ever again.

I didn't make it one step before she dropped her plate and lunged.

A wet hand wrapped around my neck as one of her legs made it around my waist. Using her own strength to hold on to me, the heat of her core came dangerously close to my dick.

"I ate, you promised," she accused. "Now tell me. *Do you like me?*"

She was either crazier than any Marine I'd ever met, or she was acting. I didn't know which, and in that moment, I didn't fucking care. I wanted to know what she was after.

Gripping her hair, I leveled her with a look. "When's the last time you knew what you wanted?"

For five seconds she looked up at me like I'd confused the hell out of her. Then her lips moved and she spoke, but the fire was gone from her tone. "What I want?"

"That's what I fucking asked."

Her chest rose with an inhale, but her voice went soft. "I want to know if you like me."

"Why?" What fucking difference could it possibly make? She didn't know me. I was nothing but hired help to her. And if she really wanted to fuck, I'd fuck her same as any woman.

"Because it matters."

"How?" If she was gonna go all needy on me, I was gonna make her spell it out. I wasn't gonna deal with any plausible deniability down the line. If she wanted my cock, she needed to know what she was getting into.

Her gaze dropped, then her shoulders. "I want you to like me."

I fought a callous laugh. "This isn't high school. I don't need to like you to fuck you."

Her muscles stiffened. "I didn't mean...." She cleared her throat and looked back up at me. "I didn't mean it like that," she admitted, sounding like a child.

Jesus. Was she that fucking emotionally stunted? "You take your clothes off, spread your legs and show me your wet pussy before shoveling food in with your bare hands like a caged animal. Then you ask me if I like you." I tightened my grip in her hair so there'd be no misunderstanding about my level of seriousness. "You want to get fucked, say the word. You want a boyfriend, look elsewhere."

Her gorgeous eyes staring up at me, she didn't even hesitate. "Fucked."

Anticipation coursed through my veins and went straight to my dick. "Fucked, what?" I asked, testing her.

"Fucked, *please*," she whispered.

One breath, two, I waited, giving her a chance to take it back.

Stupidly, she didn't.

I laid it out. "What happens after I fuck that tight pussy and come all over those perfect tits?"

She trembled and licked her bottom lip. "I shower?"

"Wrong." She wasn't gonna wash me off.

Her pulse sped up and her voice came out breathless. "I taste you?"

Fuck. "You don't get attached. You don't ask for more. You don't expect shit." I said what I needed to say, but as the words left my mouth, the thought of only having her once was already pissing me off.

"Just sex." She nodded as much as she could in my hold. "I get it."

She didn't get it. She wouldn't until after I fucked her. But my cock didn't give a fuck. I'd already grabbed her ass, dragged her the rest of the way off the counter, and was walking to the shower in the master bedroom. Her tits bouncing, her bottom lip wet from her biting it, her sweet pussy smell all the fuck over me, I was done.

No more holding back.

I was fucking her.

Still wrapped around me like the kind of trouble I had no business messing with, she held my neck tight as I turned on the shower.

She glanced at the water. "What are you doing?"

Stalling to get my shit under control. "It's not what I'm doing, it's what you're doing." I took her arms off me. "Get in."

Embarrassed heat or anger, I didn't know which, hit her cheeks, but she didn't comment. She got in the shower, stepped under the spray, then turned and looked at me questioningly.

Fuck, she was submissive.

110

"Clean up," I ordered, my tone sharp.

She flinched, but then she grabbed the soap.

Seeing her rub her tits down, my nostrils flared and I palmed my dick through my pants.

Her eyes darted to my hand.

I rubbed myself again and barked out another order. "Rinse off."

She complied, hastily rinsing the soap off before turning the shower off, stepping out and facing me with hard-as-fuck nipples, dripping wet.

I lowered my voice. "Did I tell you to turn the water off?"

Her eyes widened. "No."

I stared at her until she squirmed.

She pulled her lips into her mouth, then whispered, "I'm sorry."

She was going to be a lot sorrier. "Turn around and kneel."

For half a second, she looked at me like she couldn't believe I'd just told her to fucking kneel. Then slowly, she turned and dropped.

I yanked a towel off the rack, whipping it hard to make a snap sound.

She flinched, but then she squared her shoulders with an inhale.

I fought a smile and gently towel dried her hair. I could have done it with her standing up, but I was testing her. The length of her hair, almost all the way down her back, made me want to wrap it around my wrist and pull as I fucked her from behind.

Dragging the towel across her shoulders and over her perfect ass, curiosity got the better of me. "You give up men

111

because of a bad experience?"

She didn't say anything.

I gently wrapped my hand over her throat and tipped her head up.

Half apprehension, half desire, her eyes met mine.

I stroked her jaw with my thumb. "I asked you a question."

She swallowed, the movement flexing my hand. "I needed to concentrate on my career."

Not a yes, not a no. "You can't act and fuck?"

She didn't hesitate. "No."

Interesting. "This is acting right now." Everything leading up until I had my dick in her was pretense.

"It's not the same." She brought her arms up to cross over her tits.

My expression dark, my gaze cut to her hands.

She dropped her arms.

I thought about arching her back and shoving my cock into her mouth. "You on the pill?"

Her cheeks flushed, and she squirmed. "No."

Fucking shame. I dropped my hold on her, tossed the towel on the vanity, and stepped back. "Stand up."

Slow, but graceful as hell, she stood.

When she didn't turn around to face me, but silently waited for instructions, my dick pulsed. Calculating and measured, I circled her. She was stunning. Too thin, but still stunning.

Watching my gaze as I took in every inch of her, standing perfectly still, she whispered, "What are you doing?"

Getting off on the quiet and unsure tone of her voice. "Tell me something." I stepped behind her.

"What?"

Without touching her body, I reached around and drew my

finger over her bare cunt. "Who's this shaved pussy for?"

She shivered. "No one."

I grasped the back of her neck and leaned in. "Then why is it bare?"

"I-I'm not lying."

"Didn't say you were." Not parting her cunt, my finger circled and came away wet. "I asked why you bothered shaving if you're not getting fucked."

Women were a means to an end for me. I liked to smell them and fuck them and feel their soft bodies under me as I pounded into them. I liked a cunt constricting around my dick. But I didn't think about women beyond that. I'd joined the Marines at eighteen, and twelve years later went into personal security. I didn't have time for women beyond a night. And I sure as shit wasn't gonna end like my old man, still torn-up twenty-five years after the death of a woman who'd loved alcohol more than him.

So the fact that I was thinking about the wet pussy in front of me and the mouthy blonde it was attached to, and wondering who the fuck she'd let touch her wasn't only pissing me off, it was fucking problematic.

Circling over her cunt again, I didn't let it go. "Why's this cunt bare?"

Her back arched at my touch. "You don't like it?"

I didn't fucking like it that she was shaved before she'd met me, or that she'd fucked other men, or that her pussy being bare wasn't exclusively for my benefit. All of it was fucking with my head space, and I needed to remember who I was.

Pressing harder, I ran my finger up her soaked slit. "You waiting to be fucked?"

"Oh my God." She tried to lean back into me.

I held her neck firm, not letting her body touch mine. "Answer the question."

"Yes," she breathed.

"By who?"

"You." She ground her hips. "By you."

Right fucking answer. "Needy little bitch," I muttered appreciatively. "Hands on the counter."

Without hesitation, she leaned forward to brace on the vanity, giving me her ass.

Fuck, she was gorgeous. "Spread your legs."

She complied instantly, but then she opened her mouth. "You're still dressed."

"You want me naked?" If my dick was out, it'd be buried so deep in her, she wouldn't know her own name. "Earn it."

Gooseflesh broke out on her arms. "How?"

Not fucking touching her, I leaned over her back and spoke against her ear. "Cold?"

A tremor crawled up her spine. "A little."

Abruptly standing to my full height, I grabbed her waist and lifted.

Still holding on to the counter, she let out a shocked squeal. "What are you doing?"

"Legs up." I set her on the bathroom counter. "On your hands and knees. Head down."

"*Oh my God.*" On all fours, she looked at me. "What are you doing?"

I took a handful of her wet blonde hair and turned her head. "Head down. Face the mirror."

Her arms bent, her ass came up and she looked at me through the mirror. "Why?"

"Because you're going to watch yourself come." I shoved

two fingers into her wet cunt.

"Holy shit." Her curse echoed through the bathroom as her elbows straightened and her chest came off the vanity.

"I said head down." Holding her hair tight enough to make it count, I pulled her back down as I twisted my fingers deep inside her tight pussy.

Half moan, half gasp, she jerked. "Oh my—"

Pressing my thumb into her clit, I stroked her deep until I found the right spot.

"Ohhh fuck." She grasped the faucet and the edge of the counter and slammed her hips against my palm as her cunt started to convulse.

I yanked her hair and stilled my fingers right against her G-spot.

"Ahh!"

I looked at her in the mirror. "Did I say you could come?"

Her chest heaving, her pussy pulsing, her face contorted from ecstasy to pissed off in half a second flat. "You bastard," she spat.

I stared at her sexy-as-hell challenging beauty and shit clouded my head.

For two seconds, I thought about what it would take to not be exactly what she was accusing me of. Then just as quick, I shoved the useless thought down.

Drawing slowly out of her tight cunt, I knew who I was.

I let go of my dominant grip on her hair, lowered my voice to a nonthreatening cadence, and I gave it to her straight. "I'm worse than a bastard. I'll take every damn thing you have to give, then I'll take more. I'll fuck you until your voice is hoarse from screaming my name, and I'll fuck you until you're begging me to stop. Then I'll fuck you until you can't stand on your own." I paused for effect. "When the sun comes up, your sweet cunt will be dead to me."

Shock colored her expression.

"Understand?"

Her voice faltered. "Is that supposed to scare me?"

"If it doesn't, you're one in a million." Not that I'd fucked a million women, but I only ever got two responses from women when I told them what I was about. Fear or misplaced hope that I was lying.

I was never lying.

But the blonde in front of me studied my face like she thought I was.

Then she disappointed the fuck out of me.

Misplaced hope put confidence back in her voice. "You're lying."

"To what end?" Did I look like the commitment type?

"You're trying to scare me away." She said it like she had all the answers.

I told myself I hadn't been waiting for her to be that one in a million, that one chick who gave me a different response. Any other response. Something that told me she was different.

But she didn't.

So I told myself I was just gonna fuck her like I'd fuck any other chick—with no expectations. Two words I lived and breathed by, an utter religion I'd made out of no attachments—*no expectations*. Except for the first time in my life, those two words came up short. So fucking short that I was staring at a stunning blonde who I'd wanted to be different.

Goddamn it.

My jaw ticked, and I bit out a warning, "No expectations."

For five whole heartbeats, she stared at me.

Then she fucking threw me.

"How's this for *no expectations*? How about you don't expect shit out of me? How about you don't fuck me until I beg for you to stop. How about you don't decide before you even have one orgasm that I'm not worthy of your presence past sunrise, and how about you fuck *right off* with all of that bullshit?"

Surprise kicked me in the chest and went straight to my dick. My mind bent, and suddenly I was staring down two opposite fucking spheres of reality. On one side she was that millionth chick, on the other, she was nothing but a spoiled mouthpiece.

My head told me to test her, my dick told me to fuck her, and my emotions turned traitor.

Then I said the last fucking thing I should've. "You first."

A switch flipped. I saw it plain as day.

Her shoulders sagged, her chest deflated, and she fucking gave up.

No conviction, her tone one step away from defeat, she gave me two words that may as well have been *get* and *lost*. "Fuck you."

Perverse, I smiled. "Get up." I grabbed her by the waist.

Her wary expression turned to alarm. "What are you doing?"

"Not fucking you." I started to lift her off the vanity.

Both of her hands flew to the faucet for leverage. *"Stop."*

I smirked. "I already did, sweetheart."

CHAPTER SEVENTEEN

Audrina

A CONDESCENDING HALF SMILE ON HIS FULL LIPS, HE LET GO OF ME and strode toward the door.

"Hey!" I barked, sitting up. My naked ass on the cold vanity, I quickly spread my legs wide, reaching to put one foot in each of the two sinks because I couldn't think what else to do.

I wasn't sure what the hell just happened, but I knew he'd shut down. Or maybe he was always shut down, and I was just fooling myself at the glimpses of real I thought I'd seen in him and he was walking out that door before we'd even started this conversation.

I didn't know which it was, but I was desperate enough to take one more shot at finding out. Except all I had was spreading my legs, because that's all he seemed to respond to. I should've taken a different path, but I was so in over my head, why stop now?

Fuck it. "You forgot something."

I watched in the mirror as he paused and looked over his wide shoulder. His gun at his back waistband, his arms pushing the limits of the short sleeves of his polo shirt, his intense green-brown eyes immediately cut to my core.

But nothing in his distant expression changed.

My confidence shot, my voice wavered. "You forgot

something," I repeated, quieter than before.

Slow, like he had all the time in the world, his gaze traveled from between my legs up my stomach, over my breasts and finally landed on my eyes.

My nipples hardened to the point of pain, and my empty pussy pulsed with need. "I can make myself come." I reached between my legs.

His body predator still, he watched me. For one long moment, he kept his eyes on mine while I slowly ran a finger through my desire.

Then, without a word, he walked out.

"*Damn it.*" I scrambled off the vanity.

My indignation stronger than my dignity, I went after him.

"What the hell is your problem?" I yelled, following him down the hall.

His stride quick and sure, and shockingly graceful, he didn't even pause as he went to the kitchen. Grabbing a water out of the fridge, he uncapped it and chugged half.

"I asked you a question." My hands on my hips, crowding him in, I sounded exactly as I looked. Pathetic.

Taking another gulp of his water, looking completely unperturbed, he pushed past me. "Get dressed."

Goddamn it. "I want to have sex!"

With shocking speed and agility, he spun and got in my face. His voice threateningly low, he let his impenetrable mask slip and his nostrils flared. "I don't have sex. I fuck. Hard and long and unforgiving. You don't want to fuck me. You want to win." His jaw ticked, and he leaned closer. "Newsflash, you're not gonna."

Shit. Shit, shit, shit. "I'm not playing a game." Was I?

"Bullshit." He stood to his full height and drained the last of his water. "You want to top."

"*What?*"

He looked at me like he was superior in every way. "When's the last time you had control over anything?"

Oh my God. "You're the one trying to control me!"

"You said you wanted to fuck. I told you how it was gonna go down. You didn't like it. Game over."

"Do you even hear yourself?" Was he for real? "Who's playing a game now?"

He laughed. Deep and rumbling, it was barely a chuckle, but it made my whole body shiver with a desire I didn't fully understand.

The hint of a half smile still on his face, he squashed the plastic bottle in his hand like an accordion. "Put some clothes on, woman."

"No."

In a move that I was sure was completely out of character for him, he shrugged. Then he tossed his decimated bottle in the trash, walked to the security panel in the front hall, and messed with it. A few swipes of the finger that'd been deep inside my pussy, and he'd scrolled through real-time images of the property. When he was finished, he pulled his phone out, sent a text and slipped it back in his pocket.

Staring at him, I crossed my arms. "What are you doing?"

"My job."

Petulant as hell, I couldn't help it, my mouth went for a walk. "Was it your job to fuck with me?"

Ignoring me, he moved to the first slider that led out to the lanai. Checking the lock, he moved to the next.

After two more sliders and three windows, I lost patience

with his silence. "Are you trying to keep someone from getting in, or are you trying to keep me locked up?"

"Whichever I have to." He moved to the next window.

Naked, pissed off, vulnerable, I stood there watching. "Because that's your job?" I said the last word sarcastically as hell, but as the words left my mouth, an idea formed.

He didn't answer. He moved to the dining room and my idea grew into epic desperation. I wondered what had happened to my dignity, or if I'd ever really had any, because in the next instant, I was moving.

Aiming for the slider closest to the pool, I ran.

Literally ran.

Because I knew how quick he was.

I'd gotten the door unlocked and shoved open when I heard his curse.

It didn't matter.

Two seconds later, I dove into the sparkling aqua water that was warmer than inside the air-conditioned house but still crisp and cool. Completely submerged, my limbs reached and flexed and pulled with memory reflex, and I swam.

Underwater, free, I swam.

Stroke after stroke, my eyes open, I swam to the opposite end of the pool, and for one blissful moment, my mind cleared.

I wasn't an actress, or a desperate woman trying to get a man out of my league to have sex with me. I wasn't Dreena MacKenzie, and I wasn't a woman quitting a career people would literally kill for.

I was just swimming.

My lungs burning, I forced two more strokes and reached for the edge of the pool. My hand touched warm concrete, my eyes closed, and I broke the surface.

Air filled my lungs and my bliss collapsed.

Two large hands grabbed me under my arms and lifted.

Then I was literally tossed in the air as a tank of a man threw me up and over his shoulder. Water sluiced off my body and drenched his clothes. My hair in my face, I let out a half scream, half grunt as my stomach hit his rock of a shoulder.

His huge palm landed on my ass, and the sharp slap rang in my ears as the sting hit my backside.

"What the fuck?" I kicked out. "You asshole! *You spanked me?*"

His long strides eating up the distance between the far end of the pool and the house prison, he didn't even pause. "Scream again," he warned. "See what happens."

Enraged, I pounded both my fists on his back. "PUT ME DOWN."

The slap echoed across the pool a split second before I felt it.

And I felt it.

Oh my fucking God, all the way from my scalp to my toes. Every second of his fingers inside me rushed back in a wave of heady desire so thick, I wanted to both choke on it and hurt him. "How dare you fucking spank me!"

"Scream again," he demanded.

"Go fucking fuck yourself, you—"

He slapped me again.

My body jerked. "You goddamn *asshole.*"

Striding into the house, he paused only to slam the slider shut.

"Put me down!"

Walking in to the master bedroom, he put me down all

122

right. He threw me on the bed. I bounced once, and he was on me.

His hands around my wrists, he yanked my arms over my head as his huge, heavy body landed between my legs. "You do *not* walk out of this house naked." His body pressing into me, he increased the pressure on my wrists. "You don't go anywhere naked. You hear me?"

"Why?" I sneered. "You jealous?"

Pure alpha, ruthless intent spread across his features. "I don't get jealous, because I don't give a goddamn fuck what you do on your own time. But when you're on my watch, you don't parade your fucked-up shit naked. You don't drag me down, making me a spectacle by proxy. I will *not* be on your next viral video."

Righteous indignation mixed with suffocating humiliation. My ass stung, my pussy pulsed and tears welled. Hating him, hating everything and everyone, I bucked against his hold and lashed out. "You think you're not *fucked-up?*" I laughed a sick laugh. "Who's holding who down? Who spanked who, asshole? Nice transference," I said as sarcastically as possible.

His chest heaving, his nostrils flaring, he stared at me.

One heartbeat.

Two.

His voice, deep and commanding, dropped to a lethal warning. "Ask."

Chill bumps raced across my skin. "Ask what?"

"You wanna be fucked? Ask." His hips surged forward.

His giant cock pressed between my legs, and my pussy swelled with desire as his jeans grated against my aching clit. I couldn't stop it. The moan was low and deep and vibrated through my chest.

Oh God.

Against every reasonable thought in my head, against every ounce of sanity I still might have had left, my legs spread, my hips thrust, and three words I never, *never* should have said rushed out. *"Fuck me, please."*

CHAPTER EIGHTEEN

Tank

"**F**UCK ME, *PLEASE*," SHE BEGGED.

I thrust. Hard.

My cock driving my actions, I ground against her bare pussy, silently cursing the material of my pants between us.

"Say it again," I demanded, justifying my actions, telling myself she wanted exactly what I was offering. That she wanted my cock inside her tight pussy as much as I wanted to fucking be there. Because, *goddamn*, I wasn't thinking she was like every other woman anymore.

I was stupidly, foolishly, idiotically thinking she was that one in a million.

And I wanted a taste.

"Please," she pleaded, arching her back. "Fuck me, *fuck me.*"

I was undoing my belt before the word please finished crossing her lips. The hand that I'd let go of started coasting down my back and I grabbed it. "Arms above your head," I warned, reaching for my 9mm and pulling it out of my holster to set on the nightstand.

Writhing under me, she was acting like she wanted everything I was gonna give her, but when she saw the gun, she stilled.

I pushed off her and reached for my shirt. "Problem?"

"Is it loaded?"

What the fuck? "Is your pussy wet?" I pulled my polo over my head.

Her gaze cut back to mine, then drifted down my chest. Arms above her head, her knees bent, her cunt waiting, she swallowed. "Have you ever shot anyone?"

I kicked off my boots and tossed my cell and keys on the nightstand. "You expecting small talk?" I didn't discuss my service. With anyone. Not even my brothers who served beside me. They knew what the fuck we dealt with.

Her eyes darted back to mine. "That's small talk?"

Calculating, slow, I dragged my gaze over her full tits then her slick pussy. My dick throbbed at the thought of sinking inside that tight heat. "Turn over," I commanded. "On your hands and knees."

She inhaled. Then her voice went quiet. "I want to look at you."

For a split second I didn't fucking move. My dick hard, my mouth watering to taste that wet cunt, I stood there.

She didn't want to look at me.

She wanted to believe in misplaced hope.

She wanted to be that one magic pussy that turned me from who I was into what she wanted.

Fuck.

Fuck.

I knew what I needed to say. Fuck, I knew what I needed to do, and that was walk the hell out before I took it too goddamn far. I'd already taken it too far. But I wasn't doing a damn thing to stop it. I was fucking staring at a woman I didn't want to admit was the most beautiful woman I'd ever had naked. Except she'd get attached the second I fucked her, and I didn't do attached. But all I could think about was making that pussy mine and never letting another man look at her how I was looking at her right now.

But damn it, I didn't keep women.

I *never* fucking kept them.

My voice rough, my head fucked-up, I barked out an order. "Turn over."

She nervously pulled her bottom lip into her mouth before releasing it and inhaling. "Is that what you do?"

What the fuck? "Did I tell you to talk?"

She kept at it. "You issue orders, pretend not to care, and fuck women from behind so you don't have to look at them?"

Goddamn it. "Who says I'm not looking?"

She ignored my question. "Why? So you can stay detached? Is that your recipe for the perfect life? Mindless screwing of faceless women?"

Thirty-fucking-four years old and I didn't have a comeback for a young-as-shit, sexually inexperienced actress. No goddamn response.

And that pissed me off.

Hard core.

Shoving my pants down, I gripped my hard cock. "You wanna fucking look?" Glaring at her, I stroked myself. "Then look."

Her gaze held mine for a moment, then slow, she took me in as her eyes roamed over my chest.

My dick in my hand, I fucking waited.

Her gaze dropped lower until she finally looked at my cock.

I stroked myself.

Her lips parted on an inhale. "You're so big."

Fuck her. She wasn't going to get me to surrender that easily. Compliments meant nothing to me. I knew who the fuck I was. I stroked myself again. "Two choices," I warned.

She stared at my cock and licked her lips. "What?"

"We fuck my way, or not at all." Fuck her detachment bullshit. She'd get hers.

Her eyes shot to mine. "You're angry?"

Shit clouded my head. *She* clouded my head. "Answer the question," I demanded.

"It wasn't a question. It was a statement."

Jesus fucking Christ. "Make a decision."

Innocent and doe-eyed, but also firm, she spoke. "I already made it."

Women didn't challenge me. I used them, and they got what they wanted. I wasn't detached. I purposely kept my distance. There was a difference. I didn't have time or any fucking desire to share my bed on the regular. Being an active duty Marine left no room for it, and what I did now wasn't much better. My game plan didn't include a woman on a permanent basis. I was Falcon Gunther. I flew solo.

I always had.

But for the first time in my life, the woman on her back in front of me had me thinking about repeats. I hadn't even fucked her and I wanted more.

More of her mouth. More of her bullshit. More of her.

My mouth opened and I asked the last thing I should've. "You clean?"

Her eyebrows drew together. "Seriously, you're—"

"Because I am." I wore a condom religiously. But right now, I'd move mountains not to have to. "You ever been fucked bareback?"

Shit crossed her expression, and her chest rose and fell rapidly. "I could get...." She trailed off.

My chest tightened at the thought. "Period?"

"Um." She bit her bottom lip and closed her legs.

I dropped my voice. "Spread your legs, Audrina."

She complied, instantly.

It was the straw.

CHAPTER NINETEEN

Audrina

H

E SURGED.

His giant cock in one hand, his body a work of muscled perfection, his face a storm of anger and determination, he grabbed my ankle and pulled.

My still smarting ass slid across the bed.

He brought the head of his cock to my entrance and stilled. "Period," he demanded.

"I—*oh my God.*" My core pulsed with aching need. "Um, two weeks ago?" Maybe. I think.

His rough palm on my inner thigh, he stroked the length of me without entering. "You like that? My cock bareback against your cunt?" He rubbed hard against my clit. "You fucking feel that? From your clit all the way to your hard-as-fuck nipples?"

Holy.

Shit.

He didn't wait for an answer, because he knew. He knew exactly what he was doing to me.

"Is this what you wanna look at?" He bit out, fisting himself. "My cock sinking inside you?"

"Yes," I panted, more desperate than I'd ever been.

"Then fucking say it," he growled.

That's when it hit me.

This alpha, unwavering, dominant man needed me to give

him permission. All the back-and-forth, all the questions, all of his bluster and crude words, he was still giving me a choice. This was my call. Despite everything he'd said, *I* was in control.

My whole body shivered in that knowledge, and anticipation soaked my core. "Come closer," I whispered.

His chest rose with a sharp inhale. "Not an answer."

"Fuck me bareback, Falcon."

He thrust.

Hard and fast and punishing, he sank to the hilt, and a fullness I'd never felt stretched me to the point of pain. My hands flew to his hard thighs, and I cried out as he groaned.

One hand on my hip, the other on my nape, he forced my head up and unleashed a command. "Look."

My gaze traveled down his six-pack, to his strong, muscled thighs as he kneeled between my legs, then dropped lower to his thick, vein-popping shaft buried almost all the way inside me.

Oh my God.

My nails dug into his flesh and I shivered.

His hand fisted in my wet hair as his hips slammed into mine. "Goddamn lock and key," he muttered, staring at where our bodies were joined.

Holy shit, he was big. "What?" My voice shook.

Green-brown eyes dark with something I didn't understand cut to my gaze. Staring at me, he pulled out a few inches then slammed back in and repeated himself. "Lock and key."

His hips ground against my clit and I groaned. Lock and key. *Lock and key.* The phrase looped through my head, but his assault on my body eclipsed all its meaning, and I simply stared at the joining of our bodies.

Falcon Gunther was inside me.

Me, the farm girl who had no experience with men but could smile for the cameras and command a seven-figure paycheck. Except that money had never felt more insignificant than it did right now.

Huge and looming and alpha, and so, so dominant that I couldn't take it all in, Falcon "Tank" Gunther was all man. Except I could take it in. My poor pussy both aching and quivering for more, I wanted to drown in this. I wanted to drown in him. I wanted every single ounce of dominance he was offering and more.

Not understanding what I was asking for, I sealed my fate. "Harder."

It was as if I pulled a trigger.

He moved that fast.

His huge hands cupped my ass and he stood. I wrapped my arms around his neck and my back hit the cold wall. Grasping my thighs, he started thrusting. But he wasn't just fucking me. He was staring at himself going in and out of me like he was transfixed.

My pussy on fire from being both stretched and pounded, my nipples aching, my body trembling, I held on to his neck, but suddenly, it wasn't enough. "Tank," I panted.

His sharp gaze cut to mine.

I didn't hesitate. I leaned forward to kiss him.

He dropped his hold on one of my thighs and grasped my throat as his forearm landed between my breasts. My head against the wall, he pinned me in place.

His expression locked down. "Did I tell you to kiss me?"

Shocked, my mouth opened, but no words came out.

"Did I say you could touch me?"

What the…? "Are you serious?"

His steely gaze unforgiving, he didn't so much as blink, but his huge cock pulsed inside me.

I fought a groan. "I can't kiss you?"

He ground his hips. "You want to come."

It wasn't a question, so I didn't answer it, but I dropped the leg he'd let go of.

His nostrils flared, and he raised an eyebrow. "Change your mind?"

I didn't know what the hell kind of game he was playing, and I wasn't sure I ever would. Intuition, instinct, I didn't know which, but something was telling me that this man was either deeply wounded or completely emotionally detached. It didn't matter which. I was never going to win with him. And having him inside me was only playing with my emotions. I didn't need that kind of false hope.

"Put me down, Falcon." Despite begging him only moments ago for exactly what he was giving me, I was suddenly tired, of everything. How could I fuck a man who wouldn't even let me kiss him?

Ignoring me, he leaned closer. "What pisses you off more? That you're not in control or that I didn't let you kiss me?"

His cock still buried deep inside me, his hand on my throat, the cold tone of his voice—I should've been afraid. But I wasn't. In fact, I realized it wasn't exhaustion I was feeling. I was pissed off. "Your shiny newness is wearing off." Suddenly in touch with my anger, I let my gaze drift down his body. "Muscles or not..." I looked back at him. "Your game is played out."

"I don't play games."

I didn't hold back. "That's exactly what you do. You can't even fuck normally. You'd bleed out on a power trip before you let someone kiss you, let alone give up a single ounce of control.

And seriously? It would've been a kiss, not a commitment." I glanced down again. "Which is ironic considering you're taking the risk of fucking me without a condom. Which could lead to one hell of a lot more of a commitment than a kiss if you fuck up."

His jaw clenched. "Your wet cunt's constricting all over my cock, your nipples are hard as fuck, and you groan every time I so much as breathe near you."

"So?"

"You're bitching me out, but you're not gonna tell me to pull out?"

Indignant, I scoffed. "I told you to put me down."

"Tell me to stop fucking you," he challenged.

We glared at each other.

His chest rose and fell steadily, my heart pounded, and a thousand thoughts ran through my head. Did I win if I told him to fuck off? Did I one up him if I told him to pull out? Would I have a shred of dignity left if I let him fuck me till I came?

In the end, none of it mattered.

My traitorous pussy pulsed, and a condescending tip up of the corner of his mouth sealed my fate.

CHAPTER TWENTY

Tank

FOUGHT A GODDAMN SMILE. "TELL ME TO PULL OUT, AUDRINA." IT wasn't a warning, but it should've been. Because the second my dick sank in to her pussy, it was like a lock and key. Every lush, wet inch I sank further in, I fucking knew.

I was gonna fuck this pussy more than once.

Her size, her shape, her sweet fucking smell, I was salivating. I didn't give two fucks that I didn't get hung up on women or do repeats. I was gonna fuck the shit out of her over and over, until she begged me to stop.

No preservation, she didn't tell me to fuck off. Instead, she bargained. "Kiss me and you can fuck me."

I didn't hesitate.

I grabbed the backs of her thighs, pulled out and dropped to my knees.

"Oh my God," she screeched. "What are you doing?"

"Kissing you." I shoved her legs to her chest, and her back hit the wall as she landed at the perfect angle. My mouth closed over her clit and I sucked, hard.

Her hands sank into my hair as her feet landed on my shoulders. "Oh my God, *oh my God.*"

My tongue doing to her cunt what I wanted to do to her mouth again, my first thought was she tasted like pure fucking sin, but my second thought hit me in the chest. Not only did

I want to stay buried between her legs and never come up for air, I didn't want any other man fucking touching her. Ever.

Lock and key, she fit me like a glove.

And I was gonna make sure she knew it.

Sucking her clit, swirling my tongue, I made her fall apart.

"Oh God, Tank." She jerked against my mouth, and her legs shook as her pussy quivered. "I'm going to come."

I circled my tongue harder and she exploded.

Keeping the pressure on her clit, I rode out her orgasm. The low moans coming from her chest vibrated all the way to her pussy, but I wasn't finished.

Making her come, holding on to her, having her trust, that shit fucked with my head. Ignoring all the possessive thoughts I had no business harboring, I held on to her ass and stood.

"*Falcon!*" Her arms went around my head.

"*Audrina,*" I mimicked her tone, not even pissed she was using my real name. Which should've been a red fucking flag, but I was mission intent. My dick hard as fuck, I wanted back inside her. Tossing her on the bed, I watched her tits bounce, and I was about to give her the show she asked for of me sinking inside her when she surprised the fuck out of me.

Rolling, she got down on her knees in front of me before I could crawl over her and wrapped her sexy-as-hell lips around my cock.

Damn.

Damn.

I gripped a handful of her hair and watched as she took me halfway into her sweet mouth. "Fuck, woman."

Staring up at me, she licked the length of my shaft. "Is

that a good *fuck, woman?"*

Fighting a damn smile, I kept my expression locked. "Depends."

"Let me guess." She gave me the sexiest kitten smile I'd ever seen on a woman. "It depends on how well I suck." She took me all the way to the back of her throat.

Fuuuck.

I gripped a second handful of her hair. "You like my cock in your mouth?"

Her response was to suck so hard, I almost came on the spot.

Easing back, taking a breath, she licked up my length again then sucked hard on my frenulum.

Damn. "Where'd you learn to suck like that?" I almost didn't want to know.

"I didn't." She licked around the head of my cock. "I've never done this before." She took me all the way down her throat.

Jesus fuck. My balls tightened as I gripped her head with both hands. Thrusting shallow and tight, all the blood rushed to my dick. Hot, wet, her lips fucking perfect, I couldn't remember better head. I didn't want to. I wanted to come down her throat then eat her pussy until I recovered enough to fuck her for the next five hours.

But I wasn't dick enough to come in her mouth the first time she ever sucked a man. Taking her chin, easing her back, I pulled my cock out as I stared down at her.

Her mouth wet from her own spit, she licked her lips. "I wasn't done."

"Neither am I." I swept my thumb over her bottom lip. Flushed and innocent, but also one hundred percent sex kitten as she knelt in front of me, this woman had sunk into my head as sure as an addiction. I knew I was fucking screwed. Worse, I didn't care.

"Up." Reaching for her, I lifted her to the bed, intending to push her to her back.

Keeping her legs bent, she stayed on her knees as her eyes drifted up my chest. Looking up at me, she bit her lip.

I didn't kiss women. I'd never wanted to, not since I'd first started fucking. Cunt, tits, ass, I was interested in coming, not getting fucking intimate. But looking at her full lip between her teeth, knowing what her mouth tasted like, I wanted to kiss her. Kiss her as I fucked her.

She braced her hands on my hips. "What's that look for?"

I didn't fucking answer. I grabbed her at the waist, my fingers touching in back, and lifted until her full breasts were in my face, then I latched on to one of her nipples.

The moan coming from her throat, her tight bud between my teeth, it made my cock jump as she fell against my chest.

"Oh my God." Her hands ran through my short hair. "Your tongue is amazing."

"My cock is better." I sucked her other nipple, lifting her legs around me. "Watch," I commanded, slowly lowering her to my shaft.

She braced her arms around my neck and ground her hips against the head of my dick.

Fisting myself, I prevented her from sinking any lower on my cock. "Period," I clipped. "Tell me exactly when it was." I needed to come inside this woman.

Her eyes focused on my dick, her legs trembling, she stared as I rubbed against her entrance. "What?"

"Audrina," I snapped. "Eyes on me."

Her hooded blue gaze met mine.

"If your period was two weeks ago, I'm getting a condom."

Breathing heavily, a sheen broke out across her chest. "I've never gone bareback," she whispered.

I slammed her down on my cock.

Her head fell back, and her guttural groan filled the bedroom.

Bracing my legs, I gripped her waist and lifted her back up only to slam her back down.

Fuck. *Fuuuck.*

Tight, hot and constricting all over my cock, her pussy was fucking perfect. So goddamn perfect. "Period," I barked.

"Um, um, um...."

I ground her against my hips, hitting her clit. "When the fuck was it?"

"*Oh my God,*" she cried, still not answering.

I spun and dumped her ass on the back of a lounge chair. Shoving her chest, I grasped her ankles from behind my waist.

She fell back, inverted on the chair.

My dick slid out, and I pressed her ankles to the backs of her thighs. Her legs bent and spread wide, her slick pussy on full display, I held her there.

Slow, calculating, I rubbed my cock the length of her wet slit. "How many days since you bled, woman?"

Watching me, watching my cock, her lips moved silently like she was counting. "Seventeen," she breathed, reaching for my dick.

Fucking perfect. I grabbed her wrists and put her hands on her tits as I shoved back into her. Then I gave her a choice. "You want my come inside you?"

"Yes." She squeezed her nipples. "Oh my God, yes."

Thank fuck. I thrust. Hard.

Then I began to pound into her in earnest. Hips grinding, skin slapping, I alternately pinched and rubbed her clit. I fucked her hard, and I fucked her deep. My cock hitting her G-spot on every down thrust as I bottomed out, I wanted to fuck her forever. But a few thrusts later, a tremor went through her body, her back bowed, and she fucking detonated. Screaming my name, bucking her hips into my thrusts, she clenched her pussy around my cock in spasm after spasm.

My muscles tensed, my balls drew taut, and I fucking lost it.

Gripping her thighs, pulling them toward me as I rammed into her, I came. I came so fucking hard, and so damn much, I felt my own release around my cock as I filled her tight cunt.

Goddamn.

Goddamn.

CHAPTER TWENTY-ONE

Audrina

O H MY GOD, *OH MY GOD*.

His scent everywhere, his muscles bulging and flexing, he drove his hips into me, and he thrust and thrust and thrust. My pussy pulsed and constricted around him and his gorgeous, mesmerizing eyes held me captive in his dominating gaze.

Exertion covered his body and he thrust one more time as all of his muscles bunched. A roar, feral and possessive ripped from his chest and his hot release pumped in to my core.

He came inside me.

No man had ever come inside me.

My head in the seat of the chair, my ass high on the back, he held my ankles, pushing my calves against my thighs. Pinned, practically upside down and worked over by his size and strength and stamina, I didn't think I could take anymore. But the second his hot seed filled me, my pussy came alive again.

Sounds of pleasure I'd never heard come out of my mouth, not even when I was acting, ricocheted through my head and tumbled from my lips. I didn't know what this man had done to me. All I knew? I was writhing under him, wanting more.

So much more.

The sound of my desire and his release, wet and slick inside me, filled the room as he continued to slowly thrust after he came. With each long push into my body, his hard length hit the very limit of my ability to take him. And each one of those thrusts was a shock to my body that was equal parts pleasure and pain. I'd never felt anything so exquisite.

But then he thrust deep and stilled.

His eyes on me, his chest heaving, his nostrils flaring with each inhale, he pulsed deep inside me.

"Oh my—"

His thumb hit my clit and my words died on my lips.

But then he made a perfectly controlled circle.

"No," I cried out. "I can't, I can't…." I couldn't come again. I would fall apart, and nothing would ever hold me together again. This wasn't sex. This was mind-altering fucking, and it only had one outcome. Addiction.

Seated deep inside me, the corner of his mouth twitched. "Yes, you will." He ground his hips once.

I went off.

My pussy exploded into a thousand points of red-hot nerve endings that shot through my core and crawled up my spine. I jerked once, twice, then I shook. Everything shook. Like I was in shock, my legs trembled, my pussy quivered, my teeth started to chatter and my whole body shuddered.

But then it didn't stop.

"Falcon," I cried, suddenly scared. "Wh-wh-what's happening?"

Enormous hands slipped under my back, and I was vertical in an instant.

But the shaking didn't subside. His huge cock still inside me, I grasped at his neck as I tried to lift my legs around his waist, but I couldn't. Shaking worse, they fell to his side as he strode toward the huge bed.

One arm around my back, the other under me, his voice hit my ear. "Deep breath."

I couldn't inhale. Everything shaking like I was going into shock, I tried to respond but my teeth were now chattering in waves. "I-I...." A tear escaped. *"H-h-help me."*

A huge hand grasped my face, and green-brown eyes locked on to me. "I'm gonna pull out. When I tell you, take a breath."

I tried to nod.

"Now," he ordered. "Inhale."

Swift and sure, he laid me on my back on the bed and started to pull out.

Except his hard length didn't slide easily out my body. Hovering over me, he pulled back, but it was as if he was too big to come out, or my core was trying to keep him in, and suddenly it hurt, *really* hurt.

"Ow, ow, ow." I grasped at his bulging biceps. "Stop!"

His eyebrows drew sharply together, and he barked out an order. "Take a breath, *right now.*"

Flinching at his tone, scared of his expression, not understanding what was happening, shaking violently, I started to cry in earnest. "Please," I begged. *"Stop."*

His lips crashed over mine, and for one shocked moment, my world stood still.

Then his tongue sank deep and he was kissing me.

Violently, dominantly, expertly, he stroked through my mouth like he was crazed with lust. Forgetting to breathe, forgetting I was shaking, forgetting I was scared, my arms tightened around his neck and my head swam.

Then I felt it.

His hard length slid easily out of my body.

Wetness surged, and his release rushed out of me.

I gasped at the shocking emptiness, and his body came down over mine. As if he knew what I needed, as if he knew I suddenly felt cold and empty, his arm under my back cradled my head and he lifted me into his chest. Using his heavy, muscular thighs and one arm, he crawled us up the mattress. My head landed on soft pillows, and he settled between my legs. His body weight came down on me just enough so that I felt protected and safe, but not crushed, and he never broke the kiss.

Except he wasn't kissing me now like he did a moment ago.

His tongue still dominating, he was still controlling, but his strokes turned to a coaxing dance, and before I knew it, I was kissing him back.

And he was letting me.

His rough fingers sank into my hair, and he cupped my cheek as his hard length lay against my stomach. "Shh," he soothed, his voice too deep to whisper. "You're okay." His thumb swiped across my cheek. "No more crying."

His touch, his words, they were so achingly gentle, I dissolved into tears.

Twisting in his arms, my hands flew to my face. "I'm sorry," I sobbed. "I don't know why I'm crying." I knew. Deep down, I knew. But I couldn't admit it, not even to myself.

Without a word, he turned me all the way in his arms and brought my back to his chest. One arm slid under my head, the other circled my waist, and he pulled me close. Then he just let me cry. No words, no judgment, he simply held me until all the tears came out.

The embarrassment, the fear, it left with the tears, and

in its place a deep longing settled into my heart. I wanted this man. I wanted everything about him to belong to every part of me. I wanted to tell him where I'd really come from. I wanted to feel his arms around me every night. I wanted to have him inside me, giving me everything he had to give. I wanted him to know me, and I wanted to know him.

But I doubted anyone actually knew Falcon "Tank" Gunther.

And God, I wanted to know him.

"I'm sorry," I whispered in the quiet but comfortable space around us. "I don't know what happened."

He shifted. His hard length slid from the small of my back to between my thighs, and he settled his erection in the remnants of his release. Then he reached down and cupped me, gentle and possessive.

"Don't apologize." His masculine breath drifted over my cheek, my neck. "You weren't used to coming like that." He inhaled. "Next time will be better."

Better? Hope surged and joy spread through my heart, but just as quick, reality set in. If it was any better, my heart would stop. "I don't think I can handle you doing it any better."

His quiet chuckle filled the darkened bedroom and sank into my heart.

CHAPTER TWENTY-TWO

Tank

SMALL AND FRAGILE AND USED, SHE FELL ASLEEP IN MY ARMS.

I lay awake for hours, watching her.

Her cry for help replayed in my head like a broken record, and I couldn't let it go. I couldn't even process the shit in my head over it. Except guilt. I'd fucked her too hard. Too goddamn hard.

Fuck.

Fuck.

I rubbed a hand over my face and she stirred, so I wrapped my arm right back around her small-as-fuck waist. I needed to get the hell up and leave her alone. I'd fucked her into a goddamn panic attack, and shocked her system. Then I'd fucking kissed her and told her next time would be better.

What the ever-loving fuck was I thinking?

I wasn't thinking.

My cock, hard as fuck, was wedged between her thighs waiting to get back into her pussy.

Maybe that's exactly what she needed.

Who the fuck was I kidding? It was what I wanted, not what she needed. A chance at redemption.

I glanced at the clock. She had to be up in an hour for the damn morning show interview anyway, and she'd already had a few hours of sleep.

It was enough.
My decision was made.

CHAPTER TWENTY-THREE

Audrina

DIDN'T KNOW WHAT REGISTERED FIRST, THE WARM, CALLOUSED HAND sliding down my thigh or the masculine breath on my neck. Inhaling, I stretched and opened my eyes, but it was still dark out. I turned my head to glance at the clock on the nightstand, and his fingers caught my chin.

Falcon turned my face toward him. "We have time." Deep and rough, his voice made gooseflesh race across my skin a second before his lips landed on mine.

Sweet and gentle, he kissed me once, then pulled back.

I turned in his arms to face him. The moonlight cast a soft glow and lit up the sharp, austere angles of his face. Every time I looked at him, he was more handsome.

"Hi," I whispered.

He didn't say anything. His thumb swept across my cheek before his hand coasted down my neck and between my breasts. His palm flattened across my belly, and he held his hand there for a moment before he cupped me.

I sucked in a sharp breath.

He frowned. "Sore?"

Was I? I felt like I'd been put through a wringer. Every muscle was stretched and used and yet, his touch made my core hum with a new wave of desire so powerful it ached.

"Maybe a little," I admitted.

His lips came back down over mine, but this time, he didn't stop at one kiss. His tongue sought entrance, then he languidly swept through the heat of my mouth, tasting like mint and man. I realized he must have gotten up at some point to brush his teeth, and self-consciousness rolled over me.

I pulled back.

His thick fingers drew through my still wet pussy before one settled on my clit. "What's wrong?"

I turned my head slightly. "You brushed." Oh God, his touch felt so good.

He pulled my face back to his. "You taste like sex and sleep and woman."

I turned away again and started to get up. "I'll be right back."

"You're not going anywhere." His hand grasped the side of my face. "You taste fucking perfect." His mouth landed back on mine, and he plunged in.

His hand sank into my hair, and he grasped a handful, angling me into his kiss.

A moan crawled up my chest.

He pushed me to my back, his knee shoved my thigh wide, and he settled between my legs. Grasping himself, he rubbed the head of his cock against my entrance.

I broke the kiss and groaned, forgetting about my tight muscles and slight soreness. "More," I pleaded.

His eyes on me, his jaw set, his stare fierce like a warrior's, he slowly, inch by inch, sank inside me.

I couldn't speak. Sounds escaped my lips, my nails dug in to his biceps and my body stretched to take his fullness. I didn't want him to move, and he didn't.

Seated deep inside me, he held perfectly still, watching me.

I didn't know what dominant meant until I met this man. I didn't understand how it should feel, one body connecting with another. I didn't know there was the kind of fucking like we did last night that was so beyond sex, it transcended physical pleasure. And I didn't know there was this, right now, what he was doing to me. What he was doing to my heart.

"I don't have words," I breathed. "I didn't know just this, you inside me, that it could feel so good." More than good, he felt right. Like every moment in my life led to this... connection to him. A connection I'd never dreamed existed.

"Lock and key," he rasped.

His words from last night suddenly made sense. We did fit, exactly like a lock and key. Biting my tongue to keep my emotions in check, I reached up for his face.

He caught my wrist before I could touch him and shoved my arm above my head.

Then he began to move.

Except he didn't fuck me like last night. His movements fluid and languid, he didn't go as deep or thrust nearly as hard. His rhythm controlled, his arm holding his body above me just enough so he didn't crush me, he kissed up my neck as he slowly drove in and out of me.

His touch, his body, his hard length inside me, it didn't feel good. It felt perfect. So, so perfect that my legs spread wider and his name tumbled from my lips. *"Falcon."*

As if he was savoring me, as if he couldn't get enough of me, his lips crashed over mine and he growled into my mouth. His hips moved in a sweet, torturously slow grind against my clit, and that was all it took.

I was coming.

But this orgasm was nothing like what he'd done to my

body last night.

Wave after wave of pleasure rippled through my core and spread through my body like wildfire. My back bowed, my hands gripped his short hair, and I let out a guttural moan I didn't know I was capable of.

His thumb replaced his hips on my clit, and he swirled over my sensitive nerves. "That's it." He bit my neck just below my ear. "Come hard. Show me how much you like my cock."

As if he knew my body better than I did, his thumb swirled to the same rhythm as his hips, and a new orgasm chased the last, blindsiding me. "Oh God," I half cried, half panted. "Falcon, *Falcon*, I'm coming again." My feet planted on the bed and my hips thrust up to meet his.

His growl ripped through his chest and he surged.

Two thrusts and his muscles tensed above me. My pussy clenched around his pulsing cock, and his hot seed pumped inside me.

This time, when I started to tremble, it wasn't from shock. It wasn't fear. The shudder rippling through my body was release.

Pure, unadulterated release.

And when his mouth covered mine and his tongue started a gentle, savoring, caressing dance as he eased out of me, my heart melted into the palms of his rough hands holding me.

CHAPTER TWENTY-FOUR

Tank

M Y COCK WAS SO BIG, AND HER CUNT WAS SO SMALL, WE'D FUCKING knotted every time I'd fucked her. I'd had to kiss her to get her to relax enough to let me pull out. And goddamn, her tight cunt gripping my cock—I was hard just thinking about it. I wanted to fuck her a thousand times just to feel that grip of her body on me. And fuck if I didn't want to kiss her each of those thousand times.

But fucking her and kissing her was the last thing I should've been thinking about right now. Her ass on stage, a couple thousand in the audience and growing every minute, I needed to concentrate on the crowd.

I scanned the audience and stage again. "Collins, Sawyer, crowd control check," I spoke into the comm.

"Fucking rubberneckers," Collins muttered. "But contained."

"Status to the east is still contained," Sawyer added.

"Copy that," I replied. "Stage secure." I turned my attention back to the host who couldn't take his eyes off her.

Faking a sympathetic expression, the asshole host leaned toward Audrina. "So tell us, Dreena, what exactly did happen the other night in Miami on South Beach?"

"Well...." Audrina looked out over the crowd then met my gaze.

I tipped my chin in encouragement. She should fucking sink Payne for his bullshit.

Visibly inhaling, she turned back to the host, but he was already looking off set toward me.

Raising an eyebrow, the prick nodded at me then looked back at Audrina. "Did you want to tell us about the guest you brought with you, first?"

Fucking tool.

Audrina picked an invisible piece of lint off her skirt for effect before acknowledging the host. Feigning nerves, working the audience, I had to admit she was fucking spectacular at what she did.

"Well, Jonathan." Audrina blushed. "I did bring a certain special someone. And while I had told myself I wasn't going to talk about the... incident, or anything personal, I think my fans probably deserve an explanation."

The prick host leaned even closer to her, his expression grave. "Can you tell us what happened that night on the beach?"

Looking contrite, Audrina inhaled. "I was drugged."

A shocked, collective gasp echoed through the audience.

Audrina didn't miss a beat. "I know this is not what I am supposed to say, and I know it's not what the studios want me to reveal, but after talking to... my friend, and thinking things through...." She faced the audience. "I think it's important to let women know what can happen to them in clubs, and I think it's important for any man considering doing what my costar did to know that there are consequences."

A roar of outrage went through the crowd.

The host held his hand up. "Are you saying Colton Payne drugged you without your knowledge or consent?"

Audrina turned back to the host. "I can neither confirm

nor deny an ongoing investigation, but I will say that what you saw on those videos is nothing close to normal behavior for me, as I am sure you can attest to, Jonathan."

"Sure, sure, of course." The prick nodded diligently. "You've been on our show before and we've followed your career since your first movie. We're big fans here at *Miami Morning*. I can personally say I have known you for years, and I have never seen any such behavior from you."

Audrina gave a half smile. "Yes, well, it was not my finest hour." She looked out at the audience. "But I am hoping you all will go see the movie when it releases. I would be honored."

A cheer broke out in the crowd.

The host laughed then held his hand up again. "So, before we go to commercial break, would you care to share with us who this special someone is?" The host's face turned serious. "Who I am assuming is not your costar in this case."

Her blush returned. "No, definitely not my costar, Jonathan."

Jesus Christ.

"In fact," Audrina continued, "this person is quite opposite from any costar I've ever worked with. He's caring and dominant and alpha, and he protects me in his own special way, but he is definitely not Hollywood." Sweet, innocent, a smile spread across her face.

She turned to look at me.

My fucking chest tightened and a war unleashed inside me. I wanted her looking at me. Possessive and so fucking past unprofessional, I wanted the fucking world to know she was looking at me. But I didn't want to be seen. I wanted no fucking part of this life.

"In fact," she continued, "he's the only person besides my

lawyer who knows about the change in my life I'm about to make. A giant step, if you will." She glanced at me and smiled wide.

The host's eyes went wide as fuck. "A giant step?"

Meeting the host's surprised gaze, Audrina nodded. "Yes, Jonathan. I'm taking a step out of the spotlight." She smiled shyly. "I think it's time, don't you?"

The crowd and the host gasped.

"I... wow. I wasn't expecting this." The host chuckled before his expression turned grave. "I was hesitant to bring this up, since we have a mixed audience of all ages here and the producers have yet to verify its validity, but we were alerted to a video of you, apparently taken yesterday afternoon by a private pool, with a certain... gentleman." The host glanced at me. "I wasn't sure if you wanted to comment on that? The footage is quite revealing, in both content and nature. Would this incident, or the gentleman, have anything to do with you suddenly deciding to step away from your career?"

My heart fucking stopped.

Without missing a beat, Audrina nodded as if she were thinking. "I've known you to be such an honest and professional presence in this industry, Jonathan. I would hope that you'd be intent on maintaining your reputation rather than showing some presumed video footage of me." Her practiced smile spread across her face, but it didn't touch her eyes. Then, looking like an angel, she dropped a motherfucking bomb.

"Besides, it's no secret. I like role playing with my special someone." She turned back to look at me. Crossing her wrists like she was in handcuffs, she lifted her arms toward me in surrender. "You ready for me, baby?"

The crowd went fucking ballistic.

The cameras swung toward me, the host stood up, and the noise of the audience roared through my head. Leaning back in her seat like it was all a big joke, Audrina dissolved into actress fake giggles.

But it wasn't a joke.

Not even close.

She'd just sunk my motherfucking career.

CHAPTER TWENTY-FIVE

Audrina

TANK LOOKED APOPLECTIC AS THE CROWD ROARED.

Bile rose in my throat, but I held my fake smile.

The host shot to his feet. Whooping, pumping his fist, inciting the audience, he spun on me and said something I couldn't hear over the noise.

It didn't matter.

My heart pounding like I was going to have a heart attack, the look on Tank's face crushing me, I told myself I did the right thing.

I'd distracted and evaded.

I'd had to.

But I was sick about it. Gut-wrenchingly sick, but I didn't have a choice. Jonathan must've had a video of Tank spanking my naked ass as he flung me over his shoulder. I had to protect Tank. I remembered every word of his threat about making him my next viral video, and I couldn't let that happen. I'd lose him for sure if that happened. Not that I had him, I knew that, rationally, but I couldn't let a video surface of him. At least now I had a chance to text Peter and tell him to sue Jonathan and *Miami Morning* if they leaked anything.

But seeing Tank's face… *oh God.* I told myself I had to say what I did. I had to get the attention away from whatever footage Jonathan had.

The host shouted over the crowd, "We're cutting to commercial, but stay tuned!" He turned to the producer in the wings, laughing, making a cutthroat motion.

The cameras swung to scan the audience and the live stream cut to commercial.

Tank was on me in half a second. His hand wrapped around my upper arm and we were moving. His other arm in front of us, he plowed through the producer and everyone else in production, taking us straight toward the rear exit. The producer, the host, the stage hands, the assistants, they shouted my name, and his, but Tank didn't even pause.

The two Luna and Associates men that'd come with us suddenly appeared, and Tank moved his hand to the back of my neck.

Idiotic, unexpected heat rushed between my legs at the display of dominance and I faltered, making me misstep. My ankle twisted in my six-inch heels and I cried out as I started to fall.

Before I hit the ground, his heavy, thick arms landed behind my knees and back and I was airborne.

Knowing I shouldn't throw him under the bus anymore, knowing it was shitty, I couldn't let the opportunity pass. I looked behind us, then I did what every actress lived to do.

I gave them a show.

Blowing the entire crew, host and producer a Hollywood kiss, I wrapped my arms around my bodyguard's thick neck, threw my head back and laughed like this was all part of the show.

Tank kicked the back door open.

The three black Escalades right where we'd left them, Tank strode to the front one. "Protocol," he barked, yanking the rear door open.

"Copy," the two other bodyguards said in unison, one walking to the second SUV, the other getting behind the wheel of the front one.

Tank practically threw me in the back seat and got in behind me, slamming the door shut. "Drive," he barked at the blond man in a Luna and Associates shirt who'd gotten behind the wheel.

The driver floored it, and I was pushed against the seat. For ten terrifying minutes he wove in and out of downtown Miami traffic until he cut across to the coast and drove toward the house in Golden Beach.

The whole ride, Tank sat next to me silently fuming. His mouth set, his jaw ticking, he stared out the window.

My hands shaking, I pulled my phone out of my purse and sent Peter a text, telling him to go after *Miami Morning* for whatever video they had and spend whatever it took to get it shut down.

Fighting tears, I carefully took off my shoes and rubbed my sore ankle. It wasn't swelling up, so thank God for that, but it still hurt. Everything hurt.

The driver pulled up to the first security gate and entered the code, then drove to the gate for the house and entered that code. Before he had the SUV in park, Tank was throwing his door open and barking out orders to him. "Leave the keys. Get a ride back with Collins."

The blond-haired driver nodded, and Tank slammed his door shut.

I fought for composure. "Thank you for the ride."

The driver watched Tank crossing the front of the vehicle, then he hit the lock button and glanced at me in the rearview mirror. "You okay alone with him?"

I watched the fury in Tank's set jaw as he strode toward my door, and my heart crushed in on itself. "Yeah, fine."

The concern in the driver's face didn't ease. "You sure?"

Tank yanked on my locked door. When it didn't open, he glared at the driver through the front window even though I knew he couldn't see him and banged the side of his fist on my door. "Open up, Sawyer," he barked.

"Last chance," the man he'd called Sawyer warned.

"I'm fine." I heard the door lock release as I grabbed my shoes and purse. A split second later my door was yanked open.

Two giant arms shoved under my legs and behind my back, and Tank took me from the vehicle.

Clutching my shoes and purse to my chest, I dared to glance up at the man who'd woken me in the middle of the night to make love to me.

He didn't look furious, he looked enraged.

For a split second, I cowardly thought about the other bodyguard's unspoken offer. But as I looked over Tank's shoulder, Sawyer was already getting into the other Escalade that'd pulled up behind us, and in truth, I didn't want to run away from this man. As angry as he was, there wasn't anywhere else I wanted to be than with him.

Without a word, Tank strode to the front door, unlocked it, and shoved it open. One step inside and he kicked it shut before dropping the arm under my legs.

My bare feet hit the cold travertine floor, and I opened my mouth to apologize again.

Tank's nostrils flared and the fury in his eyes robbed me of breath. "What. *The fuck*. Was that?"

His veins popping in his neck, his jaw ticking—I'd never seen a more powerful display of emotion. And for the first time

I saw him, *really* saw him.

His dark-brown-edged eyes melted into a perfect kaleidoscope of greens and blue before a darker blue ring circled the black of his pupils. His clean shave this morning had given way to a dark stubble that made my fingers itch to touch it. Three tiny lines in each of the outer corners of his eyes made me wonder how hard-fought his years in the Marines were. The sharp edge of his square jaw tensed as he ground his perfect teeth and I didn't know if the flawless angles of his sculpted face were more Seminole or German.

I thought about every feature on his beautiful, fury-stolen face. But mostly I thought about the full, dark mauve of his bottom lip that was too masculine to be beautiful and too hard to be seductive, but had nonetheless stolen my breath when he'd kissed me so tenderly last night and again this morning right before we'd walked out the door.

And he had kissed me.

After waking me up and making love to me, he'd kissed me like he cherished me, and his hard length had slid out of my body without pain. Then he'd lifted me into his arms and taken me to the shower. He'd washed every inch of my body before he'd taken me against the wall, slowly driving in and out of me until we both came. And he'd done it all without uttering a word.

Afterward, he'd kissed the top of my head and left me to dry my hair. I was putting on makeup when he'd silently come back and stood behind me in the bathroom. Wearing only boxers, his muscles on full display, he'd stared at me in the mirror as he'd kissed the back of my neck and run a caressing hand over my breasts and down my stomach before settling between my legs. Cupping me, he'd simply stood there for a long moment, staring at my reflection and making a silent statement.

I was his.

My body was his.

He was claiming what he wanted.

Then, just as quietly as he'd come up on me, he'd stepped back and walked out. My heart racing, my core wet and aching with need for more of him, I'd taken a moment to get my bearings. Then I'd walked into the bedroom to find he'd laid out a dress, a matching lace bra and panty set, and shoes for me on his bed.

Smiling, I'd put on what he'd picked out for me then made my way to the front of the house where he'd been waiting at the door. Tall and imposing and dressed in his bodyguard uniform, he'd smelled like heaven. Then he'd pulled me into his arms and kissed me, and it'd felt like heaven.

But the formidable, angry warrior in front of me now was not the man who'd protected me, counseled me, befriended me in his own way, and kissed me without reservation. This angry warrior, he screamed dominance and control, same as my bodyguard, but the fury on his face also told another story.

It said I'd undermined him and betrayed him in every way. And I'd single-handedly destroyed his reputation.

Crushing guilt made bile rise in my throat. "I'm sorry," I whispered. "He said he had video of yesterday by the pool. I couldn't let that leak, it would've been worse. I thought some silly words would be better than that."

"Worse for who?" he barked, making me flinch. "Did you have proof he had any fucking video? He knew damn well if he showed shit, you would've sued him and the fucking network." His nostrils flared, and he shoved his free hand in his pocket, yanking out his cell phone and sweeping his thumb across to answer it without ever taking his eyes off me. "What?" he barked.

He was so close to me, I heard a man on the other end of the line swear in Spanish. "*Jesucristo.*" Then his rapid-fire Spanish was too quick for me to pick anything up, but apparently Tank understood it.

"I fucking know that," he bit out.

I heard more Spanish and picked up the word fuck three times and reputation.

Tank glared at me as he answered whatever question the man asked. "No, you're not." Tank hung up, shoving the phone back in his pocket. "You didn't just fuck me over, I was wearing a company shirt. How long before Luna's name is in the mix?"

He didn't wait for me to answer.

"I'll fucking tell you how long. Seconds. It was *seconds* before headlines hit the gossip sites and both my name and the company of my Marine brother were posted, dragged through the mud and slammed all over social media and the news outlets." Every word was bit out with a fury I'd never witnessed in my entire life, personal or professional.

And I deserved it.

I hadn't thought for one second about what he was wearing, or if my words would leak past my world into someone else's.

"I'm sorry," I whispered again. "I didn't want the press getting hold of video of you."

"*Of me?*" he roared.

Tears welled. "I'm sorry." I wanted to curl into a ball and sob. "I'll make a statement. I'll redact what I said."

"*Redact?*" he asked, incredulous. "It's fucking retract when you speak, *not redact.* And you can't ever take that shit back. You think this is some kind of fucking court case where you can have your motherfucking bullshit stricken from the goddamn record?"

A tear slid down my cheek. "Yes."

He glared so hard I faltered.

"M-maybe." No. *Oh God.* "I don't know," I lied, knowing exactly what the press was like. He'd already been tried and convicted as a sadist and his boss's company's reputation was already ruined. Which maybe wouldn't have mattered so much a few years ago, but in an industry teeming with accusations and accounts of sexual impropriety toward women? I fought tears. "I'm sorry. I'll fix this."

"Grow *the fuck* up. You can't fix shit!" He spun and strode toward the bedrooms.

Every decision I'd made in the past forty-eight hours flashed through my mind, and I panicked.

Seriously panicked.

Then I said the last thing I should have. "Falcon, wait!"

Pivoting, he took two giant steps and was on me so fast, I didn't have time to take a breath.

"Do not *fucking* call me that," he seethed. "You don't deserve to use my name."

I watched the muscles bunch and pull on his wide, strong back as he turned and stormed into the master bedroom, slamming the door shut.

CHAPTER TWENTY-SIX

I LOCKED MYSELF IN THE MASTER BEDROOM BEFORE I DID SOMETHING fucking stupid like spank the ever-loving shit out of her. Or worse, angry fuck her until I wasn't so goddamn pissed off.

My phone vibrated in my pocket, saving me from putting my fucking fist through the wall.

"What?" I barked without looking at the display.

"She still alive?" Sawyer asked.

"Go fucking fuck yourself."

He ignored me. "Did you know about a video, or have an idea what she was going to say?"

"Are you fucking serious?"

"I'm not accusing you, Gunther, I'm asking."

Sawyer was the only goddamn fuck I allowed to get away with calling me by my real name. Well, him and the fucking entitled bitch in the next room I was too goddamn pissed off at to talk to.

I hadn't corrected Sawyer the first time he'd called me by my surname because the fucker was a goddamn enigma. Rich as hell, his life set before he ever took his first breath, but the stupid fuck had given it all up to aim a government-issued M4 at fucking hajjis in a forsaken sand trap. I respected the hell out of him for it at the same time I thought he was crazy as shit. Too damn quiet for his own good, I'd never seen the fucker smile, look twice at a woman, make a personal call, or say one god-damn thing about his upbringing. In fact, he never said shit unless you asked a direct question or he was talking about work.

"What the fuck do you want, Sawyer?" If he didn't call to school me, then he needed to get to the fucking point.

"It's not like you to not see something like that coming."

Jesus fucking Christ. "I fucked her, I didn't get in her god-damn head. And for the record, I fucked her in private." I wasn't a goddamn idiot. But the second I thought it, I realized I was. The pool, the *motherfucking* pool yesterday. Visible from both the neighbors and the beach.

Goddamn it.

Sawyer didn't say shit.

"You got something to say, fucking say it," I warned. "Otherwise this call is over." I'd already gotten reamed by Luna. I didn't need Sawyer's shit too.

"I can make a call for you. Put a spin on this." He hesitated, then added, "Professionally."

Fuck me. I ground my teeth and tried to tamp down my anger. "Do I look like a goddamn Hollywood small-dicked ac-tor to you? Do I seem like I need a fucking *publicist* to handle my shit?" I'd served four tours with the United States Marines. I wasn't a fucking pussy. Let that asshole TV host release what-ever the fuck he wanted. That shit was already out there thanks to a spotlight-loving actress who held her hands up like I cuffed her on the regular.

"Don't discount what someone familiar with the industry can do," Sawyer advised.

"I'm not in the industry!" I yelled. "I don't need a goddamn handler." What part didn't he fucking understand?

Unfazed by my anger, Sawyer kept his tone like he always

kept it, this side of a fucking automaton. "Offer stands if you change your mind."

Christ. "Anything else?"

"Don't fuck the client next time."

Prick. "I don't make the same mistake twice." *Ever.*

"Good." He hung up.

I tossed my phone on the bed, and it vibrated with another incoming call. Glancing at the screen, I swore before I answered. "What's up?" Luna calling again wasn't a good sign.

"Her lawyer's not taking my call." Luna cut to the chase. "She in contact with him?"

How the fuck would I know? "No clue."

"Well, get a clue," he clipped. "From here on out, I want to be ahead of this bullshit. Get the lawyer to call me. She isn't going to ruin my reputation over this."

If anyone's reputation was fucked, it was mine. All hope of starting my own security firm was now dead in the water, but I wasn't pussy enough to bitch to Luna about it. He wanted to talk to her lawyer, fine. I'd make it happen. "Ten-four." I hung up and stormed out of the master bedroom.

I checked the kitchen and living room before backtracking and throwing open the guest room where all her shit was.

She was sitting on the edge of the bed, hands in her lap, head down.

"I'm sorry," she whispered.

I scanned the room until I found what I was looking for. I strode toward her purse on the nightstand and grabbed it. Without a word, I dumped the contents on the bed and snagged her phone.

"What are you doing?"

Ignoring her, I stormed out, slamming the door behind me.

I was dialing her lawyer as I walked back into the master bedroom.

The fucking prick answered on the first ring and launched into it. "Audrina, I've been calling you. Where are you? If you'd told me what you were planning, I would have advised against such a public display. All you did was create more trouble for yourself."

"No shit."

Silence. Then, "Mr. Gunther?"

"The one and only. Now, listen up, Stanislas. André Luna has been calling you. You're going to call him back. Then you're going to talk to your client and tell her if she doesn't want to face multiple defamation suits, she better get her shit together and make a statement. Then you're going to find her a new security detail and new accommodations. You have thirty minutes. Understood?"

I could practically hear the fuck swallow. "Thirty minutes is not a lot of time, Mr. Gunther. I understand she—"

"You don't understand shit." I glanced at my watch. "Twenty-nine minutes. Call Luna. *Now*." I hung up and walked back into the guest room.

Wringing her hands, she stood in front of the bed.

I didn't give two fucks about the duress in her posture or her bullshit remorseful expression. I was a fucking tool for thinking I could have a piece of this woman.

I shoved her phone at her. "Your lawyer's calling you. Answer."

She took the phone.

I turned to walk out.

"Are you going to talk to me?"

I kept fucking walking.

She followed me into the hall, and her small-ass hand landed on my arm. "Please, wait."

My nostrils flared, and I spun. Looking first at her hand, then at her, I said everything I needed to say, but she didn't fucking clue in.

Her mouth opened and more bullshit came out. "I'm sorry. I wasn't thinking about the consequences. I was only thinking if I preempted Jonathan's statement, then maybe…." She trailed off and inhaled nervously, looking exactly like she looked a half hour ago on camera, then more lies came out in a rush.

"I thought if I spun it a certain way, I would prevent him from showing any video of you. Of us. I didn't want you to get caught up in this. Which I know I stupidly did anyway. I panicked. I thought I was making the better choice by throwing enough of a bone to stop the release of whatever footage Jonathan had until I could text my lawyer and get him on it, which I already did. I have no words for how sorry I am. I just… after last night, I just wanted to protect you as best I could. I didn't want to screw things up. I was trying to, I thought, I mean…." She looked up at me like a fucking actress playing a part, then she dropped her voice to a whisper for the finale. "You kissed me."

I didn't say shit.

I didn't even blink.

I glared at her.

"Tank, please." Her eyes welled. "Say something. Yell at me. Do *something.*"

A better man would have kept his fucking mouth shut. I wasn't a better man. "I didn't think I was sticking my dick in a spoiled, immature narcissist last night."

Actress-practiced shock spread across her face, and the

mouth that'd sucked my cock opened.

I didn't wait for her response, because I wasn't fucking finished. "I thought I was fucking a woman."

The sound of her gasp hit the air around us and bounced right the fuck off me. I didn't have an ounce of sympathy for her.

I was fucking finished.

CHAPTER TWENTY-SEVEN

Audrina

UNYIELDING, FURIOUS, HE STRODE OUT OF THE ROOM.

I thought I was fucking a woman.

The cruel words ricocheted through my head, then stabbed into my heart. Crushing pain stole my breath, and I couldn't remember one single reason why I thought throwing him under the bus was a good idea.

He was right.

I *was* selfish. And self-serving, and so, so immature.

I should've taken responsibility for myself during the interview. I should've realized Jonathan, of all people, was bluffing about actually showing the video. I should've never said what I said, but I wasn't being honest with myself, and I hadn't been in a long time. Honesty would've been admitting that I knew Colton was a junkie, that he'd always tried to get me to take drugs, and that partying with him at a club would only lead to trouble.

I should've fired my agent years ago when I first realized he was manipulative and I wasn't happy with the path he was taking my career on or the way he spoke to me. I should've owned my choices a long time ago.

But I didn't.

And now the only man who'd ever made me feel like a real woman, hell, the only man who'd ever made me feel, period, just walked out on me.

But he didn't just walk out.

The utter disdain in his eyes took aim and destroyed me worse than any bullet from the gun he carried like an extension of himself.

Reeling, I spun in a circle and took in the four suitcases that comprised my life.

Three were full of clothes I'd never shopped for, and the fourth held all I had left of the life I used to have. A life I could never go back to, but desperately wanted.

Throwing that beat-up suitcase on the bed and opening it, I pulled out the old backpack I'd come to LA with as tears started dripping down my face. My hands riffling through my life's possessions, I didn't stop to think.

I didn't think about the day my mother walked us out of the farmhouse like she was walking me to the bus stop, only to sneak us out back to the barn where we kept the old beater car she used for her once-weekly trip to town for groceries. I didn't think about the cold expression on her face as she drove me to Ned's Diner and dragged me inside, telling me not to say a word.

I didn't think about the woman who I would later learn was a casting agent, who had legal paperwork my mother signed as she smiled and made empty promises of taking good care of me. I didn't think about the horrible feeling when my mother told me I was lucky she was giving me my dream after what I'd done. I didn't think about the first time the casting agent tried to send me home for Christmas so she didn't have to deal with me, only to have my mother say don't bother.

I didn't think about any of the past ten years of acting lessons and school tutors and living with a woman who only saw me as paycheck and booked me with nonstop publicity and back-to-back films.

I didn't think about any of it because I was already on a trajectory.

I haphazardly shoved the few pictures I had, an old baseball cap, and some jeans and T-shirts I'd bought myself into the backpack. I swept my arm across my purse's contents and pushed everything that got caught in my one sweep back inside.

My phone lit up with a call, and I glanced at the screen as Peter's name flashed.

Sending him to voice mail, I swiped through my contact list and dialed a number I never thought I would call.

Colton picked up on the fourth ring. "What the fuck do you want, *Dreena MacKenzie*?" His canned laugh was more bitter than usual. "You already took my balls."

"If you want me to drop charges against you, you're going to do me a favor."

I heard the distinct click of a lighter then a deep inhale and long exhale as he lit a cigarette. "Why should I believe you?"

"Did I ever once bitch about your nasty cigarette breath on set?"

He laughed in earnest. "No. But why the fuck would you? You were making three times what I was."

Wow. That I didn't know. "Are you going to help me or not?"

"Oh, so now it's help you? After you castigated me on live television?" He snorted out a half laugh. "Sure. Lay it out, sweet cheeks. Tell me how I can *help you*."

"I need a car."

He took another drag of his cigarette. "So buy one."

I didn't want to buy one. I couldn't wait that long. "I don't have enough time."

"Time for what?"

"None of your business. I need you to rent me a car and not tell anyone about it."

The dry humor left his voice. "Okay, for real, what's going on?"

"Nothing," I lied, reminding myself that despite the few laughs we'd had on set on the rare occasion he was sober, he wasn't my friend. Not even close. The asshole had drugged me. "I need a car, and I need it now."

"Have Janette get you one, or your asshole agent. Fuck, rent one yourself. There's a place with Lamborghinis around the corner from the hotel."

"I can't." I channeled my best sullen teenager voice. "I'm not twenty-five."

Sighing loudly, Colton held the phone away for a second. "Hey, you, wake up." I heard the rustle of sheets, then a female voice mumbled something incoherent. "Yeah, whatever. I need a favor. Here, take…." Paper rustled. "Here's two grand and change. Go rent me car… Yeah, right now. Go, giddy up. Get your ass out the door." The female voice said something. "I don't care, any kind of car. One that runs."

"Colton," I warned. "I don't want to get in trouble over this."

Colton came back on the line. "You couldn't get in trouble if you tried. Even your stunt today has your fans swooning over your new bodyguard slash boyfriend and placing bets on how soon you'll pop out little Hollywood babies." He took another drag of his cigarette. "Which, if you'd told me you were into kink, I would've been more than willing to ride that freak train with you."

"Fuck you."

He laughed. Hard. "I knew it. It was a total act, wasn't it? Did you even fuck meathead?"

"You're an asshole."

"An asshole who's getting you a car," he reminded me.

I ground my teeth. "Where are you?"

"The fuck motel, where else?"

"I'm on my way." I hung up and shut off my phone.

Thirty seconds later, I was skirting the pool and running toward the beach with my backpack.

CHAPTER TWENTY-EIGHT

Tank

WALKED OUT OF THE HOME GYM CHRISTENSEN HAD, MARGINALLY LESS pissed off. Dripping with sweat, instinct hit me. I dropped the hand towel and palmed my 9mm as I moved to the kitchen without making a sound.

My senses on high alert, I didn't know what the fuck was different, but something was. I scanned the open plan kitchen and living room, but nothing stood out. The doors were all closed, the lights were still off and the sun had just set.

Listening for any movement, I silently made my way down the hall. Bypassing the master and third bedroom, I went straight for her room and tried the door handle.

Locked.

I banged on the door once. "Audrina, open up."

One second, two, three. No response.

Shit. *Shit.*

I kicked the door right below the handle. Wood splintered as it swung open and slammed into the wall.

The second my gaze hit the room, I knew what was wrong.

Slider door open, the worn suitcase opened on the bed, shit strewn all over—she was gone.

I hit the lanai running.

Circling the pool, scanning the side yard, I ran toward the beach access and sprinted out to the sand. When I hit the beach,

I looked south and north, but I didn't see her. I didn't see anyone except an older couple with a dog a hundred yards south.

"Fuck!"

I was running back toward the house and the garage when I realized I still had the car keys in my pocket. I checked the garage for the Escalade anyway and sprinted into the house after I saw it parked where I'd left it.

I went straight to the security panel and scrolled through the video footage of the back of the house and the pool. A minute later, I saw it.

Audrina with a backpack jogging around the pool and heading straight for the beach.

My gut constricted as I looked at the time stamp, then at my watch.

Two hours ago.

Two motherfucking hours ago.

Which was a goddamn lifetime when tracking someone.

I pulled my phone out and dialed Luna.

He answered on the first ring. "This better be good. We lost three celebrity clients today."

Fuck, fuck, fuck. "She's gone."

Silence.

I inhaled, then fessed up to my fucking negligence. "Two hours ago."

"*Jesucristo*," Luna swore. "What the hell happened?"

"I was pissed. I needed a workout. She was in her room, talking to her lawyer."

"For two hours?" Luna practically yelled. "What the fuck, Tank? You do that shit on your own time."

I didn't defend myself, because he was right. I didn't have an excuse. I'd crossed every professional line I could think of.

Fucking her was child's play compared to turning my back on her. She could've been kidnapped, for fuck's sake.

"Christ," Luna swore. "Tell me what you have." He started typing on a keyboard. "I'm bringing up the security feeds there."

"She left through the slider in her room and went toward the beach. The cameras lost her after that."

"Shit, I don't have coverage on that property past the yard." He typed some more. "I'm bringing up her cell now. Hold on, I'll trace it… *Mierda*. Last ping is your location, two hours ago. She either turned it off or left it there."

Fuck me. I strode into her room, and sure enough, in the middle of the pile on the bed was her phone. "It's here. She left it."

"Damn it, hold on. Let's see who she called last."

Luna clicked away on his computer, and I fucking stewed. Rifling through the shit she left behind, I couldn't believe she'd taken off. Then again, I could. I'd been a dick. She'd deserved it, but I was still a dick. I should've fucking checked on her before working out.

"Okay, got it," Luna said absently. "I'm calling the number. I'll put it on speaker." A few seconds later, I heard a phone ringing, then someone picked up.

"Derks, you prick, that you? Where the hell are you? You said you would bring my shit hours ago."

"Mother*fucker*," I cursed. "That's Payne. Play it out."

"Copy," Luna whispered, before raising his voice. "Yeah, I got held up. I'm on my way."

"About fucking time," Payne slurred. "You get what I wanted?"

"Yeah," Luna answered. "On my way. Where you at?"

"Where the fuck do you think? The W, you moron."

"Room number?" Luna asked.

"You have a fucking seizure since yesterday? You already forget I'm in the east penthouse?"

Luna cleared his throat. "On my way."

"Hurry the fuck up, ass—"

Luna hung up on Payne. "You heard. He's at the W. You want backup?"

I was already walking toward the garage. "No. I got this. I'll let you know what I find out."

"Affirmative. And that fucking pendejo needs rehab."

No fucking shit. "Not my problem. I'm out. I'll check in later."

"Copy that."

I hung up and got behind the wheel.

Fifteen minutes later, I was riding the elevator up, ready to pound Payne's face in for the simple fact that she'd called him. I didn't know what the fuck she'd been thinking, but it pissed me off to no end that she'd reached out to him.

I pounded on the door to the east penthouse, and a few seconds later a chick in a bikini, drunk as hell, opened the door.

"Well, hello there." She grinned, holding on to the door for support. "What's your name?"

I pushed past her. "Where's Payne?"

"Fine, ignore me." She pouted.

I glanced around at a half dozen chicks in various states of undress lounging on the furniture. One was on her knees, sucking off what had to be Payne's security as he sat with his head back and eyes closed in a chair by the balcony.

Unholstering my gun, I took three strides and shoved the muzzle in to the guard's temple. "Tell her to take a hike."

179

To his credit, the asshole didn't flinch. He tapped the chick's shoulder. "Take a break, sweetheart."

His fucking dick still in her mouth, her eyes dilated as hell, she looked at him.

The guard upped the command in his tone. "Now."

Her gaze cut to my gun, and a heartbeat later, understanding dawned. Her eyes went wide, her hands went up and she fall back on her ass. "I wasn't doing anything wrong."

Jesus fucking Christ. "How goddamn high is she?"

Putting his dick back in his pants, the guard ignored me. "It's fine, sweetheart. Take a break, get something to eat."

Nodding like a fucking bobblehead, she crawled backward before scrambling to get up and take off.

I focused on the guard. "There's two ways this can go down. You and your client answer my questions." I paused.

"Or?" the guard ground out.

"I call Miami PD and tell them about Derks and the amount of drugs in your and your client's possession."

The guard sighed. "What do you want?"

"Was Dreena MacKenzie here?" I could get Luna to talk to security and explain the situation and we could review footage, but this was faster.

The guard's shoulders relaxed marginally. "Yeah. Couple hours ago."

"What'd she want?"

"No clue. You'd have to ask Colton. She went into his room and came out a few minutes later."

I stepped back, but I didn't drop my weapon. "We're going to talk to Payne, and you're going to tell him to answer my questions."

The guard stood without comment and walked toward

one of the closed doors off the living room with me on his six.

The women fell silent as they saw my gun, but I gave zero fucks.

The guard knocked once on the door, then opened it and walked in. "Colton. We got company."

Naked, fucked-up, and eyes bloodshot, Payne sat up in his bed and snorted a line on the nightstand as two naked chicks lounged next to him. "Derks better have come through. I'm almost out of blow."

"*Colton*," the guard snapped.

Payne looked up. When he saw my gun on his guard, he held his hands out. "What the actual fuck, dude? I already told you I'm sorry about Dreena."

"Why'd she come here?" I demanded.

Payne hesitated as the two women stared at me.

I pressed my gun harder against the guard's head. "Explain to him why he needs to answer my question."

"Answer him, or your drug days are over," the guard clipped.

"All right, calm the fuck down." Payne swiped the back of his hand under his nose. "She wanted a car, said she needed one pronto. She said she couldn't rent one, or some shit, so I got her one."

My jaw ticked. "What car? Where was she going?"

"I don't fucking know. I'm not her keeper." He held one nostril and sucked in deep. "You're the one fucking her, you figure it out."

I pulled my phone out and swept my thumb across to dial.

"Colton," the guard snapped. "*Answer him.*"

"Jesus." Payne lit a cigarette, then glanced at the two women next to him. "What was that other chick's name? The one who left?"

They both shrugged, but one spoke up. "I don't know, but she gave Dreena her car keys before she left."

Motherfucking shit. "She's gone?"

The chick nodded.

I looked at Payne. "Who was the girl?"

Payne threw his hands up again. "I don't fucking know!" He tipped his chin at his guard. "Ask my useless security here. He's the one who gets them."

"Name?" I demanded of the guard.

"Don't know," he admitted. "I picked her and the others up at a club last night."

Stupid fuck. "You have them sign NDAs?"

The guard's eyes cut to mine, and his expression said it all.

Goddamn it.

Holstering my gun, shoving my phone back in my pocket, I walked the fuck out.

CHAPTER TWENTY-NINE

Audrina

GRIPPING THE SHAKING STEERING WHEEL, I CURSED THE PIECE OF shit car.

I was only going sixty miles an hour, but the old sedan sounded and felt like it was going to come apart at the seams.

An SUV blew past me, honking.

"Shit." I jerked in surprise, and the right tires thumped along the lane markers.

A second later a loud bang sounded and the car swerved violently as I blew a tire.

Gripping the steering wheel, taking my foot off the gas, I got the piece of junk car to the side of the highway and coasted down a soft embankment. Breathing hard, my heart pounding, I tugged my baseball cap lower and got out of the car.

Shit, shit, shit.

The front passenger tire was completely blown.

Praying there was a spare, I went back to the driver side, popped the trunk, and held my breath as I made my way to the back.

A donut spare.

Cars flew past on the highway as I stared at what I should've been thankful for, but everything in the past twenty-four hours hit me and I couldn't stop it. I started crying. Stupid fucking piece of shit car. Stupid-ass donut spare. Stupid, *stupid* six-and-a-half-foot bodyguards, and stupid fucking me for not only sleeping with him, but saying what I did on live television.

Tears running down my face, I yanked out the spare and the jack, not noticing the lights until it was too late. Not that I could've done a damn thing about a highway patrol cop pulling up on me anyway.

Not sure if I should ignore him and start changing the tire, or just stand here like a fucking idiot, I went with option two.

The cop got out of his vehicle and took in the spare I'd hefted to the side of the car. "Tire trouble, ma'am?"

Please don't recognize me, please don't recognize me. "Yeah. It blew out. But I have a spare. I'm just going to change it quick."

His brown eyes took in my tears as his hand settled on his gun. "You okay?"

I forced a laugh and swiped at my face. "I'm good. I just cry when I get frustrated."

Staring at me, he nodded solemnly. "Understandable." He glanced at the blown-out tire. "You alone?"

"Yes, sir." Shit. Please, *please* don't ask for ID or registration. I didn't even check to see if the car had a current plate. I'd just followed the girl who could have passed for my sister out to the beach parking lot and taken the keys. I'd given her another grand and I'd made a promise to send her more money after I got to where I was going as long as she didn't tell anyone. She'd agreed, and I'd gotten on the road.

Cars flew down the highway, and the highway patrol guy didn't say anything for a moment, then an eighteen-wheeler passed and he nodded at the spare. "Do you need help with that?"

Thank fuck for growing up on a farm. "No, thanks." I moved toward the blown tire with the jack and tire wrench. "I got it. I've had lots of practice."

He looked at the rear tires. "You should get new tires, ma'am. The treads are worn down on these."

I nodded as I squatted next to the blown tire. "Next paycheck, I promise."

The radio on his shoulder squawked and a female voice issued a string of numbers. The cop touched the radio and responded in code, then glanced at me. "Be safe getting back on the highway, ma'am."

I smiled. "Thank you."

He nodded once and hustled back to his cruiser. A few seconds later he was gunning it, and I was letting out a sigh of relief. I quickly got the lug nuts off, changed the tire, and ten minutes later I was back behind the wheel, cursing my luck.

Fifteen hundred miles on a donut tire.

Fuck my life.

CHAPTER THIRTY

Tank

STARED AT THE CONTENTS OF THE FOUR SUITCASES I'D EMPTIED ON the bed.

I was missing something.

How could a chick not have one single fucking clue about who the hell she was or where she'd go? I knew her bio. The grandparents who raised her in Kansas were dead. No other family, no other friends according to the shit she'd told me in the hospital. And her ex-agent and ex-publicist were holed up at the same hotel as Payne. The same hotel she'd left hours ago after seeing Payne.

Impatient, I called Luna. I'd asked him to hack into the hotel security feeds to see what he could find and run a background check just in case. But that was thirty minutes ago.

"I'm still working on it," he answered, preempting my question. "But the hotel security cameras only showed her walking out with another blonde. I wasn't even able to capture a face shot, both of them had their heads down. They walked toward the public beach parking, then I lost them. There're no cameras on that lot. By the way, Collins is on his way over."

"What the fuck for?"

"Backup."

"For a hundred-pound actress?"

"She's gone through two of my men. She's a goddamn

elephant in my book."

"She didn't go through me," I growled.

"Around, through, behind your back, same thing—she gave you the slip. What'd you find at the house?"

Luna pissed me the hell off with his statement, but he was right. "I went through the shit she left behind, but there's nothing."

"What do you mean nothing?"

Exactly what I fucking said. "No personal items." All her shit was here, but it was as if she was a void. No prescriptions, no jewelry, no papers except screenplays, or whatever the fuck you called the print version of movie scripts. There wasn't even a single piece of paper with a sample of her handwriting on it.

"*Mierda*." Luna sighed. "So far, I've got nothing too. Her lawyer hasn't heard from her. Her agent and publicist say they haven't seen her, and neither had a clue about where she'd go. Her license has the studio listed as her address. She's got no property listed under her name, no living relatives according to her bio, and no vehicles registered to her. How can a famous actress be a ghost?"

No fucking clue. "I need something." I needed to fucking find her.

"Working on it." I heard typing. "But we may need to call this one."

"Fuck that." She fucking threw my rep and Luna's. "I'm finding her and she's gonna retract what she said."

"To what end?"

"What the fuck? What do you mean to what end?" What she did was bullshit.

Luna exhaled tiredly. "Look, I'm the first to admit I'm pissed as hell. Mostly at myself for not seeing what a loose cannon she was. But the damage is already done. Fallout happened. We'll fucking adjust."

"I'm going after her," I warned.

Luna didn't say shit.

"What?" I demanded after a few seconds.

"Why do you want to go after her? Real answer."

Fucking Christ. "First Tyler, then me, then your company. She fucked us over." What the hell? "You need more reasons?"

"No, but it sounds like you got more reasons you're not letting on to."

What the actual fuck? "Like being accused of being a sadist on national television?"

"Are you?"

"Jesus fucking Christ." If I hadn't served with him, I would've been pounding his face in.

Luna didn't let it go. "Did you handcuff her?"

"Not when I fucked her," I snapped.

Silence.

"That what you want to know? Anything else, *boss*?"

"*Jesucristo*, Gunther." Luna let out a string of curse words in Spanish. "Do I need to call our fucking lawyer?"

"For what?"

"Did you handcuff her?" he asked, incredulous. "Because I'm not getting my ass sued for wrongful imprisonment, or whatever the fuck you did to her."

"I'm gonna pretend you didn't just insinuate I had nonconsensual sex."

"Well, did you?"

"Fuck you." Adrenaline pumping, livid, my head a goddamn mess, I walked back out to the front hall and pulled up the video footage again.

"Tell me to fuck off all you want, I wasn't the one hand-cuffing and fucking a client."

"For the record, those events weren't simultaneous." I was a grown-ass man, I wasn't gonna explain shit to him. "Not that it's any of your business." I scrolled through the footage of her leaving, hoping to see something I missed the first ten times I watched it. But all I accomplished was watching her ass running away from me again.

"None of my business? You fucked her on my payroll," Luna practically yelled.

Jesus Christ. "Just get me a lead. I'll find her."

"Which brings us right back to where we started."

The front door opened and Collins walked in. "Yo!"

I nodded at him and walked back to her bedroom. "Call her lawyer again, see if he knows if she has a permanent address." That was the best I had. I was out of ideas.

Collins followed me into the bedroom and whistled low at the mess. "Chick's got more clothes than a damn mall."

Luna snorted. "Her lawyer isn't going to tell me shit. He gets paid not to."

Collins bent over by the bed and snatched something off the floor. "Damn. This isn't a bleeder," he muttered, holding up an old photo. "This is trouble."

Even more jaded about women than me, Collins catego-rized women into two types, bleeders and trouble. The sick fuck said bleeders were women who bled your checkbook dry, but I suspected his nickname was twofold. The other category was trouble, which he classified as a whole new level of living hell.

I snatched the photo out of his hand. "Luna, hold up." I stared at the picture. It was her on a horse at full gallop. She was young in the picture, ten, twelve maybe, but she looked almost the same. Her long blonde hair was blowing behind her, her smile was unguarded, and she looked like a younger version of the woman I'd had in my bed. The one without makeup or pretenses.

Collins pointed at the top left of the photo. "What's that say?"

My gaze cut to the background.

There was a street sign. Oak. The road part was faded out. Or lane, or street. I didn't fucking care. How many dirt roads called Oak could there be in Kansas?

"We got a lead," I told Luna.

CHAPTER THIRTY-ONE

Audrina

THREE DAYS.

Three long, insufferable days to drive to Iowa, and this was my reception?

I stood in my parents' kitchen staring at three strangers with my backpack on one shoulder.

"Well look what the cat dragged in," my mother muttered, going back to chopping vegetables.

My father looked at my wrinkled dress. "That what they wear in Hollywood these days?"

My brother leered at me. "That's probably what you wear when you're broke." He punched my dad's arm and laughed before looking back at me. "You broke, ain't cha, sis?"

My mother dumped the zucchini in a frying pan. "Broke or not, everyone's gotta pull their weight around here." She nodded toward the table. "Wash up, girl. You ain't no better than any of us. Set the table while the boys take the horses back to the barn."

Speechless, I stupidly did exactly what my mother said.

CHAPTER THIRTY-TWO

Tank

NINE MOTHERFUCKING DAYS.

Countless Oak Roads, Streets, Lanes, Avenues. All of them dead ends. None were dirt roads, and none had farms with horses on them.

Pitch fucking black, in the middle of nowhere southeast Kansas at almost midnight, I sat in the SUV wondering what the fuck I was doing. Chasing a goddamn woman I'd fucked once. Three times if you wanted to get fucking technical.

I didn't want to get technical.

I wanted to find her ass.

And spank it.

Fuck.

Fuck.

But that wasn't gonna happen.

I had to call it.

Inhaling, I dialed Luna.

He answered on the first ring in a hushed voice. "Luna."

"You can't talk?" He knew it was me calling.

"Affirmative."

"Copy that. Just a heads-up, I'm coming back in. No results, I'm calling it."

"Negative."

"What?" Tired, I rubbed a hand over my face.

"Calling back." Luna hung up.

I sat there a minute looking at my phone. Then the minute turned into five, and I threw the SUV into drive. As I pulled back on the road, my cell rang.

I pushed the button on the steering wheel to answer. "What's up?"

"I didn't call you earlier because it was only a hunch. I needed time to confirm it, but something came up two days ago."

Two fucking days ago? I pulled back over and threw the Escalade in park as my heart rate rocketed. "Confirm what?"

"Did you know her first agent died?"

"No." And I didn't care.

"Me either, not at first, until I did some searching a couple days ago, trying to tie up loose ends. She died five years ago. She was single, never married, no kids, her clients were her life, but she didn't have any that were nearly as successful as Dreena."

I hated her nickname. "So?"

"So, guess where she grew up?"

"No fucking clue."

"Kansas."

So she grew up in the same state as Audrina, so fucking what? "You going somewhere with this?"

"No siblings, she was raised by her grandparents."

Frowning, I sat up straighter. "Okay."

"They died a year apart."

"Shit," I said quietly. That was Audrina's bio. Word for word.

"And guess what her middle name was?" He didn't wait for me to reply. "MacKenzie."

"Jesus fuck." Who the hell had I been chasing for nine god-damn days? "Then who the hell is she?"

"I don't know. I've searched name changes using her screen name, and I can't find anything. Usually those are public record, but you can request they be sealed for safety purposes. Or?" He paused. "For minors."

Fuck me. "So how do we find out who the hell she is?" And where she went?

"I have a few ideas, but I need to be back at base and on my machine there. I've been with a client for two days, but I'm wrapping it up."

"Have someone else do the search."

Luna snorted. "It'd take me longer to explain how to do it than if I did it myself. Give me an hour to get back in the office and run a search. I'll call you then."

A fucking hour? This was the first lead I'd had in nine days. I didn't want to wait an hour. "Tell me what to search for." I pulled back on the road and headed for a hotel I saw earlier. "I've got my laptop."

"Give me an hour," he repeated.

"Fine." *Fuck.*

"Later." Luna hung up.

I drove to the hotel parking lot then sat in the SUV and stupidly did a search on my phone for Audrina's first manager. The first shit that popped up was the South Beach video. My dumb ass watched it five times, fluctuating between a jealous rage at Tyler carrying her naked and remembering every inch of her body I'd tasted.

For nine days I'd replayed the shit I'd said to her in anger, and I was fucking pissed at myself. I remembered what I'd said to her about not being her next viral video. I should've cut her some slack for trying to keep another video out of the media.

Luna had told me he'd gotten it out of her lawyer that there was in fact a video. A neighbor had filmed the shit by the pool and sold it to someone on *Miami Morning*'s staff. The lawyer had been able to get the footage destroyed with threats of lawsuits, but it didn't make me feel any fucking better.

She was still out there somewhere.

Fifty-seven minutes later my cell rang and I answered.

Luna cut right to the chase. "I can't believe I didn't think of this nine days ago."

I was out of patience. "Think of what?"

"To look into her previous agent. Before you left nine days ago, when I called her agent and her publicist to tell them she'd split, the publicist gave me a bullshit line about respecting her privacy, but her agent was livid. I asked if he knew where she'd go, or what friends she might turn to. He'd told me she didn't have friends unless you counted her useless previous agent. When I asked him for the contact information, he'd told me she was dead, so I'd let it slide.

"But two days ago when I was reviewing my notes to close out the case, I remembered his comment about the dead agent. I ran a background check on the woman, and that's when I found out what I told you."

Goddamn it. "And now?" What the fuck did he have now?

"And now, we hit pay dirt," he said proudly.

"Tell me what the fuck you found," I ground out.

"At first, nothing. But then I found an old court filing. She'd become the legal guardian of a thirteen-year-old female minor ten years ago. The name of the minor on the paperwork was sealed, but the parent who signed the papers wasn't. Lorna Jensen, aged forty-three."

My heart was fucking pounding. "Goddamn it, Luna."

Ignoring me, he went on. "But I couldn't find a Lorna Jensen that age anywhere. Not in California, not in Nevada, Arizona, or Oregon. Nothing. No birth certificates, no driver's records, no legal documents, nothing. So on a hunch, I checked Kansas."

I held my fucking breath.

"Nothing. So as one last ditch attempt, I checked the neighboring states."

Jesus fucking Christ. "And?"

I could practically hear him smile. "I found her. Inadvertently. Twenty-three years ago, listed as the mother, Lorna Daisy Jensen gave birth to a healthy baby girl named Magnolia Audrina Jensen. Town? *Drinaville*, Iowa. Address?" He paused for effect. "Nineteen eighty-nine Oak Road."

I quickly plugged the address into my phone's GPS. "Motherfucker, that's twelve hours from where I'm at."

"You're welcome."

I ignored his sarcastic ass. "Her parents are alive?" Besides the obvious greedy reason, why the fuck had her mother signed over guardianship to an agent?

"And kicking apparently," Luna answered. "Because the address on the property records is a farm with thousands of acres."

"I'm heading there now."

"Copy that."

"I'll report in tomorrow."

Luna chuckled dryly. "Just get your woman and come the fuck home. I've been short a man for nine days."

"She's not my woman. I'm going after her because—"

"Gunther," Luna snapped, interrupting me.

"What?"

"Shut the fuck up and admit you got it bad for this chica."

My back teeth ground. "I don't *get it bad*."

Luna laughed loudly. "Right, Marine. Keep telling your-self that." He hung up.

I drove to fucking Iowa.

CHAPTER THIRTY-THREE

Tank

O AK ROAD.

Dirt, dust and one street sign with the road letters so faded you could barely see them.

It was the exact same as in the picture.

Crops on either side, I drove down the single lane until it widened in front of an old farmhouse and barn. Not a soul in sight, nothing but the sound of wind, I got out of the SUV.

Land as far as the eye could see, there were acres and acres of it. It was remote and isolated and so fucking quiet, the place made my skin crawl.

The crunch of gravel sounded behind me a split second before he spoke.

"Figured there had to be something that drove her back here."

I turned around.

An old man with a shotgun casually held in one hand eyed me. Bright blue eyes, blond hair gone gray, he looked too old to be her father, but she sure as hell resembled him.

"Figured that something was a man," he added.

I glanced at the twelve gauge. "You got a problem with wildlife here, or just strangers?"

He ignored my question. "I don't know whether I should shoot you or shake your hand."

I took a calculated risk and held my hand out. "Tank Gunther."

He eyed me skeptically but took my hand. "That a name or a statement?"

I didn't bullshit him. "Both."

He glanced at my height. "Don't suppose I can argue with that."

"Not sure you'd want to." I wasn't being an asshole, I was just letting him know I wasn't gonna sit here and waste my time shooting the shit.

He nodded slowly. "She back for good?"

So she was here. "Ask her yourself."

He scratched the gray stubble on his chin and looked out over his fields. "Made a lot of mistakes in my day." His shrewd gaze made its way back to me. "You probably know what I'm talking about."

Fuck. He was going to do exactly what I hated. Crossing my arms, I leaned back against the SUV. "If you're implying I've made mistakes in life, you'd be right. Doesn't mean I don't learn from them."

He nodded again, then looked back out at the farmland that stretched for miles. "My daughter one of them mistakes?"

"I'm here in a professional capacity, if that's what you're asking."

"Bedding my daughter is a professional capacity?"

Jesus Christ. "I'm not sure what your daughter told you, but whatever it was, it was one-sided."

His eyes narrowed as he frowned. "She didn't tell me anything." He looked at me like he could see right the fuck through any bullshit I could dish out. "She never does."

I merely tipped my chin because I didn't know what the

fuck went on between them. "She around?"

"That depends."

"On?"

"Why you're here."

Fuck it. I told him the truth. "She needs to do something for me."

He eyed me again. "You don't look like you need any woman to do your bidding."

"You're right." I didn't. "I want her to do something for my boss."

"Something for you, or something for your boss, which is it?"

I scanned the old house in the distance and the barn off to our right. "Does it matter?" Where the fuck was she?

"Not to me," he admitted.

"You gonna tell me where she is?" This was a big fucking property. It'd take me a day to search it.

"Still deciding."

"Can't fault a father for protecting his daughter." Not that I knew shit about being a dad.

He let out a grunt. "I protected her too much." His gaze met mine. "Lost her ten years ago because of it."

Ten days ago, I was so fucking mad, I would've told the old man to fuck off and get his daughter's ass out here. But I had to admit, the shit I went through to find her had me curious about how she'd gotten from point A to B. A thirteen-year-old farm girl didn't often break into Hollywood.

"She never told me about that," I admitted.

The old man looked pensive. "I'm sure there's a whole lot she never told you. Women are like that."

I smirked. "I'm sure you're right."

"Well." He inhaled deeply. "Not my place to tell it."

I didn't say shit. I waited him out because the second someone told you they shouldn't say something, it meant they were looking for any excuse to tell you. And nothing made people talk like keeping your mouth shut. They'd rush to fill the void. Me? I lived in that fucking void. But apparently the old man didn't.

Thirty seconds later, he was opening his mouth and dumping his regrets.

"I didn't send my kids to school. Had no use for it myself. Nothing beats learning how to do an honest day's work." He nodded at his fields. "Been farming this land since I could walk. Figured my kids would have the same life. It didn't matter one of 'em was a girl. You ask me, girls got two good hands and two good legs same as boys. Both can learn to farm. Figured my boy and girl would learn how to work the land together and it'd give 'em an easier time of it than I had after my daddy died." He kicked the dirt. "Ain't a one-person job. Not even with a heap of farmhands."

I didn't know shit about farming. "I imagine not." Give me a gun over a shovel anyday.

"Well, I didn't account for a girl growin' into a woman." He raised an eyebrow at me. "No idiot box, no proper schoolin', no time wasted sittin' in front of a computer that tells you about the world instead of you seeing what's right in front of you. I kept them kids honest. Step off your front porch and you got life. That's how I always saw it, and that's what I taught 'em." He looked past me toward the house. "Didn't realize it was all for naught." He paused, scratching the back of his neck.

I kept my mouth shut.

He abruptly changed the subject. "You ever tried to hold

on to a spooked horse?"

I shook my head.

"It's impossible. A man's strength ain't no match for a horse when he's behaving, let alone when he's got the fear of God in him." He nodded slow, like he was agreeing with himself. "Never was good at taming those wild beasts. You can't do nothin' but get outta their way when they get like that."

"I've never ridden," I admitted.

"I reckon you'd enjoy it, so long as you got yourself a horse that wasn't stubborn enough to throw you the second you told him to do something he don't wanna do." He shook his head. "Women ain't no different than a stubborn horse."

"Stubborn I can handle."

He lifted an eyebrow. "You sure about that?"

I didn't have time to answer.

She walked out of the barn with a horse.

CHAPTER THIRTY-FOUR

Audrina

Holding Peony's reins, I walked out of the barn only to abruptly stop in my tracks.

Holy shit.

Holy fucking shit.

He was here.

On the farm.

Larger than life, Tank looked even bigger than I remembered, and worse, emotions I'd been fighting to keep down just so I could breathe through the day came rushing back at the sight of him. He literally took my breath away.

Peony whinnied and kicked the dirt.

"Easy, girl," I murmured. "Easy."

His gaze cutting through me, Tank took in every inch of my body without his eyes ever leaving mine. "I need to talk to you."

My stomach lurched, and my knees almost buckled at the sound of his deep, unforgiving voice. A dozen thoughts flew through my head with a dozen more responses I wanted to say. *I miss you. I want to talk to you too. I'm sorry. I can't breathe. I want your arms around me. I need you. I fucked up. I never meant to hurt you. Please,* please *kiss me.*

But I didn't say any of it. "I'm busy."

Daddy looked between us, and for a second I thought he'd

come to my rescue. But we weren't that family. We never were. If there was anything I'd learned from my father, it was that the Jensens fended for themselves.

"Audrina," Tank warned.

My father grunted and stepped forward, taking Peony's reins.

Tank glanced at him before looking back to me. "You can take five minutes to talk to me." He tipped his chin toward the path that led around the side of the barn before heading toward it without even looking to see if I followed.

I glanced at my dad, but he was already leading Peony in the opposite direction.

Shit.

Nerves licking up my spine, my stomach flipping, I was trying to breathe through my pounding heartbeat when a breeze kicked up and I got a lungful of his scent. Man, soap, musk, laundry detergent, it all blended together and smelled about a thousand times better than I remembered.

Fighting a groan, I was thinking about making a run for the house and locking myself inside when my mom came out on the front porch, glared at me, then went right back inside. She still hadn't asked why I'd come home. Neither had Dad. In fact, they hadn't asked me anything, not about my career or what I was doing here, or if I planned on staying. They hadn't asked a thing. They'd just put me to work.

I'd walked in the house at dinnertime over a week ago, had insults thrown at me, then we'd all sat down and eaten off the same plates with the same silverware that I'd grown up with, as we discussed the same issues with the farm. It was as if time had stopped.

But it hadn't.

Nothing was different, except everything had changed.

In seven days I'd learned my brother was divorced and living in a trailer on the other side of the apple orchard. He and a few hired farmhands tended to the cornfields, and Dad took care of the apple orchard, which was opposite of how it worked before I left. My brother and I had always taken care of the apple trees. Those trees, the ones Tank was walking toward, had been the best part of my childhood.

I was trying to decide if I wanted to taint those precious childhood memories with a giant beast of a man who was no doubt still angry with me, when he turned around and gave me a warning look.

My first instinct was to rush toward him and all of his alpha bossy bullshit and beg for forgiveness. Thankfully it was immediately followed by the stubborn streak that'd motivated me my entire life.

My hand went to my hip. "How did you find me?" My mother had given me over to a D-list casting agent all those years ago, complete with a legal name change and guardianship papers. She'd buried my identity, and my family had kept their mouths shut for ten years. It'd worked. No one had figured out who I really was. Until now.

Predator slow, Tank walked back toward me. Looming over me, expression impenetrable, he stared at me for two heartbeats. Then he reached in his cargo pocket and pulled out a photo. Using his first two fingers to hold it up, fingers that had been inside me, he flipped it to face me.

I dropped my gaze to the picture.

It was me, on Peony's mother, Daisy. Gripping two handfuls of her mane, riding bareback, a smile wider than I remembered how to make, I was holding on for dear life as she ran full tilt. My long hair behind me, the sun setting, I remembered the day like it was yesterday.

I cleared my throat against the memory. "My brother took that picture. So what?"

We'd snuck my parents' new camera the night before after they'd gone to bed. Daddy had bought it to take pictures of the horses because he was going to sell them. It was the only piece of technology in the house, and my brother and I had been forbidden to use it, but we were kids and we were curious. My brother had taken pictures all day, and we'd used the small screen to look at them until the battery ran out.

It'd been the best day ever until Daddy caught us. Then we'd both gotten a beating and were sent to bed without dinner. That was the first night my brother had come into my room. A week later I'd caught Momma looking at a pile of printed copies of the pictures before breakfast, before anyone had been up. She'd shoved the pictures in a drawer, and I'd stupidly not thought more of it.

"Look closer," Tank commanded.

I peered at the picture my mother had sent to the casting agent all those years ago. It was one of the only mementos I had of my childhood. "Where did you get this?" I thought I'd gotten all the pictures when I'd left.

"Background, right side," he said ignoring my question. "What do you see?"

I looked closer. Our mailbox, right next to the street sign.

"Do you know how many streets in the US are named Oak?"

Road, I mentally corrected, looking closer at the picture he was still holding up. But the photo was old and the RD was blurred out, same as it was on the actual sign. "No idea."

"Almost seven thousand."

"Who knew," I said dryly, reaching for the picture.

He snapped the photo back and shoved it in his pocket.

"Hey, that's mine." I stupidly reached for his pocket.

Grabbing my wrist faster than I could blink, he pulled hard. My chest slammed into his, and his voice dropped to a warning. "Did I give you permission to touch me?"

It was instant.

Desire surged between my legs, and need so sharp it was painful crawled across my skin. My mouth watered, my pussy clenched at emptiness, and I wanted to ride him like I'd ridden Daisy.

If his brand of dominance was a drug, I was addicted.

"Answer me," he demanded.

His unforgiving gaze held me hostage, but I didn't have to give in to my addiction.

Steeling my resolve, I straightened my shoulders. "What are you going to do, Falcon?" I purposely used his name. "Turn me into your *needy little bitch*? Throw me down and fuck me right here in front of the stables?"

Not a single muscle moved on his face, but his voice turned lethally quiet. "Fantasizing about my cock?"

"You wish," I taunted, lying. He was all I'd been thinking about.

He grasped my jaw as his fingers closed over my neck in dominance. "You sure you wanna keep up that attitude?"

"Or what?" I forced myself to pull back. He let go of my face, but not my wrist. "In case you haven't noticed, this isn't Miami Beach."

"It's not fucking Hollywood either," he countered.

"Meaning?"

"Cut the bullshit." His grip on my wrist tightened. "You know why I'm here. You know what you need to do."

My stomach bottomed out, and the last ounce of hope I'd been stupidly, *stupidly* holding on to was crushed into the dirt of my family's farm. "Go fuck yourself." I wrenched my wrist free, stormed into the stables, and started mucking out Peony's stall.

Tank stormed right in after me. "Two choices," he warned. "Put the pitchfork down or I make you put it down."

"Go ahead and try." Fighting back tears, I made the mistake of not even looking at him.

A second later, I was airborne.

One arm around my waist, Tank ripped the pitchfork from my hand, threw it down, then spun me. My back hit the side of the stall, he grabbed my wrists and he pinned my arms over my head.

I kicked him.

His nostrils flared, but that was it. No flinch, no grunt, no change in expression.

So I let loose.

My back arched, my legs kicked out, and I fought against his hold as I threw my whole body into a headbutt. Twisting, kicking, seething mad at him, at myself, I didn't even realize I was crying until my guttural scream filled the stables and Peony's sister, Daffodil, started kicking her stall and neighing.

"Let me *go!*" I futilely yanked to free my hands, but managed to get a solid kick to his upper thigh.

That's when he moved.

Dropping my arms and catching my waist, he spun me to face the wall as he grasped my wrists again. Bringing my arms up, my palms hit the rough wood of the barn wall as he held me captive with my hands on either side of my head.

His hot breath touched my ear as his voice grated across my frayed nerves. "If you ever try to kick me in the balls again, I will give you a spanking you'll never forget. You hear me?"

Fighting to hold back a sob of humiliation, I bit the inside of my cheek.

"You fucking hear me?" he barked.

Ashamed, enraged, despondent, I somehow managed to nod.

His hand left my wrist only to slam against the wall a second later with his cell phone. "Call your publicist. Make a statement. Unfuck your goddamn mess."

"I don't have a publicist anymore." My voice hitched.

"She's waiting for you to call." He dropped my other arm, shoved his phone into my hand and stepped back.

My heart shattered, my hands shaking, I didn't make the call.

I stared at his phone.

His smell all around me, it felt more intimate holding his phone than having his hands on me.

But I didn't have an intimate relationship with this man.

I'd never have anything with him.

Steeped in regret, I dropped his phone and walked out.

CHAPTER THIRTY-FIVE

Tank

GODDAMN IT.

I snatched my phone off the horseshit-smelling ground and went after her.

Striding toward the house, she crossed her arms protectively in front of her.

Guilt hit me in the chest before I fucking stomped it down and barked her middle name. "Audrina!"

Ignoring me, she kept walking.

I threw down my one play. *"Magnolia Audrina Jensen."*

She froze.

I closed the distance and lowered my voice to a warning. "I know your real name. I know what you did to protect it, and I know where your family lives."

"Is that a threat?"

Yes. "Make the fucking call."

A screen door squeaked. "Who are you?"

I snapped my head up.

A woman, barely twenty years older than Audrina, with the same hair and same eyes, stood on the porch of the house. Except unlike her daughter, she wasn't beautiful. She could have been, if she didn't look like decades of hard living and hatred had eaten her alive.

Audrina sucked in a stilted breath. "He's no one. I was

just coming in to help you, Momma."

Her mother openly stared at me. "I don't need help. Supper's ready. Are you going to introduce your friend?"

"He's not my friend. I'll call Daddy." Audrina put two fingers to her mouth and whistled.

My hands on my hips, I should've introduced myself, but instinct and the ten shades past crazy look on her mother's face made me keep my mouth shut.

The mother kept staring at me, but addressed her daughter. "Weather's coming in. Did you put Peony back in her stable?"

"Daddy has her."

Her mother nodded. "He knows she doesn't like the storms." She glanced at her daughter. "Who is he?"

Audrina sighed as she looked out over the cornfields, but she didn't say shit.

Fuck this. I tipped my chin at her mother. "Tank Gunther. Personal security. Nice to meet you, Mrs. Jensen."

Her gaze cut to her daughter and she ignored me. "You need a bodyguard?"

Audrina half laughed, half snorted. "Not anymore."

The sound of galloping hooves cut off the fucking bizarre interchange a few seconds before a male version of Audrina rode up on the horse she'd brought out of the barn and dismounted.

Tying the horse's reins to the front porch, his tone was hostile as fuck as he glared at me. "Can I help you?"

He was half a foot shorter than me and seventy pounds lighter. I could take the wiry prick down in a fraction of a second. I nodded toward Audrina. "I'm here to talk to her."

"We're done talking. He was just leaving." Audrina

stepped up to the horse to pet her.

The mother glanced at the sunny sky. "Storm's coming. He's staying for supper."

"No, he's not." Audrina glanced at the asshole who had to be her brother. "Where's Daddy?"

"You know Peony won't let him ride her." The guy pet the horse on the back hind leg. "Ain't that right, girl?"

The horse whinnied.

"Magnolia, James, go wash up for supper." She issued the command like she was talking to two insolent children instead of two adults.

Audrina crossed her arms and glared at me. "I'll come in once he leaves."

Before she had the last word out, her brother had grabbed her arm. "You do what Momma says." He started to drag her up the porch steps.

Every protective instinct I had kicked in, and it was instinctual. One stride and I had the asshole's wrist in a crushing grip. "Let go of her. *Now.*" I'd bury the motherfucker.

The horse neighed, and for one heartbeat James glared at me.

Then he dropped his hold on Audrina and held his free hand up. "All right, big man, you win. I ain't touching my sister no more. You still wanna fight me?"

Audrina scoffed. "Shut up, James."

Her father walked around the corner of the house. "Why isn't supper ready?"

"It is." His wife didn't hesitate. "We were just going in." She eyed Audrina. "Take Peony back to her stable. James, go wash up." Not waiting to see if anyone followed her instructions, she went back inside.

Audrina took the horse's reins, her father walked in to the house, and James followed after him, giving me one more glare.

"What the hell do you think you're doing?" Audrina whisper-hissed, taking the horse back toward the barn. "You're making everyone mad."

Alarm bells went off like a fucking five-alarm fire. "Your brother always push you around like that?"

"Oh my God, *seriously?*" She dropped her voice to an angry whisper again. "You *pinned* me against the barn wall, and you're going to ask me about my brother? *Screw you.*" She held her hand up and the horse neighed. "On second thought, forget it. Been there, done that."

Still pissed at the way her brother had handled her, I grabbed the horse's reins and stood in front of her. "We're not talking about us right now. I'm still pissed the fuck off at what I just saw and, worse, your reaction to it. Give me one good reason not to throw you in the SUV and get you the fuck out of here." I leaned down to her to make my point. "Because I've seen a lot of fucked-up shit in my day, and, sweetheart, your family takes the cake." Not to mention my instincts were going fucking ballistic. There was a goddamn reason she hadn't been back to this place in a decade.

Incredulous, she scoffed. "You're a piece of work, you know that?" She yanked the horse's reins from me and led the beast into the barn.

I followed her. "Is anyone in your family fucking glad you're here? Because from where I'm standing, all I see is hostility." And some seriously fucked-up dynamics.

"Like you're not hostile?" She closed the door to the horse's stable. "Do you even hear yourself?"

"I have a fucking reason to be pissed at you right now." She'd fucking left me. I tipped my chin toward the house. "What's their excuse?"

"Oh, I don't know," she said, sarcastic as hell. "Ten years ago I left three people to do a four-person job and never came back? *What the fuck?*" She looked at me like I was the crazy one. "Life isn't a fairy tale where every family kisses and makes up." She threw her hands out. "So I don't have a perfect family, so what? They're mine, and I sure as hell don't have to stand here and justify shit to you." She spun and started for the exit.

I reached out to grab her, but realized I was doing the exact same shit her asshole brother had done, so I slammed the side of my fist against the wall instead. *"God fucking damn it, Audrina. Stop!"*

She flinched and froze, but she didn't turn around.

My head a fucking mess since I laid eyes on her, I wanted to fuck her as bad as I wanted to throw her over my goddamn knee. Inhaling, trying to calm the fuck down, I stepped in front of her.

She crossed her arms, and her head dropped.

"Look at me," I demanded.

"Go home, Falcon," she said quietly, her voice hitching.

Jesus fuck. I tipped her chin, and when I saw the tears, I knew it wasn't an act. "You're right," I admitted. "I'm still mad about the bullshit you pulled on *Miami Morning*. I'm angry Luna and Associates took a hit from the bad press. But I'm pissed as hell you took off on me."

A tear rolled down her cheek as she kept her eyes averted. "I'm sorry."

I swept at the tear with my thumb, and for the first time

214

I understood just how fucking alone she was. "You said you were drowning that night. You remember any of that?"

She nodded, barely, and her hair fell over her face.

I brushed the strand back. Jesus Christ she was beautiful. "This isn't coming up for air, sweetheart."

She burst into tears.

CHAPTER THIRTY-SIX

Audrina

BURST INTO TEARS, AND HE PULLED ME INTO HIS IMPOSSIBLY HUGE arms.

"Now you're my knight in shining armor?" I fought a sob and lost. I hated him. I hated that he came for me only to tell me to fix my mess, then he swiped at my tears and tucked my hair behind my ear. I hated that he was here for two seconds and he knew all my dirty little secrets. And I hated that he saw me drowning. "Go. *Home.*" I wrenched out of his grasp.

He dropped his arms, but he didn't step back. "Come with me."

My hand flew to my mouth to stifle the sob and I didn't have a choice.

I ran.

I ran out the barn door.

I ran across the dirt driveway.

And I ran past the house.

My legs pumping, my chest feeling like I was having a heart attack, my stomach threatening to heave, I kept running.

I ran past my mother coming out the screen door and calling my name in disgust. I ran from the mistake I'd made on *Miami Morning*, and I ran from the man whose heavy footsteps I heard gaining on me.

I ran from the truth.

He was right. I was drowning, and this wasn't coming up for air. I didn't belong here. I didn't belong anywhere, but for one night almost two weeks ago, I felt like I did, and that hurt more than anything else. I wished I'd never gotten a taste of Falcon Gunther's own special brand of attention. And I wished I'd never heard him call me sweetheart.

Bile rising in my throat, I kept running.

I ran all the way to apple orchard.

But when I got to the first row of trees, the nausea I'd been fighting all day became too much, and I bent and vomited. But I didn't just vomit. Wave after wave convulsed my stomach, and I kept heaving until I was on my knees and nothing but bile was coming out.

My hair was swept back, and a strong hand landed on my back. "Easy. Take a breath."

Heaving, fighting panic, I tried to suck in a breath and choked.

"Hey, hey, hey." The hand holding my hair gently pulled till my head was upright. "In through your nose. Deep breath."

Tears streamed down my face, but I managed to inhale.

"Good girl," he murmured. "You're okay."

Oh my God, he was watching me vomit. "Why are you being nice?" My life hit a new low.

"You want me to be a dick?" He swept the rest of my hair out of the way.

"I'd trust it more." I shoved at his hand.

Ignoring me swatting at him, he pulled me to my feet. "Jesus, woman."

"What the fuck is that supposed to mean?" Desperate for water, I wiped my mouth on my sleeve.

Making sure I was steady before he let go of me, he slowly

dropped his hands. "It means I'm not a complete asshole."

I snorted and immediately wished I hadn't. Choking on the vile taste in my mouth, I spit on the ground like a fricking animal then moved the hell away from my own vomit.

Following me, Tank reached into the trees, casually plucked an apple, and rubbed it on his thigh before whipping out a switchblade from his pocket. Cutting the apple first in half, then one of the halves in quarters, he deftly cored and skinned it before holding the piece out to me. "Suck on this."

The thought of putting anything in my mouth made my stomach turn, but I was desperate to get rid of the taste of puke, so I took the apple and ate a bite. The sun-warm slice tasted shockingly good.

"If you're gonna eat it, chew slow," he warned, popping a piece into his mouth in one bite.

Ignoring his advice, I ate the rest of my slice. It was the first thing that'd tasted good in days.

Coring and peeling the rest of the apple, he handed me another piece. "You always puke when you run?"

"No." I bit into the second piece and wondered why I'd been here for a week and hadn't been eating the apples.

"You got any other symptoms?" he asked casually. "Fever, upset stomach?"

"Are you a doctor now?" I walked down the row of trees that were planted before I was born.

He picked another apple. "Have you been throwing up before today?"

What the fuck? "You worried I'm too sick to fix your boss's precious reputation?" Screw him. It was handled, but I wasn't going to tell him that.

"No." His knife sliced through the apple with practiced

ease. "You late?"

I froze.

Then the nausea came back with a vengeance, and I clenched my jaw, taking shallow breaths through my nose. "Just because a woman throws up, you think she's pregnant?" Forcing the last word out, I sucked in a deep breath and reached for deniability. I wasn't pregnant. I couldn't be pregnant. *I was not pregnant.*

"No. But a woman I had unprotected sex with who doesn't show any signs of the flu, but starts heaving?" He looked me in the eye. "That I fucking think about."

Fighting panic, fighting nausea, and fighting stupid tears that came at the drop of a hat the past week, I turned and aimed for the house. "I'm going home."

"You think that's your home?"

"Screw you."

"Answer my question," he demanded, tossing the apple and pocketing his knife.

"It's the only home I've got." Because I'd stupidly never put down roots and bought myself a place.

"The other question."

I stopped and spun. "Leave me alone. Leave the farm. Go home and stop pretending you give one shit about me other than to get what you came for. Which isn't fucking happening, because I'm not calling Janette or anyone else. *So leave.*"

"*Jesus fucking Christ.*" He lost the calm, detached composure to his tone.

"Are you blind?"

I threw my hands up. "Do I look blind?"

He pointed toward the house. "Do you see your brother or your father coming to your rescue?" Veins popped on his neck.

"They didn't even fucking ask if you were okay. I could be a goddamn serial killer for all they know, and they left you to fend for yourself!" Every word came out louder than the last.

I glanced at the house, and when I saw them all sitting at the kitchen table through the window, shit sank in my stomach. All of them eating, not one of them checking outside. I looked back at Tank, ready to tell him he was wrong, but it was pointless.

Following my glance, he saw exactly what I saw.

Gutted, I stood there.

He dropped his hands from his hips and lowered his voice. "Come on, babe. Get your shit. Come with me. You don't belong here."

That was the problem. I didn't belong anywhere. Seven days with the three strangers who were my only family, and not one of them had asked me why I was here. Not even my mom. Especially not my mom.

No one asked me anything because they didn't want me here.

They didn't care that I'd paid off the mortgage on the farm, or bought the adjoining parcel and rolled it into their land. No one thanked me for the extra equipment I'd bought. No one had even talked to me except to bark orders, ask what I was going to handle that day, or tell me to come to supper.

Tell me to *wash up*.

Like I was dirty.

Like I'd always been dirty.

And suddenly, I saw it for what it was.

I represented all of their mistakes.

My brother's sickness, my mother's resentment, and my father's anger at a situation he was trapped in.

Tank studied me like he knew my thoughts. "You got a better offer?"

"Stop it," I barely whispered.

"Stop what? Pointing out the obvious?" He stepped closer. "We both know you don't want to be here."

"You don't know me," I argued.

"I know plenty."

"Bullshit." No one knew me.

"You really wanna test me like that?" The six-and-a-half-foot unwavering beast of a man didn't wait for an answer. "You been gone so long from this place, those people in there either don't give a shit about you anymore, or they never did. You were running from the bullshit fame because you were drowning in a life where you had no control. You wanted to make decisions for yourself, but all you accomplished was winding up right back in the passenger seat. Don't fucking bullshit me about wanting to be here. The woman who sat buck ass naked on my counter and spread her legs in front of my food isn't a woman who wants to take shit lying down."

I blinked.

He wasn't finished.

"I don't know what your goddamn favorite color is, or what the hell you eat besides vegan shit and apples, but five seconds after finding you, I knew the only thing holding you here was an old horse."

"She's not old." She was middle-aged.

"Get a new horse." Except he didn't just mean get a new horse, he meant get a new life.

Mad, sad, angry, hurt, I reached for the only defense I had left. "Fuck you. Don't pretend like you give a shit about what I want or what I do. You're only here because you want me to make a statement and save your friend's reputation."

"Jesus fuck," he growled.

I turned to go inside.

"Goddamn it, woman. *Wait.*"

I paused, but I didn't turn around. I couldn't. I would burst into tears, because him standing here, telling it like he saw it, was the closest thing to a friend I'd ever had. "What?"

He stepped in front of me, and his expression was one hundred percent alpha, but I also saw the dark circles under his eyes. "I've got a hotel in the next town over. I've been looking for your sweet ass for ten goddamn days, and I'm fucking hungry and tired." He dropped his voice. "*Come.* With me."

My chest tightened and my core pulsed.

Desperate longing filled every inch of my soul as he stared at me with his gorgeous green-brown eyes, and I realized something.

I had nothing left to lose.

He already owned my heart. He'd come for me. Did it matter why? Being with him, even if it was only to ride back to Miami and figure out what I was going to do next—that'd be a thousand times better than staying here.

And I would be with him.

At least temporarily.

I sighed like it was a difficult decision, then the real me, the woman who wasn't a complete pushover, she came out after hiding for seven days. "I'm not sleeping with you."

The corner of his mouth twitched. "Go get your shit, woman."

I crossed my arms. "And then what?"

As if he knew me, as if he knew every pathetic thought in my head, he gave me his own brand of honesty. "Then we eat some food, you get your vomiting ass horizontal, and we reassess in the morning."

A thread of doubt surfaced. A minute ago he'd told me to come with him. I assumed back to Florida. But now he was telling me we'd reassess in the morning? "You said—"

"Stop." He cupped my cheek. "I know what I said."

I threw out the other problem I'd avoided so far. "People will recognize me." I'd been safe here because I was isolated, but out there in the world, all I'd have between me and being recognized was a six-and-a-half-foot, dominant, trigger-happy bodyguard.

"Trust me." This time, half his mouth tipped up. "I'm a professional."

"Magnolia!" my father bellowed from the porch. "Get in here. Your mother's food is getting cold."

Tank's smile dropped and his nostrils flared, but he didn't say anything and he didn't take his eyes off mine.

I exhaled and moved out of his grasp, stepping toward the house.

"*Audrina.*" Half in warning, half in question, he said my name short and fast.

"I'm going to brush my teeth." I hoped like hell I wasn't making the second-worst decision of my life. "Then I'm getting my backpack."

CHAPTER THIRTY-SEVEN

Tank

FOLLOWED HER INTO THE HOUSE, WONDERING IF I'D LOST MY goddamn mind.

I'd spent ten days looking for her because despite all the technology in the world and the shit you saw on TV, people weren't easy to find. She hadn't touched any of her bank accounts, not the ones we knew about, and we'd never even gotten a lead on what car she was in.

I made it two steps into the front hall and her father came out of the kitchen.

He glanced at me then his gaze trailed after his daughter as she took the steps two at a time. "Where you going, girl? Food's on the table."

Ignoring him, Audrina disappeared into her room.

"We're not staying." I crossed my arms on purpose.

His gaze cut to my biceps, then my eyes. "She ain't yours. You don't speak for her."

Anger surged, and I glared at him. I'd misread the old fuck as mostly harmless earlier. I wasn't going to make that mistake again. "You think you speak for her?"

He puffed his chest. "She's my daughter."

"Yeah?" Fucking asshole. "Was she your daughter ten days ago? A month ago? Was there any time in the past decade that you gave a shit about her?" My temper flared and my voice dropped low in warning. "Was she your daughter when your wife signed away custodial rights to a casting agent?" The greedy fuck. The house was old, but the barn and the equipment in it were new.

"That ain't none of your business."

The fuck it wasn't. "I'm making it my business, because you haven't said one decent word to her since I've been here."

"You come sniffing around my daughter, you don't know the first thing about being decent."

The son pushed his chair back from the table and came to stand beside his father. "You need to leave."

What a fucking joke. I could take both of them without breaking a sweat. "I'm gonna." I glared at her brother. "As soon as your sister comes back downstairs with her stuff."

"She ain't leaving," the father postured.

She sure as hell wasn't staying here anymore. "You know what you seem to forget, old man?" I heard her footsteps coming back downstairs.

"I don't forget nothing," he barked.

Addressing her father, I took Audrina's backpack. "Yes you do. You forgot one crucial fact."

Audrina looked between us. "What's going on?"

Her father ignored her. Her brother ignored her, and her mother sat at the kitchen table with an expression of disgust.

I put my arm around her shoulders and looked her old man in the eye. "You forgot she's a fucking person." I hustled her out the front door.

"You stop right there, girl," her father bellowed.

"Ignore him," I muttered, ushering her to the passenger side of the SUV and opening the door before I threw her backpack in.

"That's it," her father warned. "You leave now, you don't ever come back. Not even with your tail between your legs."

Her ass in the seat, one foot on the running board, Audrina froze.

"Do not engage," I warned low so only she could hear me. "It's not worth it."

Holding on to the door, glaring at her father, she pulled herself up and out of the seat. "Is that what you think?" she asked, incredulous. "That I came back here with my *tail between my legs?*"

"You sure as hell ain't here with no dignity," he spat. "You ain't known dignity since you was thirteen."

"I paid your precious farm off," Audrina seethed. "I bought you all new equipment. And you're calling *me* undignified?"

Taking a step toward us, her old man pointed his finger at her. "Don't you dare mouth off to me, girl."

I didn't want to have to hit the old man, but I fucking would if he took one more step. "Back off," I warned.

"Or what?" The old man challenged me. "You gonna throw some of that useless muscle around you got in one of them fancy gyms? You ain't worked an honest day in your life."

The son stepped beside the old man. "Let her go, Pop. She ain't worth it. She's trash. She always was."

Rage surged. Barely holding it back, I took her arm. "Get in the car, Audrina." Asshole or not, the piece of shit was still her brother. I told myself I wouldn't fucking hit him.

But then she opened her mouth and let the cat out of the bag. "Is that how you justify yourself, James?" She laughed bitterly. "That I'm trash? That I always was? That you tried to climb into bed every night with a piece of *trash* ten years ago?"

I spun and my fist flew.

The first blow hit him in the ribs, and when he doubled over, I aimed a perfect uppercut. He dropped to his knees like the piece of shit he was, and I kicked him.

"Falcon!" Audrina yelled before I could kick her asshole brother again.

Adrenaline and rage pumping, itching to fucking end him, I glared at her old man then rounded the front of the SUV as Audrina got back in the passenger seat.

Five seconds later, I was gunning the heavy engine down the dirt road, pissed off I didn't commit murder.

CHAPTER THIRTY-EIGHT

Audrina

WHITE KNUCKLING THE STEERING WHEEL, JAW TICKING, TANK WAS silent as he drove twice the speed limit down the county road.

"If you don't slow down, you'll get a ticket." If the sheriff was still out for the day, and not at the one bar in town.

"He touch you?"

"What?" I asked, stalling. I knew who and what he meant. I just didn't want to think about it. I was too busy being pissed off at the man who was supposed to be a father to me. But he never was. Neither of my parents had ever been nurturing, or even kind. I'd always chalked it up to living the hard life of a farmer, but there was more to it than that. None of them were happy. In fact, they were all intent on fostering unhappiness.

"Your brother." Tank's nostrils flared. "He touch you?"

"When?"

His hands twisted on the steering wheel. "Since you've been back."

"No."

He inhaled. Twice. "Ten years ago?"

"Yes." I didn't see any point in lying now. I'd already aired my dirty laundry.

"Give me one good reason not to turn around and fucking end him."

For some reason, Tank's words made the consuming anger and betrayal I'd felt a few minutes ago toward my father and the sheer hatred toward my brother ease somewhat. Not that I wanted my brother dead, but the fact that I wasn't alone in my anger made it more… tolerable.

I gave Tank the only reason I could think of. "Because I don't care anymore."

"You went back there," he accused.

I looked out the window at the endless acres of farmland that I used to consider my home, but now seemed like a lifetime ago. "I thought it would be different." I realized that was a lie. "No, I wanted it to be different."

"What happened?"

"Nothing. I showed up and it was as if I never left. It was assumed I would carry my weight, and I fell back in to the old routine of mucking out the stables, getting ready for harvest, moving the horses, and whatever other chores needed to be done. No one asked me why I was there. They just…." Jesus. "They just assumed I was there to work."

Tank abruptly slammed on the brakes and pulled over. His chest rose with a deep inhale, and he looked at me with determination. "What happened ten years ago?"

My stomach dropped, and the nausea came roaring back. I turned to the window. "It's nothing." I regretted saying what I did in front of him, but I didn't regret saying it to my brother. "It's not what you think."

He exhaled, and when he spoke, his voice was softer, quieter. "Intent's just as bad in my book." His hand landed on my nape. "Talk to me."

Suddenly, I was angry. And incredulous, and mortified, and humiliated, and about a hundred other uncomfortable emotions I never wanted to feel or deal with. *"Talk to you?"* I asked viciously. "So what? You can tell me I was justified, or lecture me about going back? Or tell me all the things I did wrong, or the shit I should've done right that I didn't?"

His face an impenetrable mask, he held my angry glare. Then he said one word. "No."

I waited, but that was it.

One damn word.

"No?" *What the fuck?* "That's it? Just a *no?*" I threw my hands up. "Anyone ever tell you that you're shit for pep talks? Because that one sucked." Crossing my arms, wanting out of this SUV, wanting to be away from him and all his soapy, musky man scent, I turned toward the window again. "Just drive. You can drop me off in the next town over." I'd figure something out. I had money. I could go anywhere.

My seat belt released and huge arms were around me, pulling me halfway over the center console.

His breath landed on my cheek, and his hand buried in my hair as he brought me to his strong chest. "Tell me what he did to you."

I could feel the coiled tension in his muscles. I could hear his faster than normal heartbeat. I could taste the scent of his anger. But what I couldn't feel was judgment.

He was angry.

Incredibly angry.

But not at me.

Tears welled. "He touched me." My breath hitched and memories I had buried deep came to the surface. "With his hands, night after night, for over a month, he came into my room, and I couldn't stop him. He was two years older and bigger than me, and he threatened to tell Mom and Dad I was the one touching him. One night he must've made too much noise because my mom walked in and caught him."

His arms tightened around me. "What'd she do?"

For the first time in my life, I saw the whole thing through an adult perspective. My own mother had walked in to my bedroom late that night, and when she found her son on top of her daughter with his hands down her daughter's pajamas, she'd chosen sides. My own mother had turned against me.

She didn't yell at James. She didn't beat him or even scold him. She'd yelled at me. Why did I let him touch me? Why did I tempt him? What the hell was wrong with me? She whisper screamed horrible words at me in the dead of night while my brother, a foot taller and fifty pounds heavier, stood over my bed smirking.

A week later I was in Los Angeles with a stranger, and my mother's parting words had been how now I could follow my dreams.

I swallowed back impotent anger, and tears fell. "She blamed me for tempting him. Then a week later, she drove me to the only diner in town to meet a stranger. She signed guardianship papers over to a casting agent and gave me away." I choked on a sob of anger. "She told me I could *follow my dreams*."

He pulled back and took my face in his hands. "You know she was fucking wrong, right?"

I barely nodded. Ashamed, angry, I knew my mother had been wrong, my brother was sick, and my father was an abusive enabler. I'd had ten years to process the grief of losing a family that never wanted me, but that wasn't what was racing through my mind and making my nerves fray.

My past wasn't controlling my thoughts, or driving me to make more money or be the best actress I could be. I wasn't even thinking about any of that.

I was staring at a man holding my face in his hands who wasn't paid to act out his affection, and I knew I wasn't worthy of him. He'd spent ten days of his life looking for me, and I'd greeted him with anger and told him to leave. But he hadn't left. He'd sized up the situation in seconds, told me he was getting me out of there, then he'd punched my brother on principle.

He'd defended me.

Defended my virtue.

Defended my dignity.

And stood up for me simply because it was the right thing to do.

Feelings, thick and heady with a longing so intense I was choking, swallowed me whole. But then I was drowning in shame and guilt, because I didn't have any virtue left. I wasn't worthy of the man who defended me when I'd destroyed his reputation.

The same intense amber-green eyes that had stared down at me almost two weeks ago while his body had driven into mine were holding me hostage now, and I wanted to disappear into their depths. More, I wanted to be the woman worthy of his intensity and attention.

But I wasn't.

Sick, I pulled out of his grasp, and he let me.

Leaning back in my seat, I stared straight ahead. "You can drop me at your hotel, or in town. Whichever is easiest."

He sat back in his seat. "What the fuck just happened?"

"I don't know what you mean." Trying to keep my voice even, I prayed like hell he would drop it. I didn't want to have this conversation. I didn't want to have any conversation. I wanted to go somewhere by myself and hide for a decade.

"You know exactly what I mean."

Inhaling, I chose my words as carefully as I could, because he had defended me to my shit family. "Look. I know why you're here and what you want." My hands twisted in my lap, and the next words hurt far worse to say than I could've ever imagined. "You don't have to pretend to be my friend or defend my virtue to my shitty family just to get what you want. I'll take care of your friend's business." I already had, but for some reason, I didn't tell him that.

His nostrils flared, and for one whole minute, he didn't say anything. He just stared at me.

Then he threw the SUV back in drive and muttered, "Put your seat belt on."

CHAPTER THIRTY-NINE

U N-FUCKING-BELIEVABLE.

Did she think I didn't have any fucking self-control? That I punched her piece-of-shit brother out because I had a fucking temper? That I was defending her *virtue*?

What the actual fuck?

I floored the engine and drove toward the nearest shit-smear town. I didn't know if I was more pissed at her for being fucking blind or myself for actually giving a shit about this girl.

And she was a girl.

She was too damn young for me, and I had no fucking business thinking about the goddamn what-ifs. If she was pregnant, I'd deal with it. I'd be there for my kid.

My kid.

Jesus fuck, the thought alone made my chest tight and anger surge. I'd never been so fucking stupid with a woman before. *Never.* But a goddamn Hollywood pain in my ass spread her legs in front my of plate and I'd had to fucking have her.

Goddamn it.

A half hour later, two towns over, I was pulling into a brand-name pharmacy, thankful I didn't have to deal with some small-town shit. I pulled into a parking spot and threw the engine into park, but I didn't turn it off.

"Wait here," I ordered. The last thing I needed was

someone recognizing her right now.

She smirked. "Where am I going to go?" She gestured across the parking lot. "The dollar store?"

Who fucking knew with this chick? It'd taken me days to find her. "Lock the door after I get out. Don't open it until I come back."

She saluted me. *She fucking saluted me.* "Yes, sir."

I shoved the door open.

"Hey."

I glanced back at her, raising an eyebrow. "What?" Christ, she was beautiful with no makeup.

For a second she looked at me and I would've sworn I was looking at the real woman, not the actress. Then her expression hardened and she fake smiled. "Don't bother getting any condoms." She waved a finger between us. "It's not happening."

Pissed off, I threw her shit right back on her. "Who says I was getting them for you?" I slammed my door and pounded my fist once on the window. "Lock up."

I didn't wait to hear if she followed my instructions. I strode into the store and went looking for something I never thought I'd be buying in the middle of fucking Iowa, let alone any state.

Five minutes later, I was in over my head.

"Do you, um, need any help, sir?"

I glanced toward the voice, and a barely legal, blonde-haired, blue-eyed chick who could've been Audrina's cousin blushed at me. "I mean…" She pointed at the pregnancy tests. "Do you have any questions?"

"You gonna answer them for me if I did?" Christ, she looked about an hour past her eighteenth birthday.

She blushed harder. "Well, I mean, not that I have any personal experience using them." She laughed uncomfortably.

"But I know, um, which ones, people, um, usually buy."

Jesus fucking Christ. I grabbed the one that promised early results. "Where's the soda?"

She exhaled like she was relieved I hadn't asked her something else and pointed across the store. "The cold case toward the back. There're lots of choices."

Fucking great. I strode over, grabbed a soda, and went to the checkout. The jail-bait chick quickly hustled behind the register and smiled.

"Do you need anything else today, sir?"

I fished my wallet out, threw down some cash and leveled her with a look. "Don't get any personal experience," I warned.

Her cheeks heated again. "Excuse me?"

I held up the pregnancy test before shoving it in my cargo pocket. "Wait till you're married before you need one of these."

She laughed uncomfortably again. "Don't worry, I don't plan on it, sir." She handed me my change. "But thank you for the advice."

I tipped my chin and walked out. Two strides before the SUV, Audrina glanced up and unlocked the door. I got in and handed her the damn soda. "Here."

She took it and looked at it strangely. "You got me ginger ale?"

"Yeah." I backed out of the spot.

"Well." She sighed. "Now I feel like an ass."

She should. I didn't say shit.

"Thank you," she said sincerely.

"Welcome," I muttered, pulling back onto the only road through town.

She opened the drink and took a sip. "Where are we going?"

Back to Miami. "Motel."

"Because that's a solid plan."

"You're ready to drive back to Miami, I'll keep going." I was tired as fuck from driving all night, but if she said the word, I'd man up.

"That's an even worse plan."

My jaw ticked. "Why?"

She threw her hands up. "I don't live in Miami, okay. I don't live *anywhere*. And you just took me from the one place I did live, so what the hell do you expect me to say? Yay, road trip?"

Goddamn it.

I pulled over. I didn't want to have this conversation on the side of the road, but fuck. *Fuck.*

I threw the SUV in park and looked at her. "I found out your real name last night at midnight when I was in fucking Kansas, after spending nine goddamn days reconning every damn street named Oak. I was twelve hours away, and I drove through the night. I'm fucking tired. We're going back to the dump of a motel I checked into an hour ago so I could shower, then we're gonna take a fucking nap. When we wake up, if you don't feel like puking, we're gonna eat a goddamn meal together. Questions?"

She hesitated only a fraction of a second. "Will french fries be involved?"

CHAPTER FORTY

Audrina

E BLINKED. TWICE.

"And a milkshake?" Because I really missed dairy.

He stared at me a moment longer. Then he gave me a clipped single-word answer. "Yeah."

I inhaled deep and let it out slow. "Okay." Milkshakes I could handle.

He pulled back on the road, and a half hour later we were in a town south of where I'd grown up that I'd never spent any time in. Not that I'd spent time anywhere growing up except the farm.

Maneuvering the giant Escalade into a lot built long before giant SUVs, Tank parked and cut the engine. "Wait there." Getting out and rounding the front of the vehicle, he scanned the almost empty lot and dark sky before opening my door. "Come on."

Thunder cracked overhead as I got out of the SUV.

Tank grabbed my backpack and put his arm around my shoulders as he ushered me up rickety stairs and down the length of the outdoor corridor barely wide enough for the two of us. The motel was a long way from the hotel penthouses and suites I'd lived in for the past decade, but I didn't realize how different until he opened the door at the very end with an actual key.

I looked around the small, drab room that smelled faintly like mildew as he locked the dead bolt and threw the chain. "There's only one bed."

"I'm not gonna try and fuck you right now." He tipped his chin at my feet. "Jeans and boots off. Get in bed." He tossed his keys and cell on the nightstand then took his gun out of his back waistband and set it down.

I stood there, just taking in the sight of him. "You're bossy."

He pulled his T-shirt over his head as he stepped out of his own boots. "You have no idea."

My pussy tingled, because I had a really good idea. I eyed the uncomfortable-looking side chair. "I'm not that tired."

He stepped up to me, but he didn't touch me. "Clothes off, or I take back what I said."

Nerves and anticipation coursed through my veins. "That seems kinda backward—take your clothes off so I *won't* fuck you."

His intense gaze ratcheted up a thousand degrees. "Do not test me right now, Jensen."

Hearing him call me by my last name instantly killed the tingle between my legs. Kicking off my boots, I undid my jeans. "You know what's not sexy?"

"You taking off to fucking Iowa?" He yanked the bedspread that'd seen better days off the bed.

"No." But I took note of his tone and statement and filed it away to think about later. Much later. When I had a plan to get away from him so I didn't fall right back in bed with him. The irony wasn't lost on me as I slid my jeans down my legs. "You calling me Jensen isn't sexy."

"Wasn't meant to be." He took his pants off and threw them over the back of the side chair. "Get in bed."

"Yes, sir." Thankful I'd worn underwear today, I saluted him and crawled on to the queen-sized bed that looked way too small for him alone, let alone the two of us.

Without hesitating, he got in beside me, angled my back to his chest, and slid one giant arm under my head and the other over my waist.

His unique scent, all power and man and soap, washed over me. Inhaling deep, I curled into him as I wrapped my hands around his forearm. Not realizing how tired I was, I exhaled and my eyes fluttered shut.

For three heartbeats, I was in heaven.

Then he took me completely off guard.

"I didn't spend ten days of my life looking for you just so I could tell you to make a phone call."

Shocked, I turned and glanced up at him. "Then why did you come for me?"

Incredulous, he shook his head. "Fuck, woman. Seriously?"

Yes. No. I didn't know. Not knowing what to say, I stared at him.

He shook his head again, then closed his eyes. "Go to sleep."

That was it? "You're going to drop a loaded statement like that and not follow it up?"

"You don't want me to follow that up," he replied, not opening his eyes.

"Why?" I stupidly asked.

"Because…" His eyes opened and his intense gaze focused on me. "The only way I'm gonna follow that up is by sinking so deep inside that tight pussy of yours and pounding out my frustration for as long as it took me to get here."

I sucked in a sharp breath as liquid desire pooled between

my legs.

"But before that happens, you and I have a lot of shit to talk about. And right now, I'm too damn tired, so we're sleeping."

Shocked, miffed, elated, horny, I was all of it. But the only thing that came out was a whispered protest. "What if I'm not tired?"

"Go to sleep, Audrina," he warned.

Holding his gaze for a moment, I fought a smile. Then I closed my eyes.

A second later, he exhaled and I felt his head shift on the pillow next to me.

"Old man," I whispered.

"Watch it," he growled.

I dared a peek at him and all of his shirtless glory. His eyes were closed, but the corner of his mouth twitched up.

I gave in to the smile I'd been holding back.

Then I snuggled into his strength and safety and fell asleep.

CHAPTER FORTY-ONE

Tank

SHE SLEPT LIKE THE DEAD.

I'd woken up a few hours later, and she'd still been out. I'd extracted myself, thrown my clothes back on, and run out in the pouring rain for fast food. Now I was back, and she was still sleeping. I wanted to crawl in bed with her, but the milkshakes were getting warm.

I sat on the edge of the small-as-fuck bed and fingered a strand of her soft hair. "Audrina." She was fucking gorgeous, always, but asleep like this, she was stunning.

Inhaling, she stirred, but she didn't open her eyes. "I smell french fries."

Grabbing the bag off the table and snatching a fry, I held it to her lips. "Open."

She opened her clear blue eyes, but not her mouth.

"Eat," I commanded.

She studied me as if looking at me for the first time. "You like to tell me what to do."

I didn't deny it. "You like to challenge me."

"Not all the time." She ate the french fry. "Shit, that's good."

I grabbed the carrier with the drinks and leaned back against the headboard. "Chocolate, vanilla, or strawberry?"

She looked at the drinks on my lap. "What's the fourth one?"

"Diet Coke."

She smiled. "Kinda ridiculous, don't you think?"

I didn't drink sugared shit. "Pick a fucking milkshake, woman."

She snatched the chocolate one. "Did you really get all three flavors for me to choose?"

"Yeah." But next time I'd get the fucking chocolate. I pulled the two large fries out and handed her one. "You still not eating meat?"

She did the cute little snort thing. "I was forced to eat chicken a few times or starve." She took the lid off her shake and dipped a fry in it.

"How'd your stomach handle it?" Maybe that was why she'd hurled.

"By the third time, it wasn't too bad." She ate the nasty shake-drenched fry.

I took the chicken sandwich out of the bag and held it out to her. "I also got a burger with the works, minus the burger." I pulled it out too.

She took the burger-less burger. "Thank you, but I think I'll confine my culinary adventure to dairy overload today."

I nodded and took my double burger out. We ate in silence and shared the diet soda. For the first time in ten days, I felt like I could fucking breathe. But as I sat there and ate food in a comfortable silence with this woman, I realized I hadn't felt this kind of peace since before I'd enlisted. Hell, since before my mom died.

I never thought about finding a woman I fit with. But this blonde-haired strong-willed woman? She fucking fit. Lock and key, she more than fit.

And I liked it. A whole damn lot.

I watched with satisfaction as she polished off half the fries, some of the sandwich and most of the shake. Then she lay back down and put her head on my lap.

"Okay, that was more junk food than I've eaten in five years." She rubbed her stomach and looked up at me. "What did you want to talk about?"

I set the soda on the nightstand and cut right to the chase. "I want you to take a pregnancy test."

Her hand rubbing her stomach froze and her muscles tensed. "Why? Just because I vomited?"

"Yes." And because I'd come inside her, and I couldn't fucking stop thinking about it.

She laughed uncomfortably. "I'm not pregnant, Falcon."

I brushed her hair off her face. "Then take the test."

She sat up and pulled her knees to her chest. "What are you doing?"

I hesitated, trying to gauge the look of alarm on her face. "Do you want kids?"

Her hand went up and she scrambled back. "No. No, no, no. We are not having this conversation." She got off the bed. "Don't sit there and pretend like this is anything except you clearing your conscience by getting me to take a stupid test." Her voice and her attitude ramped up, and she snatched the food wrappers off the bed and crushed them into a ball. "Well guess what? Mission accomplished. You found me, you fed me, you're free of obligation, on every level. You can go now. No strings. Have a nice life." She tossed the trash and walked into the bathroom, slamming the door behind her.

I was off the bed before she had a chance to lock the door. I threw it open and was ready to let loose about her attitude and bullshit defenses, when I found her sitting on the edge of the tub, crying.

Goddamn it.

I picked her up.

"*Hey*," she screeched. "Put me down!"

"No." I strode back into the dump of a motel room and sat on the bed.

The second my ass hit the mattress, she was fighting to get off me. "Let me GO."

I held her tighter. "No."

Her fist hit my chest, and more tears fell. "I said, *let me go*."

"Stop crying."

She looked at me like I was fucking insane. "That's the best you've got? *Stop crying?* Don't ever tell a woman to stop crying! That's not how you calm someone down. Don't you know *anything?*"

There was something wrong with me, because I fought a smile. "I know you're scared."

She looked away, but she stilled. "Let me go, Falcon. I'm begging you."

I put my lips to her ear and gave her the single thought I'd been fixated on since I sank inside her. "What if I don't want to?"

A silent sob shook her shoulders. "Don't do this to me."

I grasped her chin and brought her face back to mine. "Would it be so bad if you were knocked up?" Everything about this was fucked. We didn't know each other. She drove me fucking insane. But God help me, I wanted every inch of this challenging woman.

Her voice pitched high. "Are you crazy?"

Certifiable. "I'll take care of you," I promised.

"And a kid?" she asked, incredulous.

I didn't hesitate. "Yes."

She stared at me for a long moment. "You're serious."

"Every word." But I'd only said half of what I needed to say. "I want you to take that test, so we know what we're dealing with, but I want something else first."

"What?" She bit her bottom lip.

I fucking jumped. "I want you to come back to Miami with me, no matter what the results are."

She frowned. "Why?"

Inhaling, I said to her what I'd never said to another woman. "Because I want you to move in with me."

Perfectly still, her eyes so clear, the blue was translucent, her blonde hair falling down her back and over her shoulders in a just-slept mess, she was so damn gorgeous and innocent, she made my chest hurt. But she was also strong-willed, sexy and infuriating, and the thought of letting her go made me want to crush shit with my bare hands.

So when she didn't say shit in response, my jaw ticked and my nostrils flared. "If you're not interested, tell me now."

CHAPTER FORTY-TWO

Audrina

MY HEART IN MY THROAT, I COULDN'T EVEN SWALLOW.

Falcon "Tank" Gunther, an impossible, uncompromising beast of a man in bed and out, had spent ten days looking for me... so he could ask me to move in with him?

"Fine," he growled, lifting me off him like I weighed nothing and setting me on the bed.

"You want me to move in with you?" I asked, dumbfounded.

"I asked," he grunted, swinging his legs over the side of the bed. "But you're not fucking answering."

Oh my God.

Oh my God.

He was *nervous*.

"But the whole thing with *Miami Morning*." My cheeks flamed in embarrassment and my voice got quiet. "Everything I said. Everything you know about my past."

He looked at me, and as if he were allowing it, allowing me to see his emotions, I watched his expression change.

He looked at me with more patience than anyone ever had. "Your past wasn't your fault. It doesn't change a single damn second of this dialog, or have any influence on what I'm asking. I'm not gonna lie and say I don't want to put your brother six feet under, but that doesn't change shit between me and you. Understand?"

I nodded, too anxious to feel relief. "But *Miami Morning*… I said—"

"I know what you said." He studied me for a moment. "I get why you thought you didn't have a choice."

"I didn't. He said he had footage of us." I had to protect him from that.

Tank nodded. "He did, and your lawyer took care of it. But if he hadn't, I would've." He leveled me with a look. "You don't need to protect me. I know how to stay out of the tabloids."

Suddenly, I was miserable. "If you're around me, you're not going to be able to avoid it."

He stared at me for a long moment. "You done being in the spotlight?"

I let out a humorless half laugh. "I'm in dozens of films. I don't know if I'll ever be done being in the spotlight." I mean, eventually I would. The popularity of my films would wear off, but I didn't know when.

He didn't say anything.

I cocked my head as something occurred to me. "You don't act like most men do around me."

He held my gaze. "Good."

"Have you ever seen any of my films?"

"No."

No hesitation, no emotion in his answer, I felt like I was missing something. I made a joke. "You don't like chick flicks?"

"I don't do movies."

I tried to hide my shock. I wasn't upset he'd never seen my movies, in fact, I think I preferred it. "Ever?"

The one time my mother had taken me and James to see a movie when we were kids, it'd changed my life. After the movie, I'd told my mother that I wanted to be an actress when I grew up. Little did I know at the time how that one statement would change my life.

A few years after my first movie, I realized I should've probably thanked my mother for my career, but she hadn't given me to the casting agent out of love. She'd wanted to get rid of me.

Falcon shook his head once. "No."

"Why not?" I asked the question, but never in a million years could I have predicted his answer.

"Four tours in Afghanistan cured me of ever wanting to sit in a dark room with flashing lights and loud noises."

My heart broke for him at the same time as it swelled with the knowledge that he'd trusted me enough to share that. But more, I was humbled by the sacrifices he'd made. "I'm sorry," I said quietly. "Thank you for telling me."

He tipped his chin in acknowledgement.

I suddenly remembered there hadn't been a TV in his bedroom. "Do you listen to music?"

He shook his head. "Not much time for it in the Marines. Never picked up the habit."

"Of course." I felt like an idiot. "What do you like to do in your downtime?"

He rubbed a hand over his face and closed his eyes as he exhaled. Then he leaned over, grabbed a book out of his bag and set it on my lap.

I picked it up. "An encyclopedia of hand guns? Should I be worried?"

"You think I don't know how to use a gun?"

"No, I mean of course not, you were in the military."

"The Marines," he corrected.

"So you know about guns."

"Yeah."

"Then why read about them?"

"Downtime. You asked." He took the book back and put it in his bag. "You done with acting?"

"I am." I was. I didn't have to think about it. "Despite being around my family the past seven days, it wasn't all bad. I love Peony and being on the farm, and not putting on costumes or makeup or trying to remember lines. It's a simpler life, and I was missing that."

"That's what you want? A simple life?"

The way he gave me all of his attention, the way he asked pointed questions without any preamble, I liked it. I more than liked it. But he also made me feel incredibly shy. "Simple would be good. Perfect, in fact." I looked away and noticed the time on the clock on the nightstand. Shoot. "What about you?"

He didn't answer.

Seven minutes past the top of the hour. I looked up.

His voice turned to liquid sex. "You know what I want."

Oh God. I wanted him so bad in that moment, but I had to tell him. "I need to show you something," I blurted, glancing back at the clock.

His intense gaze followed mine to the nightstand, then cut back to me and his eyes narrowed. "What?"

The interview was airing today, and it'd already started. I glanced at the clock again, then I reached for the TV remote.

"You're turning on the TV?" he asked as his cell rang.

"Just bear with me." I fiddled with the remote.

Eyeing me, he answered his phone. "What?"

I tuned in the network that carried the most popular afternoon TV host. Maybe the most popular TV host ever. She'd been doing her hour-long show for decades, and everyone who was anyone in Hollywood had been interviewed by her.

Knowing what I'd needed to do ten days ago, I'd used Colton's phone before I left his hotel, and I'd called the famous TV host.

"Yeah," Tank said into the phone as he stared at me. "Copy that." He hung up. "When were you going to tell me about the interview?" he accused.

"Just…" I bit my lip and turned the volume up. "Just listen. Please."

I was wearing the silk blouse Tank had picked out for me to wear to the hospital as I sat in the hotel suite Gerri Johanna had flown on her private jet to meet me at halfway between Miami and Iowa. I looked small and shell-shocked, and she looked as put together and professional as she always did.

"To all of our fans who are just tuning in after the commercial break, we have a very special airing of the *Gerri Johanna Show* today. We're here with Dreena MacKenzie in a secret location, because as you can imagine, the press surrounding her recent events has been quite the spectacle." Gerri looked at me. "Thank you for meeting with me, Dreena. I'm honored you chose me to help share your story."

"Thank you for having me, Gerri, especially under these special circumstances."

Gerri nodded. "Before the last commercial break, we talked about the incident on the beach, but now I would like to hear about your appearance on *Miami Morning* in your own words."

His expression like stone, Tank glanced at me.

"Just watch," I whispered.

"Well…" I pushed my hair behind my ear. It was a nervous gesture I hadn't even realized I'd done when we'd been recording. I'd practiced for years to break that habit. "It was a difficult time. I was still reeling from the incident at Club Frenzy and my subsequent beach streaking, but more, I was in a position I've never been in before." I looked up at camera. "I was falling in love. But I didn't understand the feelings at the time. I thought it wasn't possible, and frankly, I was pushing through with my plan to leave acting. I decided a few years back that I needed an end goal. I've been so incredibly blessed to be in this industry and to have the unimaginable success I've had. I've been more than fortunate, and I am so very grateful. But I've also thought for a while that it's been past time to step down and let someone else take the spotlight. I was ready to move on to the next phase of my life. I just never expected all of these events to come crashing together and coincide at once.

"Frankly, I panicked when Jonathan on *Miami Morning* said he had footage of me from the previous day. The only person I had been in the company of was the one person I wanted to protect from the spotlight."

My recorded self looked directly at the camera. "I'm so very sorry for the false things I said, and about the implications toward Mr. Gunther, and for the ramifications to his employer, Luna and Associates. I take full responsibility for everything I said, and I would like everyone to know that I made it up."

"It sounds like you were under quite a bit of stress all around," Gerri said sympathetically.

"I was, but it was no excuse for my behavior and I apologize."

Gerri smiled. "Would you like to talk about the special man in your life?"

I cringed at the image of myself on TV forcing a nervous laugh. "No, I would not." My face fell. "And unfortunately, things did not work out how I had hoped."

"I'm so sorry," Geri said with the trademark sincerity that

had made her a favorite of both her fans and the people she interviewed.

"Yes, well." I looked at the camera and smiled a screen-worthy smile. "I would like to thank my studio, my agent, my publicist, and most importantly, all my fans over the years who came to see my movies. I will be forever grateful." I looked back at Geri. "And thank you, Geri, for meeting with me and airing my story."

"You are most welcome, Dreena."

The show cut to commercial.

I turned off the TV and looked at the man who was too good for me. "I'm sorry."

Without a word, he reached into the cargo pocket on his pants, pulled out a box, and set it on the bed.

I looked at the box.

An early response pregnancy test.

"When did you get that?"

"When I got you the ginger ale," he answered, no intonation in his voice.

My stomach in knots, a slew of thoughts ran through my head, but all of them were wrong. I shouldn't want to be pregnant. I shouldn't want to be tied to a stranger. I shouldn't want a man who bossed me around and took no prisoners.

But I did.

I wanted him.

I wanted the man who fucked me like a warrior, then held me in his arms and made slow love to me like he couldn't get enough. I wanted the man who stared at me and gave me all of his attention, not because I was famous, but because he was just being himself. I wanted the man who'd spent ten days relentlessly looking for me. And I wanted the alpha ex-Marine who was man enough to tell me he would take care of me and his baby.

I wanted the man I felt safe with.

I wanted Falcon Gunther in every way a woman could want a man.

But I was terrified to take that pregnancy test.

What if I wasn't pregnant? What if what he'd said about wanting me to move in with him no matter what was a lie? What if he changed his mind? What if I was pregnant and he was only with me out of honor?

I stared at the pink-and-white box, then I did something I'd never done with anyone. I admitted my fears. "I'm scared."

With all of the practicality I was beginning to realize was pure Falcon Gunther, he gave me four realistic words. "What's done is done."

I looked up at him. "I shouldn't want it to be positive."

He met my gaze and held me captive in his green-brown stare. "Neither should I."

Oh God. "So… you're saying—"

"I want you pregnant, Audrina."

I loved hearing him call me that, but I had to be honest. "You know that's not my real name."

"You legally changed it?"

"Well, my first agent did, but yeah…" I half laughed. He was right, what was done, was done. "Audrina MacKenzie is my legal name now."

"You prefer Magnolia?"

The name sounded strange and foreign coming from his lips, and I realized I wasn't Magnolia Audrina Jensen. I hadn't been for a long time. That girl died ten years ago. I may not be *the* Dreena MacKenzie anymore, but I was Audrina MacKenzie.

"No." I shook my head. "I don't prefer it at all."

"Any other secrets you're hiding?"

If I didn't know better, I'd think he was fighting a smile. "No. What about you?"

"What you see is what you get."

I didn't only doubt that, I knew he was full of it. "You're so full of shit."

The corner of his mouth tipped up as he smirked. "Get your ass in the bathroom and piss on the goddamn stick."

My stomach bottomed out. "Oh?" I raised my eyebrows to try to cover the soul-crushing jealousy I was suddenly drowning in. "Sounds like you have experience with how this works."

His expression turned deadly serious. "I never fucked a woman without a condom before you because this is the exact situation I was trying to avoid."

Cautious relief spread through my veins, but I still questioned him. "Then how do you know what to do?"

"I read the back of the box." He gave me a challenging look. "I can fucking read, sweetheart. I'm not just a dick with muscles."

Oh my God. "I wasn't implying you were stupid."

He half smiled again, and my heart melted. "Just giving you shit, babe. Come on." He stood and snatched the box off the bed. "You and me got a date with a stick and a toilet." Quick and agile, he scooped me off the bed.

"Wait!" Holy shit. "I'm not peeing in front of you."

Shaking his head, he looked down at me as he took two strides toward the bathroom. "You think I've never seen a woman take a piss before?" He set me down in front of the toilet and opened the box.

The jealousy came back tenfold.

When I didn't say anything, he set the box down and looked at me. "What's wrong?"

"Nothing." It was a knee-jerk response, but I didn't want to tell him that thinking about him with other women made me want to curl in a ball and cry.

"It's not nothing, but I can't address what I don't fucking know."

"You swear a lot."

"Get used to it. I'm a Marine."

"I didn't think you were active duty anymore."

"I'm not. Once a Marine, always a Marine. Now quit stalling and tell me what the hell made you upset."

That was all it took. My words came out like vomit. "I have no idea if you've ever seen another woman use the toilet, because I don't know you. But for the record, I don't want to think about what you have or haven't done with other women. It makes my stomach hurt and my eyes well, and frankly, it makes me feel a little stabby and a whole lot jealous." The more I said, the more shit spilled out. "So I don't want to ever hear you say 'you think I haven't done this with a woman,' or 'you think I haven't done that with another woman,' or a dozen women, or shit, the way you fuck, *hundreds* of women." I threw my hands up. "I can't even think about that. I don't want to think about that. Ever, ever, EVER." I sucked in a breath. "Not even if this stupid test is negative and you leave me for some other woman who actually *is* pregnant with your child, and then you see me again, alone and hoarding cats and snacking on bacon—even then. *Do not tell me about other women.*" I glared at him. "Ever."

His smile was wide and full and so devastating, I kinda hated him. "Copy that." He leaned down and gave me a soul-crushingly sweet kiss on my cheek before whispering in my ear. "Piss

256

on the stick, gorgeous. I need to know if I've got my work cut out for me."

Before I could catch my breath, he stood to his full height, pivoted and left the bathroom, closing the door behind him.

"Holy shit," I whispered, leaning against the sink for support.

CHAPTER FORTY-THREE

Tank

HEARD HER CUSS THROUGH THE BATHROOM DOOR.

Shaking my head, I fucking laughed.

"This isn't funny!" Her voice muffled, I still heard the trace of fear in it.

I pushed the door open.

She jumped and dropped the box.

I picked it up and stepped into her personal space. "Not a joke to me, babe."

"I know." She looked anywhere but at me.

I tipped her chin. "I'm not gonna let you go through anything alone."

"There isn't anything *to* go through."

There was a fucking pregnancy test on the counter. I stared at her, silently calling her on her bullshit.

She snatched up the box. "Fine. Point made."

I touched my lips to her forehead and reiterated my promise. "Not alone." Stepping back, I turned toward the door.

"How'd you know?"

I looked over my shoulder at her. "Know what?"

Looking vulnerable as fuck, she shrugged like this wasn't a loaded fucking conversation. "How I feel… about being alone."

I was an eighteen-year-old kid shooting an M4 in Afghanistan before she was making movies. I had my brothers downrange, she had her costars, but the irony wasn't lost on me that we both flew solo. This shit, her and I, it was the last thing I was looking for. But standing here, I didn't want to be anyplace else.

Her question, my reasons, the situation, all of it—I could sum it up in three words. "Lock and key."

"Lock and key," she whispered, biting her bottom lip.

I had to step back before I said fuck it with the damn test and took her.

"Take the test," I quietly ordered. Ten fucking days. I needed to be inside her.

With a nod, she shut the door.

Inhaling, I walked across the room, grabbed my cell, and fired off a text to Luna.

Me: *Need another week*

I rationalized I needed time to bring her back to Miami and get her settled, but in truth, I just wanted to fuck her, sleep next to her and watch her eat with her hands.

Luna replied instantly.

Luna: *Copy that. Tell her thanks for the interview*

Me: *Copy*

Luna: *You good?*

Me: *Yeah*

Luna: *Too early to haze you?*

Me: *Fuck you*

Luna: *LMFAO*

I didn't reply. A few seconds later, he sent another text.

Luna: *So. Love, huh?*

Me: *Not having this convo*

Luna: *That interview was viewed by millions. You ready for this?*

Jesus fuck.

Me: *Again, not having this convo*
Luna: *She ok?*

I didn't have time to answer. She stepped up behind me and placed the pregnancy test on the table in front of me.

My heart fucking stopped and I stared.

She was pregnant.

With my kid.

"I, um—" Her voice broke.

I turned and wrapped my arms around her as I let loose with a fucking roar.

She started in surprise then her arms went around my neck and she held me tight.

I stood to my full height and her feet came off the ground. Burying my face in her neck, I fucking breathed her in. Flowers, woman, sleep—she smelled like a perfect dream. "Fuck, woman." Openmouthed, I kissed her neck. "You're gonna look sexy as hell knocked up."

"Falcon." She burst into tears.

Putting her legs around my waist, I sat on the bed and took her face in my hands. "Hey, hey, hey." I swiped at her tears. "Talk to me."

"Do you even want kids?" she cried. "Or are you just saying that to make me feel better?"

I couldn't fucking help it, I smiled. "You want the sanitized answer or the truth?"

Her breath hitched. "Truth."

I pushed her hair behind her shoulder. "Two weeks ago, no. I didn't want kids, let alone a commitment to a woman."

She inhaled sharply and her back stiffened.

I cupped the back of her neck. "But then I met a fucking hot mess of a woman who'd created the scandal of all scandals, sunk her good-girl rep, and found out she'd been drugged. Which, by the way, that fuck Payne is in rehab, and you need to call your lawyer. He told your asshole agent you wouldn't press charges against Payne if your agent took whatever severance deal you offered him. Payne being his next biggest client after you, your agent took the deal."

She looked surprised. "You talked to Peter?"

"Yeah." Fucker had been calling me daily wanting updates. "I have your phone. You should call him later."

"Thanks." She tried to pull out of my grasp.

I held on to her. "I'm not finished telling you about the hot mess of a woman I met two weeks ago."

"I changed my mind. I want the sanitized version."

I fought a smile. "You're not getting it, but I will tell you this. A lesser woman would've cracked under the pressure of what happened. But the woman I met, you know what she asked me after she woke up in strange place, with a strange man and couldn't remember shit?"

"Don't forget handcuffed," she added dryly.

I'd never forget that. "She asked me how her ass looked."

Sighing, she rolled her eyes. "For the record, I was joking."

"I know." I swept my thumb across her cheek. "That's my fucking point. Because that hot mess of a woman I met? She was actually ballsy and mouthy, and best of all?" I gripped her hair and held her tight. "She's fucking brave."

"Oh," she said quietly.

"Yeah, *oh*."

Her gaze dropped. "I have a confession."

"You didn't care how your ass looked." I'd already figured that out.

"No." She barely shook her head then looked up at me. "I

still haven't watched that video. I don't want to see it."

"Smart move."

"Oh God." She covered her face with her hands. "It's that bad, isn't it?"

It was worse, for someone who wanted a career in acting. "You done for good with movies and acting?" I pulled her hands down so I could see her eyes.

She didn't hesitate. "Yes. Even if I lost all my money tomorrow, I couldn't go back. I don't want to. That life was always tainted by the way it began for me."

I didn't touch her last statement. If I had my way, we'd have a lifetime to fucking hash that shit out. But right now, I was focused on her admission. "Then the video means nothing, and you don't need to ever see it."

She exhaled, but she didn't look relieved.

"What?"

"What if I go back with you and—"

"No if," I corrected. "You're coming with me."

"What if you don't like me in a week? A month? What if you don't want to be with me?"

I smiled. "I've got a hot-as-fuck younger woman who sucks dick like a goddess and she's carrying my kid. What the hell would I have to complain about?"

Worry etched across her features. "I'm being serious."

I sobered. "Growing pains, stupid shit couples argue about, that shit's gonna happen. We'd be lying to each other if we said otherwise. But I'm not gonna let that shit come between me and the woman who's carrying my kid."

"But it's not just about learning to get along as a couple."

"You're right." I brushed my hand down her arm and took her hand. "It's about chemistry, trust and honesty. The first we have in spades, the second we're working on and the last we need to always remember."

"You make it sound so simple."

"Life is only as complicated as you make it, sweetheart."

She leaned forward and put her forehead on my chest. "I think I really like you, Falcon Gunther."

I rolled her to her back, pushed her thighs apart with my knee and settled between her legs. "Only like?" I kissed her once. "What happened to falling for me?"

CHAPTER FORTY-FOUR

Audrina

MY HEAD SPUN.

I was pregnant. *Pregnant.* With this giant, dominating beast of a man's child. And he wanted me to move in with him, and I'd never even had my own place.

I should've been freaking the hell out, but his huge body was over me and his hard length was pressing against my panties, and he smelled so incredibly good that all I could think about was being naked.

His lips landed on my throat then traveled to my ear. "Still not answering?"

The sound of his deep voice made gooseflesh race across my heated skin. "What were we talking about?"

"Brat." He nipped my neck.

I shivered. Then I gave him the only truth I felt safe enough in that moment to give. "I missed you."

"Ten days is too damn long. I want inside you."

His mouth crashed over mine, and his tongue plunged in.

Then it was as if we'd never been apart.

Gripping my hair, angling my face, and taking what he wanted, he dominated me with his long, drugging kiss. But he didn't just dominate me. His hand slid over my body, gentle and caressing, as if reacquainting himself with every inch he'd missed. His chest vibrated with moans that swallowed the distance between us. And he showed me with his body how much he wanted me.

I'd never felt more like a woman.

I didn't just like this man, and I wasn't merely falling for him. I'd already fallen. Totally and completely.

His arms on either side of my face, caging me in, his hips pressing into mine, his desire hard against my core, he groaned, but then he pulled back.

Staring down at me with hooded eyes swirling with determination, he gave me his deep, sexy voice. "You need to decide." His expression darkened. "But know this. You run again? I'm coming after you."

I dared to put my hand against his cheek. "I'm not running."

He didn't pull back from my touch. "You want this?"

I loved how honest he was. How he didn't fear talking about the future, and how he didn't see any obstacles we couldn't overcome. "I want you."

He held perfectly still. "And my kid?"

All at once, it hit me. It'd never crossed my mind that I wasn't keeping the baby. Not once. Overwhelmed, shocked, terrified, I felt it all, but I didn't even consider an alternative. Except he didn't know that.

I took his face with both of my hands. "I never even considered not having your baby."

His shoulders relaxed, his chest rose with a deep breath and the heavy line between his eyes softened as he exhaled his tension. Then he said the absolute last thing I ever expected this alpha, *alpha* man to say.

Quiet and stoic, he gave me his gratitude. "Thank you."

The last of my reservations shattered into a million pieces as my heart filled with a joy I didn't know was possible.

My eyes welled, and I kissed him.

Soft and gentle, my lips against his, I wanted to show him my heart. I wanted to give him a piece of me I'd never given to anyone else. I wanted him to know how much he meant to me.

But the second our lips touched, the heat between us exploded.

We weren't gentle. Or subtle, or reserved. We'd crashed into each other's lives, and the sexual tension had detonated then like it was detonating now.

Dominant and aggressive, he took over the kiss and I let him. His mouth on mine, then on my neck and down my throat, he latched on to my breast.

My back arched, and he ripped my panties down my legs.

His thumb circled my clit, and he sank a finger inside me as I frantically reached for his pants. Beyond talking, there were no words between us. I needed him inside me, stretching me, filling me, and he knew exactly how to deliver.

Shoving my hand away from his pants, he quickly freed himself and sat up. Leaning back on his knees, his finger stroking in and out of my needy core, he stared down at me. "So fucking beautiful."

"Please," I begged, reaching for his cock.

"Arms above your head," he commanded.

My hips thrusting against his hand, I complied.

Fisting himself, fingering me, circling my clit with his thumb, he stared at me for a long moment. Then he slowly added a second finger. "What's your simple life look like?"

Oh my God. His fingers were magic. My eyes fluttered shut.

His hand stilled. "Answer the question."

My eyes popped open, and I desperately tried to think. Because I knew this man enough to know I wasn't coming until

I gave him the words he'd asked for.

"Um…." Simple life. What did I want?

"Don't think," he ordered, rubbing his cock against my inner thigh. "Just tell me."

As if my body and my mind were made for his brand of dominance, my thoughts turned into words and spilled out of my mouth. "I want a house on the beach, and I want lots of kids, and I want to fall asleep in your arms every night. I want our kids to ride horses, and I want to love you like you've never been loved before."

My alpha, dominant, ex-Marine bodyguard surged.

His hard length plunged into my core, and he thrust all the way to the hilt.

He growled, and I cried out.

Then his lips were on mine and he was moving. Hard and deep, then gentle and shallow, he drove into me, over and over.

Desire, soul deep and relentless, built up in layer after escalating layer of need until my body bowed off the bed.

Crying out in shock, elation, and pure, mind-altering joy, I came apart. *"Falcon!"*

My pussy clenched around his impossibly huge length, and every muscle in his body went rigid. A roar ripped from his chest, and he filled me with his love.

EPILOGUE

Tank

I'M NOT SIGNING THE PRENUP!" SHE SLAMMED THE DOOR IN MY face.

"Then I'm not fucking marrying you!" I yelled back, pounding my fist on the door.

"*Fuck off.*"

"Open the goddamn door and I will!" I'd fuck off and fuck her right in this goddamn hallway.

Collins chuckled. "I told you, *trouble.*"

"Go fuck off with that shit," I ground out. "Don't call my wife trouble." Why the hell had I asked him to be my best man?

Collins grinned. "She isn't your wife yet."

"Because she won't *fucking sign the prenup!*" I yelled at our bedroom door.

"Because signing it gives this marriage an end date," she yelled back.

I threw my hands up. "See what the fuck I have to deal with?" *Goddamn it.* "Pregnant women." I shook my head.

"I still wouldn't sign it if I wasn't carrying your kicking, who-needs-sleep-at-night, I'm-a-holy-terror son!"

"*Jesus Christ.*" I leaned my forehead on the wall.

"Quit swearing," she barked.

"Trouble in paradise?" Talon Talerco, the SARC assigned to our Marine unit, chuckled as he came up the stairs.

"See?" Collins crossed his arms. "Trouble."

Talon looked at me but tipped his chin toward Collins. "He still spoutin' that bleeder versus trouble shit?"

"Yeah." I pounded on the door. "Open up, woman."

She stood her ground. "I'll open this door when you tear up that prenup."

Fuck me. "No."

Talon chuckled. "She ain't budgin'. You wanna put a ring on it, you better man the fuck up."

"I don't want her goddamn money." I had my own.

Collins smirked.

Talon laughed in earnest. "You're in a fuckin' mansion on the ocean in the highest-priced zip code in the state." He tauntingly raised an eyebrow. "Your money buy her this?"

I growled at Talon. Combat medic or not, my respect for him wavered when he was being a prick.

"Exactly." Talon smiled, as if proving a point. "She wanted it, she bought it, you benefitted. Seven bedrooms is plenty a room for little Tanks and Dreenas. Who fuckin' cares where the funds came from?"

"Audrina," I corrected. "My woman's name is *Audrina*."

Talon reached over and casually grasped the door handle and turned. The door swung open and my woman stood there with tears on her cheeks.

"Hey, darlin'." Talon smiled at her. "How ya feelin'?"

"Mad." She swiped at her face then put her hand on her bump. "And fat."

Grinning, Talon shoved his hands in his pockets. "Well, you look gorgeous as hell. I'd marry you."

It was reactionary. My arm was up and my hand was on Talon's throat before he drew his next breath. "Watch it," I warned, shoving him against the wall.

Talerco smiled his fucking smile, and Collins muttered, "Trouble."

"Let go of Talon," Audrina ordered.

"Sign the prenup," I demanded, giving Talon one more shove before dropping my hand.

"Marry me because you love me," she threw back.

"I do fucking love you!" I roared. "That's why I had the goddamn paperwork drawn up. *I'm protecting you.*"

Her face softened, and she smiled. "Okay."

I stilled.

I'd fallen for this emotional pendulum shit before in the past six months. Pregnant women could flip on a dime. "You're signing it?"

"No." She grinned and rubbed her belly. "But I love you back and I'm marrying you."

"*Jesus fucking Christ.*" I wanted to throttle her. Then fuck her. Then kiss her.

Talon chuckled. "We'll go tell the preacher and guests to have a few more cocktails while y'all fuck and make up." He winked at Audrina. "Don't worry, darlin'. I'll make sure the bar tab's on him." Talon went downstairs and threw open the door to the lanai. "Drink up, everyone! The soon-to-be newlyweds are gettin' one more screw in."

Collins shook his head. "I'm grabbing a beer." He disappeared down the stairs.

"You fucking do that," I said, staring at my woman.

"Don't be rude," Audrina defended him.

"He called you trouble. I'll be as rude as I fucking want."

"You like trouble," she shot back.

"You're right." I fucking loved her smart mouth... on every

other day but our wedding day when she wouldn't sign a damn piece of paper that'd protect her money. Not that I'd ever take shit from her. She'd more than paid her karma dues with her fucked-up family. "Just sign the prenup." I sighed. "Please."

Her voice went quiet with hurt. "I don't want to sign any paperwork that gives you a clear conscience to leave me."

Jesus. I couldn't fault her abandonment issues, but fuck, she was crushing me. "I'm not leaving you. Ever. I'm doing this to protect you. I want you to feel safe."

"I feel safe when I'm with you."

"I'm always gonna be here," I promised.

She looked at me with doe eyes. "Then don't make me sign anything."

"Jesus, woman." Pregnant, pouting and in a wedding dress. I didn't stand a fucking chance. "Am I ever gonna win an argument with you?"

Sweet and innocent and so fucking gorgeous it hit me in the chest, she smiled. "Only in the bedroom."

Fuck, she knew how to work me. "And don't forget it," I muttered, knowing I was going to drop the prenup thing.

"Are we done arguing?"

"Yeah." I reached for her.

She stepped back. "It's bad luck to see the bride before the wedding."

Quicker than her, I moved. "I don't need luck." I lifted her into my arms. "I already knocked you up, woman."

She smiled her real smile. "Yeah, you kinda did."

I kicked our bedroom door shut. "You loved every minute of it."

She wrapped her arms around my neck. "Yeah, I kinda did."

I narrowed my eyes. "Kinda?"

"Well…" She bit her bottom lip and glanced at the closed door. "I kinda forget how it happened." She blushed. "Maybe you should remind me."

I was already walking toward our bed. "Forget, huh?"

She nodded. "I think you might've kissed me."

I laid her down and pushed the silky material of her dress up her thighs. "Yeah, I kissed you." I shoved her dress up to her waist.

Damn.

Damn.

No underwear.

My already throbbing cock got so fucking hard, all my blood rushed south and I surged. My mouth latched on to her sweet fucking cunt, and I sucked. Hard.

Her back bowed off the bed. "Oh my God, *Falcon.*"

I licked her entire length. "Whose pussy is this?"

"Yours. Yoursyoursyours."

Damn fucking straight. I drove my tongue into her.

Her hands gripped my hair, and her hips thrust up to meet me. Her desire filled my mouth as her pussy started to detonate. Sucking her clit between my teeth, I gave her one more lick before unbuckling my belt and unzipping my pants.

My cock sprang free, and I pulled her to the edge of the bed. Fisting myself, I looked down at my woman. "You're mine."

Her delicate hand grasped my thigh as her hotter-than-sin, sex-rasped voice washed over me. "I love you."

I thrust deep in to my soon-to-be wife and stilled. Cupping her face, I gave her what I never thought I would give away. I gave her my heart. "I fucking love you."

THANK YOU!

Thank you so much for reading SCANDALOUS! If you were interested in leaving a review on any retail site, I would be so appreciative. Reviews mean the world to authors, and they are helpful beyond compare!

And make sure to check out the other books in the Alpha Bodyguard Series!

MERCILESS – Collins's story
RECKLESS – Tyler's story
RUTHLESS – Sawyer's story
FEARLESS – Ty's story
CALLOUS – Preston's story
RELENTLESS – Thomas's story
SHAMELESS – Shade's story
HEARTLESS – Ronan's story

Have you read the Uncompromising Series?
TALON
NEIL
ANDRÉ
BENNETT
CALLAN

Have you read the sexy Alpha Escort Series?
THRUST
ROUGH
GRIND

Turn the page for a preview of the other exciting books in the Alpha Bodyguard Series!

MERCILESS

Bodyguard.

Mercenary.

Gun for hire.

I didn't care what you called it, the end result was always the same.

You paid me for a job, you got results. The Marines trained me to shoot, but life taught me to aim. Working for the best personal security firm in the business was a stepping stone. Put in my time, build the résumé, then move on. I didn't do attachments on any level.

Until a smoking-hot former one-night stand crossed the street in front of me, holding hands with a kid who was my spitting image. She tried to play it off, deny he was mine. She said she didn't remember me, right before she picked her kid up and ran. She thought she'd made a clean escape.

But she was about to find out how merciless a bodyguard could be.

RECKLESS

Bodyguard.

Escort.

Bad boy.

I didn't come from the wrong side of the tracks. I was the wrong side. Every cliché you could think of, my family embraced. The only advantage I had was being the best-looking out of all my brothers. Except when I joined the Marines, looks didn't count for shit downrange.

I wasn't active duty anymore, and working for the best personal security firm in the business, my looks were getting me in more trouble than they were worth. I just didn't realize how much trouble until a princess from a country I'd never heard of asked for me by name. Her request was simple—me, my gun, and an art opening. But she recklessly failed to mention one crucial part of the assignment... pretend to be her new fiancé.

Now she was about to find out how reckless a bodyguard could be.

RUTHLESS

Bodyguard.

Protector.

Security Detail.

I wasn't supposed to join the Marines and serve three tours. I'd been groomed to be another kind of warrior. Since I could walk, I'd been primed to take over the family business. Build the real estate empire bigger, ruthlessly fight my way to the top—make everyone richer.

Instead, I'd enlisted. Wanting to protect my country, not a bank account, I'd turned my back on the family business and given the Marines eight years. Now I was a bodyguard for the best personal security firm in the business, and life was perfectly uncomplicated... until an innocent redhead smiled at me and destroyed everything.

Now she was about to find out how ruthless a bodyguard could be.

FEARLESS

Bodyguard.

Sniper.

Morally corrupt.

I didn't care who I aimed at. You paid me, I pulled the trigger. I sold my skills to the highest bidder, and trust me, I had skills. The Marines trained me to aim a sniper rifle, but life taught me to get the job done—at any expense.

Except hostage recovery wasn't on my short list. I didn't care that the personal security firm that'd hired me was paying double to get some rich businessman's daughter back without casualties. I didn't negotiate with terrorists. Ever. I had my own plan. Take out anyone in my sights, recover the hostage, and get out. But then I laid eyes on the half-naked, bleeding brunette, and I changed my mind. I was gonna do a lot more than simply pull the trigger.

Now they were going to find out how fearless a bodyguard could be.

CALLOUS

Bodyguard.

Tracker.

Silent observer.

Life was in the details. The weight of a government-issued rifle, the trajectory of a bullet, the speed of the wind—those details were crucial in the Marines. But outside the military, that level of observation was currency, and I was selling my skills to the best security firm in south Florida.

Except I wasn't on a job when I noticed the nervous brunette pushing through the crowd. Her hair loose, her shirt borrowed, she stumbled in too-big shoes before looking over her shoulder. I didn't follow her glance. I didn't have to. I'd already spotted the muscle after her. The question was if I was going to do anything about it. Before I could decide, her pursuer took aim. It was the wrong move.

Now everyone was going to find out how callous a bodyguard could be.

RELENTLESS

Resourceful.

Resolute.

Bodyguard.

A single diagnosis, and I wasn't good enough. Not for college ball, not for my family, and not for the Marines. Medically discharged before I finished basic training, I was determined to prove myself.

Landing a job as a bodyguard for the best security firm in the business was a second chance. It should've been my focus, but a sophisticated blonde walked through the lobby and dismissed me with a single glance.

Now she was going to find out how relentless a bodyguard could be.

SHAMELESS

Bodyguard.

Shadow.

Warrior.

The Marines trained me to be a weapon. Tactical warfare was in my blood. I didn't think twice when I was deployed for the fifth time because I was born battle ready. Then a mission went south and left me with a medical discharge.

Too many years downrange, I didn't fit in the civilian world. Taking a job with the best security firm in the business seemed like a solid plan… until I was assigned babysitting duty for a spoiled little rich girl. The only thing worse than the assignment was the client's mouth. She thought she could run it—all over me—and not suffer the consequences. She was wrong.

Now she was about to find out how shameless a bodyguard could be.

HEARTLESS

Bodyguard.

Sentry.

Explosives expert.

There was a reason I was the only Explosive Ordnance Disposal technician in the Marines who'd never sustained any injuries. I didn't take chances. Ever. My actions were precise. My thoughts were controlled, and I lived by one creed—no second chances.

Except serving my country as an EOD in the Marines had a shelf life. Promoted off the front lines, I didn't want to ride out my career behind a desk. A civilian job with the best security firm in the business seemed like a better solution… until a frightened client with haunted eyes lied to me about everything.

Now she was going to find out how heartless a bodyguard could be

ACKNOWLEDGMENTS

I don't just have heroes in my books, I have these amazing, unsung heroes that make up my tribe. Without them, I could not do what I do.

Kristen—I can't tell you enough how much you rock, because you totally do! Thank you so much for putting up with me and beta reading all these bad boy alphas. Your insight is invaluable to me and I adore you!

Virginia—I don't even know how many books you've slogged through for me anymore, LOL. All I know is that you're stuck with me forever. Thank you for making me look like I actually know how to use a comma!

Olivia—It's official, you're the frosting on my cake! And even though I STILL have no clue what a dangling whatchamacallit is, and a comma splice sounds more like a dance move than grammatical error, I am beyond thankful that you know how to whip me into shape, LOL. Thank you for always making everything pretty!

Clarise—My cover ninja. You make everything beautiful and sexy and perfect and I love laughing with you!

Stacey—I am so thankful you know what you are doing, because you make the prettiest formatted books EVER! Thank you!

Hubby—Last but definitely not least! For all the countless conversations about everything book related, and all of your help—thank you SO much. But mostly, thank you for being my partner. I could not do this without you!

XOXO -Sybil

ABOUT THE AUTHOR

Sybil grew up in northern California with her head in a book and her feet in the sand. She now resides in southern Florida, and while she doesn't get to read as much as she likes, she still buries her toes in the sand. If she's not writing or fighting to contain the banana plantation in her backyard, you can find her spending time with her family, and a mischievous miniature boxer.

To find out more about Sybil Bartel or her books, please visit her at:

Website: sybilbartel.com

Facebook page
www.facebook.com/sybilbartelauthor

Book Boyfriend Heroes
www.facebook.com/groups/1065006266850790

Twitter
twitter.com/SybilBartel

BookBub
www.bookbub.com/authors/sybil-bartel

Newsletter
eepurl.com/bRSE2T